WI

DANTE'S CYPHER

IW

DANTE'S CYPHER

T. STEPHENS

TATE PUBLISHING
AND ENTERPRISES, LLC

Published by Tate Publishing & Enterprises, LLC
127 E. Trade Center Terrace | Mustang, Oklahoma 73064 USA
1.888.361.9473 | www.tatepublishing.com

Tate Publishing is committed to excellence in the publishing industry. The company reflects the philosophy established by the founders, based on Psalm 68:11,
"The Lord gave the word and great was the company of those who published it."

Book design copyright © 2013 by Tate Publishing, LLC. All rights reserved.
Cover design by Junriel Boquecosa
Interior design by Caypeeline Casas

Published in the United States of America

ISBN: 978-1-62854-940-9
1. FICTION / General
13.10.30

DEDICATION

To my wife, Carla—without her I would truly be nothing. I really do mean that. She loves me in spite of myself.

To my parents, Louis and Suzanne—they framed who I am and stayed the course for the long haul. Thank God for them.

From the bottom of my heart, thank you. Each one of you.

To Mason, Sarah and Kenneth-you know who you are, thank you so much!

T.

ACKNOWLEDGMENTS

- Leonard Coe, a veteran patrolman for eighteen years
- Troy Tumpney of Troy Built Construction, Nashua, New Hampshire
- Nicole Boudreau for the Spanish Translations
- Jim G. Baroud, a veteran patrolman

I wanted to thank these folks mentioned above for helping me understand some of the technical issues of my research, from terminology, to phraseology, to applicability. They aided me tremendously in understanding the real world applications, situations, and outcomes of different scenes, not just a stiff representation of the story information I was trying to provide to you. They helped me give the real life feel that is so very important in telling a good story.

Thank you very much to them for their help. I am deeply appreciative.

KLANG IN THE NIGHT

"Can we just backtrack to that dirt road we crossed about fifteen minutes ago and set up camp? We're not going to pick the trail back up in this thorny, swampy hellhole tonight. Admit it, you're lost," the brunette hiker insisted to her stubborn partner.

"Will you just can it? We've been in this type of situation before, and I've always got us out. You know I'm right," the other woman replied, not looking up from the map she stared at in the light of her headlamp.

The map reader was a solidly built woman in her midforties with close-cropped dirty blond hair that the straps of the headlamp had matted around her head. It was her idea to hike the entire Appalachian Trail, and she had planned all of the details of the trek: the south-to-north route, so they would finish during the beautiful New England summer; the sights they wanted to see along the way; the logistics and rations—everything. The trip was something she had wanted to do since college, and she had prepared for it for years. When the time was finally right, and she thought she had a partner who could do it with her, she took a sabbatical from work, left her cat with her mother, and started the journey of her lifetime. Her name was Abigail.

The brunette was in her midthirties and built like an athlete, but with appealing feminine curves, long, strong, and lean—the exact type of woman Abbie liked. She was smart, considerate, passive, and a little high-maintenance. She was the "lipstick" of the two. Her name was Rachel.

The women were about twenty feet apart. Rachel was examining their current surroundings in the light of her own headlamp.

"No. You're right," Rachel conceded, as she usually did, "but we've been hiking off-grid for two days now, and I would love to find a pond or river to just rinse off in. I'm sure as hell not hopping into this smelly swamp to wash off the trail grime. I know we're close to Route 77. I saw it on my map, and every once in a while, if it's quiet enough, I can hear a truck way off to our west. Tomorrow night, I want to stay in a B and B and take a decent shower and sleep in a soft bed. It's been almost a week for both, and I feel it."

Her large pack thumped to the ground as she unclipped it. The pack was a soft respite for her sore, tired bum as she settled down on it.

"And we are not making camp here for the night. The ground is soggy, and the air stinks like rotten swamp."

"Okay. Just hush for a minute so I can get our bearings," Abbie said as she shrugged off her framed backpack next to a huge web of thorns. She wanted to sit down and compare her map to her compass. Abbie chuckled to herself, thinking it was a good thing Rachel was a great piece of ass. Otherwise, Abbie would have happily lost her months ago back in hillbilly country.

As she sat down on her pack, it rolled backward, sending her awkwardly flailing her arms and somersaulting in slow motion into the thorn bush. She felt the thorns pierce her skin through her fleece coat and T-shirt and was surprised that she kept rolling once she made contact with the patch of thorns. She had not seen that the viny thorn bush she had dropped her pack next to extended out over the black swamp water. What she thought was spongy ground was an optical illusion; part of her pack was actually suspended above the water, held up by the thorns of the thick bush. Her legs flailed up in the air as she flopped and splashed backward into the deep, rank, pitch-black water.

Rachel scoffed out a large laugh she barely tried to conceal.

"Serves you right, you pushy bitch," she muttered to herself, giggling.

The splashing and fumbling lasted only a brief moment, and then everything was still. Rachel expected to see a very irritated Abbie rise out of that stinky water like Godzilla, but there was only silence.

"Abbie? What the hell are you doing in there?"

Nothing. No sound emerged from the darkness.

"If you think you're going to sucker me into getting ambushed, you've got another think coming, sister! And you are definitely sleeping out of the tent tonight!"

Silence.

Rachel didn't like the silence at all.

Abbie was tough, but she wouldn't have spent an extra second in that stink. With that thought, Rachel was up and moving toward the spot where she had last seen her partner. She went over to Abbie's pack and shined her light down into the dark water. No trace of Abbie anywhere. Rachel frantically screamed her lover's name into the night.

"*Ab...bie! Abb...bieee!*"

In desperation, she waded waist-deep into the black murk.

"*Ab—*"

She was halfway through her final scream when her feet slid out from under her as she was sucked down into the black abyss.

Somewhere off in the dark woods, unheard by a living soul, a metallic *klang* resounded through the night.

HEADING TO CAMP

Shining steel, double-edged, like lumberjacks used back in the old days and reminiscent of a medieval battle weapon—polished and smooth with a long hickory handle, the axe was twice as expensive as the other models in the store. Steve had a huge amount of wood to split, and he wanted an axe that would hold an edge. It was perfect.

"Like you need another piece of outdoor gear," a mildly annoyed female voice said from the other side of a shoulder-high aisle.

"It's not gear. It's a tool and ultimately a gift," Stephen Babin replied, "one I'll be doing a ton of work with this weekend. When I'm finished, I want to leave it for Mason to thank him for his generosity and all he's done. He's let me hunt with him at his camp for years without ever asking for a thing. This is the least I can do for him. It's why I want to get the best one."

With a roll of her eyes, Carla responded, "Whatever," as she nonchalantly perused the knickknacks on the shelves of the multifaceted convenience-clothing-hardware-hunting-food store and post office in the backwoods of Maine.

In the refection of the high-polished steel, the stunning beauty of his wife of five years was still remarkable. He watched his petite yet curvaceous (in all the right places), long brown curly-haired bride stroll through the aisle in the reflection of the axe and mimic false outrage to herself. She could render him speechless just by looking at him, and he knew it.

Steve was literally stunned by Carla's beauty the first time he saw her. He was running to catch an elevator at the University of Connecticut, not paying attention to how fast he was going, knocking her off her feet to the elevator floor. She was so livid at that moment that she wouldn't acknowledge his existence.

He was silent. He didn't even try to apologize. It was not because he was arrogant or embarrassed; for the first time in his life, he was dumbstruck in the presence of a woman, rendered speechless by her beauty.

As Steve came to know her, he realized there was more to Carla than physical attributes. She was smart, very smart, and she understood just how to play him. Years later, completely aware of the power she had over him, he loved her even more.

The thought of how much he loved her caused him to smile, and he felt a "Spanish moment" coming on.

"¡Te amo, Mi amor! No puedo vivir sin tigo!" Steve said in an overly gallant, horribly fake Spanish accent as he reached for Carla.

Here we go again, she thought as he whisked her off her feet into an exaggerated sweeping dip.

At UConn, Steve was a communications and marketing major. He also minored in Spanish, which didn't sit well with his parents, who were of Canadian descent and wanted his minor to be French. He actually spent a semester abroad in Seville, Spain. At one time, he was quite fluent. Every so often, he liked to flex his Spanish muscles and recite some overtly embarrassing, very dramatic, very public proclamation in Spanish of his deepest affections for his wife.

When he first started with his theatrics, she was embarrassed because he made such a scene of it. Then for a while, she became annoyed because he never cared who was looking or where they were. Steve's Spanish moments were always performed in some grandiose fashion that would end in her being dipped and then kissed passionately.

One time, after Steve had performed his act in a Walmart back home, Carla was about to chastise him for creating such a scene in public when she noticed something in the faces of some women who had witnessed Steve's performance. She saw envy and longing in their eyes—they wished their husbands would show them a public display of affection once in a while. From that moment, she never again complained about his Spanish the-atrics. She feigned indifference, but deep down, she was always thrilled Steve loved her so much that he didn't care where they were or who was around when he publicly proclaimed her his own Spanish rose.

They were heading to Mason Macfarlane's hunting camp in Beldon, Maine. Built on the remnants of a two-hundred-year-old farm, it was situated deep in the middle of the woods. The original name of the old place was Long Shadows Farm, and it had been quite a spread in its heyday. Mason had adopted the name for the camp that was to be Steve and Carla's destination.

The camp had no electricity, running water, telephone service, or cell-phone reception. It consisted of one hundred acres and a log cabin that was one large room with a bunk bed in the north-west corner and a queen-size bed in the northeast corner. A round kitchen table sat in the middle of the room with four wooden chairs around it that was used more for card games than eating. Along the western wall were two old reclining camp chairs and the largest window in the cabin, which caught beautiful sunsets. A woodstove and a metal storage cabinet for dry goods lined the eastern wall, and along the southern wall were the corner door, counters, cabinets, and sink. Above were coat and gun racks. The support beams consisted of rough-hewn logs, seven feet up, laid every three feet perpendicular to the eve of the roof.

Lighting was provided by gaslights fed by quarter-inch copper piping that ran along the supports to the eastern wall and outside to an eighty-gallon propane tank. Antique gear ornamented the walls—wooden skis, a toboggan above the foot of the queen bed, a huge beehive, and an old game cart. The antique pieces added to the allure and ambiance of the hundred-year-old structure.

For Steve, who enjoyed going there in the fall year after year to hunt, even though he had never seen a deer on the property, it was a perfect place to get away.

He spent many days in the woods and not just at Mason's camp. Being out in the woods was more of a religion to Steve than the Roman Catholic faith in which he had been raised. The outdoors was the only place he felt completely at peace. This was the kind of place that sent him into the woods almost daily in the fall and made him a student of the outdoors.

Their shared appreciation of the outdoors bonded Steve and Mason. Both worked for a large biotech company in high-stress jobs. They found common ground and became close friends, despite the twenty-five-year difference in their ages; they shared a mutual sense of contentment in going back to the same camp year after year, not just to hunt but to be there.

Mason was a Mainer's Mainer who loved the outdoors for its own sake and was not fond of tourists or outsiders. He was a certified Maine Guide, which was the most difficult to attain among all of the state guide certifications. Mason didn't find it necessary to speak often, but when he did, it was to the point, and Steve was one of the few people who found that to be a refreshing quality. Mason was a generous, honest, and sincere man, who loved his wife, Sarah, without question. Few people in Steve's life had these qualities and were still so unassuming. He was a refreshing change from the BS and stress of corporate life.

In anticipation of the coming winter, when Mason used the cabin to get away, Steve had asked him if he could go to the camp and split some wood. He wanted to show his appreciation for Mason's letting him use the camp by splitting and stacking a few cords of wood.

Mason appreciated the gesture.

"Absolutely! Why don't you take Carla up and sneak away for a long weekend? I could never get Sarah out there, but it would be a great getaway weekend for a young couple, alone," he said with a wink. "Plus, it would give me an excuse to go to camp. I could tell Sarah I'm going to 'supervise' your progress and come visit for a while."

"That sounds great!" Steve said enthusiastically. "I'll do just that."

He knew Mason's motivations were twofold—he sincerely wanted to visit, and he was very particular about his things and how they were organized.

This trip was turning out to be a win-win-win idea for everyone involved. Steve would put some sweat equity into the camp, as a form of thanks to Mason. Steve, Mason, and Carla would get to spend time together at the rustic camp. Mason would be able to have the wood just the way he wanted it. And most importantly, Steve would get some much-needed free time with Carla.

This trip will be perfect, he thought.

MACABRE HISTORY

All was going smoothly as the delighted couple sped toward their weekend of rest and relaxation. In the back of their capped pickup, they had all of the materials they would need, thanks to the multifaceted Maine store. Steve had the tools needed to do his work. Carla had everything she wanted—a good book to read, a lounge chair, some wine, accouterments for romantic meals for two, and the undivided attention of her lover man. She had even brought a few provocative ensems, if the mood was right.

Steve turned the 4x4 truck off of Route 77 north onto Long Shadows Road and started down the dirt road that went five miles eastward to Mason's camp. Long Shadows Road itself went ten miles deep into the backwoods, intersecting with some old logging roads farther back. Steve wasn't sure where the road came out, if it did at all. Whenever he went down the road, it was to get into the woods around Mason's camp and recharge his soul.

After ten minutes, they pulled up to a rough-cut crossbar that spanned the dooryard (the old New Englander's word for "driveway") to Mason's camp. A No Trespassing sign hung from the crossbar.

"Mason is pretty particular about his stuff. He doesn't want anyone on his land," Steve said. "He used to have it open, but then some of his things were stolen, and he closed off access to the place. He posted the entire hundred acres."

"Yeah. I saw the signs for the last couple of minutes along the road. I figured we were getting closer," Carla replied.

Steve got out and moved the crossbar. He moved the truck thirty feet forward, hopped out, and rehung the crossbar. When he hopped back into the four-door pickup, he turned to Carla with an awkward grin and said, "Mason is pretty particular about his stuff."

The camp was just as Steve had described it. The quaint log cabin had a little front porch with long granite steps. It looked like every picture ever seen of an old woods camp, and it was topped off with the obligatory rusty smokestack.

Towering pines lined the far side of an impressively manicured front lawn. The lawn looked like a perfect place to lie out and sunbathe. The dooryard, which was about ten yards away from the west side of the cabin, was a dirt road that ran north past the cabin and out into the open woods.

"What do you think?" Steve asked Carla.

"I think it's cute, and if the inside is as charming as the outside, this is going to be a great little weekend!" she said cheerily. "I love the lawn. It looks professionally manicured."

"Whoa, whoa, whoa, whoa! This is a hunting camp! We don't use words like 'cute' or 'charming,' and most of all we never ever say"—Steve falsely bristled in disgust—"'manicured.' Have you lost your mind, woman?"

"I think you'll make it through the inadvertent use of adjectives there, Jungle Jim. So put a lid on it, and get my stuff! And be quick about it!" She double snapped her fingers in jest.

Steve thought again delightedly about how much he loved her.

As he let the dogs out of the enclosed bed of the silver truck, Carla went up to the log cabin for a closer inspection and to look in the side window. At first glance, everything looked neat and orderly. It was much cleaner and organized than she would have expected from some smelly, old hunting camp. She was interrupted in her thinking by a dog nose poking into her butt.

"Yes, Nick. It's still me. Now can you get your nose out of my bum?"

Nick was their seven-year-old male Rottweiler. He was a very good dog and Carla's "first child." He was about a hundred pounds, quite a hefty load when he sat on someone's lap. With a maternal smile, Carla turned around to pat her "first child." Meanwhile, their other dog, Stella, was sniffing around in the yard. Stella was also a Rottweiler, Nick's daughter, in fact. They had got her as part of the stud fee for breeding Nick a few years back. She had the cutest face ever on a Rottweiler, Carla and Steve were convinced. Stella was more rambunctious than her dad, however, and occasionally swiped snacks off a table and climbed onto furniture. Aside from these few indiscretions, she was a good girl (who also weighed about a hundred pounds).

As Steve made repeated trips from the rear of the truck to the porch with their gear and supplies, Carla walked around to the front of the building that was supposed to be their haven for the weekend. She noticed a large metal oval, hanging under the eave of the gable end of the roof, above the small porch.

"What is that for?" she asked Steve as he approached the porch with the last of their things from the truck. To his dismay, she was pointing to the large metallic oval hanging under the roof of the front porch.

"You don't want to know," Steve replied with the pained expression of "Oh no." in his eyes.

"No. Tell me," she replied, eager to know.

"Trust me, honey. You don't want to know."

Now impatient, Carla reaffirmed her original question and added, "Tell me, or I will kick you in the shin."

He loved when she got fiery. Anything could happen, and it was usually pretty exciting.

"Okay. But just for the record, I tried to warn you."

"This land became available through a foreclosure about fifty years ago. The original farm had been in the same family for about two hundred years but had fallen into disrepair and ruin. The bills and taxes piled up for years. On the day the foreclosure was to finally take place and the bank would take control, this creepy old farmer named Dain Longshadow, who was the last owner of the bankrupt farm and also the last surviving member of the original family, committed suicide inside of that oval out on the front grass."

"Oh my god!" Carla exclaimed in morbid fascination.

"Wait! You haven't heard all of the details. It gets better. When the deputies from the sheriff's department arrived to evict Dain, they found him kneeling on the ground in the front yard, facing westward, away from the camp. The deputies said that when the old man saw them approaching on foot, he screamed something that sounded like 'I'm coming with you, Father!' And at that moment, right in front of their eyes, the kneeling man raised an axe and buried it in himself. He chopped into the juncture of his own shoulder and neck, instantly killing himself. The horrified deputies ran up to him, but it was too late. They saw he was kneeling in the very same rusted oval that's hanging over your head." With a flippant, "I told you so" grin, Steve then said to his appalled wife, "Aren't you glad you asked?"

"That is absolutely morbid! Why the hell does Mason have it hanging over the front door of his cabin?"

"He feels it's part of the history of this old place."

"A twisted and macabre history, if you ask me," Carla said with a foreboding shudder.

FIRST-NIGHT CREEPS

After a dinner of grilled steak and summer corn on the cob, they cleaned up and settled in to enjoy the beautiful early summer Maine evening—warm, relatively free of bugs, and with a spectacular sunset. It was cozy and romantic—perfect. A sense of romance to come was in the air, and they were both quietly looking forward to it, enjoying wine and light reading. Steve had split a fair amount of wood. The exertion was helping him wind down and putting him in a mellow, relaxed mood. He was kicking himself for not thinking of doing this trip to Maine with Carla before. He never thought she would be so agreeable about rustic camp life, but she seemed to be doing just fine. She seemed to be actually enjoying herself.

Damn, she is beautiful! he thought.

After about an hour, they started to turn in. Steve let the dogs out for their evening outing; Carla started to get the bed ready. He threw a log in the small fire he had started in the wood stove after dinner, let the dogs back in, went over to the bed, and slid in next to Carla, who was nice, warm, receptive, and, most importantly, naked. They intertwined like they were made of fluid, not flesh and blood.

Things are moving along perfectly, he thought.

At that very moment, as if to prove him wrong, a violent gust of wind shook the camp. With the creepiest moan, it rattled the dishes in the cabinets and slammed against the west wall of the camp. The squall sounded tortured and angry—and unnatural. The sound intensified with the heightening blast of the air rushing in.

For a moment, Steve thought the camp would collapse under the pressure of the gale or at least the windows would shatter.

Stella started to howl and bay at the freight train-like gust that was assaulting the camp.

Then it just stopped. Nothing. Silence. No residual wind, and no wind through the trees. Nothing. Just silence.

Steve and Carla were clutched onto each other like vices. Without realizing it she had sunk her nails into his back, deep enough to draw blood. He did not notice it at first. He had one arm around her back, and the other was in a half-pushup position, suspending both of them up off the bed about four inches. They were frozen in position when they heard a loud metallic *klang* on the front porch. Carla let out a stifled shriek when she heard it. Stella yelped and scurried under the bed.

"What the hell was that?" Carla gasped.

"I think it was the big ring that was hanging over the door. It must have fallen off of its nail and knocked crap over on the porch, if I had to guess," Steve replied with a little grin.

"Not that, you jerk! What the hell was that gust of wind?" she said with a touch of impatience and a tad of fear.

"I have no idea or experience with such things, but I have heard of these things happening in the mountains sometimes. They're called microbursts, and they're like mini tornadoes or hurricanes. I have no better guess for you than that," he explained as he climbed out of bed and realized his back was sore in a couple of places.

"What in the hell did you do to me when you grabbed onto me?"

As he turned to the door, she saw what looked like eight little crescent moon-shaped wounds on his back. Some were actually weeping small trails of blood.

Thank God he has a high tolerance for pain because that has got to hurt, she thought, snickering to herself.

Steve made his way over to the door and opened it slowly. He peered through the door and grabbed a flashlight that one minute before was swaying from the nail it was hanging on next to the door. He turned on the light and shined it onto the small front porch. Everything seemed normal, and he stepped out onto the front porch to assess the damage. Nothing seemed to be destroyed, just a little disarrayed from the ring crashing down onto the porch. He shined the flashlight into the front yard of the camp and saw the ring was out on the grass about twenty yards from the front porch.

It rolled a long damn way, he thought. He flashed the light around the yard. Nothing was awry, as far as he could tell.

"What's going on out there?" Carla said from the confines of the bed inside.

"Nothing really, believe it or not. There's nothing out of place except the ring out here on the grass. I'm just going to hang it up and come back in," Steve replied.

"Well, get your naked butt back in here and warm me up!" she yelled.

Until that moment, he did not realize he was naked in the front yard of the camp. There was no nip in the air to speak of and not a cloud in the sky. He could see all of the stars. It was so crystal clear he thought he could see every star in the universe.

Steve picked up the ring and carried it onto the porch. As he was carrying it, he noticed something he thought was unusual. He expected the ring to be a little colder than the surrounding environment, but it felt warm, just a little warmer than the current temperature. Not being a metallurgist, Steve could not remember if metal conserved energy and the heat that it was exposed to or if it dissipated quickly.

It must have reserved some radiant heat or something it was exposed to during the day, he thought. *Maybe it was in direct contact with the sunlight. Who knows? Who cares? This thing creeps me out.*

He climbed up onto the railing and hung the ring back up on its nail. Just touching the ring gave him the heebie-jeebies, never mind carrying the thing.

He jumped down and went inside, then turned around to check the front yard one last time from inside the safety of the cabin. He noticed something that seemed peculiar: no branches on the grass in the front yard. Not one.

A gale like that should have broken something off of the pine trees that border the eastern and southern edges of the front of the camp, he thought. *Hell, a force like that should have snapped a few of the trees themselves, never mind some of the branches.* But nothing seemed disturbed in the beam of the flashlight on the front yard. Not a pencil-thin branch. It didn't even look like there were any extra pine needles in the front.

That's odd, he thought. He decided to give it a more thorough inspection in the daylight of morning because he was sure there must have been some damage or something down after that little "Long Shadows hurricane."

He didn't know why, but he felt compelled to put both of the locks on the door, just to feel safe.

As he walked back to the bed, he told Carla about the first microburst he had ever heard of over at Waterville Valley Ski Resort in New Hampshire. It came down and knocked over every tree on a three-acre swath right on the side of the mountain. That happened back in the early eighties. The microburst didn't bother anything else. Some witnesses said it looked like a mini tornado right there on the side of the mountain; others said they just saw this huge gust of wind come and blow down the trees like they were matchsticks. All of the witnesses said it lasted fewer than ten seconds. Some said it lasted fewer than five. They all said it made an awful noise that most described as it sounded like a freight train. Steve read all about it in an article in one of the local publications at the mountain. He was so interested in it because he saw firsthand the devastation it created, and also because he thought it should be impossible for tornadoes to form in mountainous areas. Tornadoes need wide-open flat areas like those in the Great Plains and the tornado alley of the US Midwest.

His quasi explanation was working, even though the sound of this microburst event was not like a freight train, but more like some agonized demon from hell with hemorrhoids, broadcast on one of the loudest intercom systems in the world.

He could see that Carla was starting to relax again. She had a look in her eyes that he was familiar with and liked to see.

Just as he was about to climb into bed, he heard Stella whimper from underneath the bed. He got down on his knees and looked under there.

"Come on, girl," Steve said. "It's all over. There's nothing to be worried about anymore."

Stella wouldn't budge. He reached under the bed to pat her, and something happened that he would never have expected in a million years: Stella bared her teeth and snapped at him viciously. Steve was caught so off guard, he barely got his hand out of the way in time.

That would have sucked, he thought. He was amazed at Stella's behavior. He didn't know whether to whip her ass or to let her be. He decided on the latter.

"She must be really shook up," he told Carla.

Carla's eyes were the size of saucers; she could not believe that Stella had snapped. Stella was always the mellowest dog. Steve could read Carla's mind from the look on her face.

"Don't worry about it too much, honey. She just had a good scare. In the morning, she'll be back to normal. You watch," he assured her. "Now where were we before all of this excitement started to happen and derailed my efforts to collect me a piece of you?" he said with a smirk. "Oh, and by the way, if you could leave the rest of my flesh on my body and not use your fingernails as individual filet knives, I would be all right with that."

"I thought you liked the rough stuff," she quipped.

He smiled broadly and grabbed hold of her. He was about to make her his woman again and burn off some of the adrenaline and testosterone in abundance after the wind event.

Carla responded energetically in a heightened state of arousal in the throes of their lovemaking. Everything was more intense and responsive.

When they finished and were intertwined in a perspiring postclimactic heap in the bed, she said in a gasping voice, "That was the most intense experience I've ever had in bed. I don't know how you did it, but it felt like I had ten hands all over my body at the end there. I hope you can duplicate that little trick again. That was awesome!"

As Steve lay on top of her trying to catch his breath, he thought she must have really been wound up from the wind incident because his hands were on the bed frame trying to get leverage. She sure outdid herself tonight.

As they lay together slipping gently into sleep, they heard *snap!* There were snap sounds in the kitchen, obviously from mousetraps.

"What is that now?" Carla asked plaintively.

"Just mousetraps," Steve said, yawning. "This camp is over a hundred years old. Mason has never mentioned a problem with mice, but it's to be expected in a building this old in the middle of the Maine woods. Just go to sleep. They won't hurt you. They were probably upset by our little wind event and are trying to get resettled. I have got to hand it to this little camp, though. This old girl is built tough. She just took a mighty shot to the ribs, and she stood through it without a problem. I expect the same out of you when you get to that age." Steve snickered.

Carla's reply was to elbow him in the ribs and roll over, taking all of the covers with her to her side of the bed.

She is crazy about me, Steve thought, chortling to himself as he lay completely naked with no covers on his side of the bed.

Steve woke with a start to Carla kicking the blankets off and screeching.

"Something just went right across my body while I was sleeping. I felt it go from my breast down toward my crotch when I realized there was something in the bed," she screamed.

"It was probably just a mouse. Let's go back to sleep," Steve mumbled.

"No. It was heavier than any damn mouse that I ever felt. It felt bigger than a rat, for Christ's sake, and it was under the covers. I was half-asleep, but I still felt it plain as day."

"Are you sure you weren't dreaming or something? I mean, we have two full-grown Rottweiler's here at our feet. Don't you think they might have noticed something as big as a rat sneaking around two feet away in the same room they're sleeping in? If a moth farts outside at home, they'll bark like it's Armageddon."

Steve was tired and starting to get irritable. Plus, he was lying right next to her, and he didn't feel or see anything. Just to be sure, they took off all of the covers and shook them out. Then they thoroughly inspected the bed. Nothing, just as Steve expected.

It must have shown on his face as they were remaking the bed because just as they were lying back down for the third time that evening, Carla said as if to justify her actions, "Maybe you're right, and I was just dreaming it, but it still felt very real. If one more thing like this happens tonight, we are going to the local motel. I don't care how tired you are, what time it is, or how much it costs. Understand?"

"If I agree, will you just go back to sleep?"

"Yes," she huffed.

"Good. Good night, honey," he said. "Don't let the bed rats bite."

"You idiot," she growled.

Goddamn, do I love her! Steve thought, as he drifted back to sleep.

CARLA WALKS THE DOGS

After their creepy night, Steve and Carla somehow managed to sleep and didn't awaken until nine. Carla was quick to shake off the events of the night before and get moving. Steve was still groggy and rolling around under the covers, hoping not to be disturbed.

Carla popped out of bed.

"I'm going to take the dogs and go for a walk around the land," she announced. "There are plenty of trails, and I shouldn't get too lost. What do you think there, sleepyhead? Do you want to join me?"

"No, thanks. I still have a lot of wood to split and would like to get ahead of it. If you want, this evening, I could take a walk with you and show you some beautiful places off of the property," Steve replied sleepily. "Just be careful of bears," he warned. "You shouldn't have any problems having the dogs with you. Just keep talking to them, so if there is something out there, it will hear you coming and leave before you would have any encounters."

"Are you kidding me? Are there really that many animals out here that I have to worry about? Is this Maine's *Wild Kingdom*? Should I expect to see Tarzan or something?"

"Don't overreact. I just like to be prepared, and I want you to be prepared and as safe as possible. The chances are pretty slim you'll see anything more than a cricket. And if you should bump into Tarzan out there running around in a loincloth, I fear more for his safety than for yours. He's going to have to run for his life if you get him in your crosshairs out there."

Her response was to hit him in the face with a pillow. "You're an idiot, but I love you despite yourself," she said in a feigned maternal tone.

Carla set about tidying up the cabin. Steve hopped out of bed and groped her rigorously from head to toe before he started getting dressed.

"I think we're probably going to have to have a repeat performance of last night's romp if you keep looking this good to me," he said with a devilish grin.

"Without the camp blowing over and mice doing a conga line across my torso, yeah, I could possibly be interested, *if* you behave," she mockingly admonished. *As long as you do that hands-all-over-the-body thing again, you can have me whenever the hell you want me*, she thought.

Stella was underfoot as Carla was going out the door.

"That's a good girl. I didn't notice you were out of your little bed cave. You're a good little girl, aren't you, baby? It's good to see you back to your old self."

Stella was wagging her entire butt and body; she was so happy to be getting attention.

"She seems to be back to herself," Carla said.

"Yeah, she just needed to sleep it off, like we all did, actually," Steve responded.

As soon as Carla opened the door, Stella and Nick charged out into the front yard for their morning constitutionals. They were good dogs. They listened well, stayed close, never took off, and were excellent companions to one another.

As Steve surveyed the dogs through the open door, he noticed that even in the bright morning sunlight, there were no extra branches or limbs down in the front yard.

Everything seemed fairly normal, for now.

"I'm going to follow the major logging roads and try to climb that little peak out there," Carla said, pointing her finger to the southwest at a little knoll about a quarter mile away.

"Just stick to the major logging roads, and don't wander off any clearly marked paths," Steve said. "These are big woods, and you can get turned around pretty easily if you stray too far. If you stick to the trails, you should be just fine. It looks like a beautiful morning for a walk, and besides, with you not bothering me constantly, I might actually be able to get some work done around here."

She shot him a look and said, "Thanks a lot, Mr. Smooth."

"Seriously. Stick to the trails, and I'll expect you back around noon," he said with a tone of concern.

"Yes, Dad," she groaned.

As Steve watched her heading up the trail, with the dogs running around and sniffing everything, he was struck again by how naturally beautiful Carla was and how she was everything he was looking for in a woman, wife, and partner. *Goddamn, do I love her!* he thought, smiling to himself as he turned around to prepare for the day's work.

Carla was enjoying stretching her legs in the Maine woods. She was moving along briskly, working up a little sweat and breathing in the clean, unspoiled air. The dogs were leading the way about twenty feet in front of her. Occasionally, one peeled back to get a quick pat of attention and reassurance that all was well.

After about twenty minutes, they were just about to start climbing the little knoll when something caught her attention in the woods off to her left, about seventy to eighty yards away. She wondered what it was, thinking that it better not be a goddamn bear. As she quietly peered through the woods, the dogs stopped as if they had been given a command and faced the woods in the same direction in which she was looking.

Then it happened. She saw movement. Whatever it was, it was big.

GONE

In the twenty minutes that Carla and the dogs had been gone, Steve had been able to produce a sizeable pile of split wood. He was in a full sweat and enjoying the experience more than he expected he would. It was a combination of being able to see the fruits of his labor in the growing pile of split wood and the fresh Maine air, which was very different from what he experienced in his sales job. Every workday, that job took him in and out of the stuffiest, antiseptic-infused, bacteria-saturated hospital air. Plus, the outdoor work pushed his muscles in a way that was more useful and different from what any gym equipment in the world could do, and the pure physical labor didn't have any bullshit attached to it. All of it contributed to Steve's sense of well-being. It was just a great morning to be alive, and he was getting the most out of it. Last night's toss in the hay didn't hurt any, either.

He had worked up enough of a sweat in the short time he had been working that he had to take a break to remove his T-shirt. As he was wiping the sweat from his brow, he saw the ring over the porch fall from the eave again with a loud *klang* and roll out into the front yard to almost the exact spot it was in the night before. He noticed there wasn't the slightest hint of a breeze in the air.

I'm going to get another nail for that pain in the ass ring before I leave, he thought. *Still, all is right with the world.*

———◆———

Dead silent and still, Carla peered into the woods, trying to see what was moving through the brush. Whatever it was, it wasn't moving toward her, but it seemed to be moving in the same direction she was. She could see only movement, not shapes or colors.

What is that? she wondered.

Then she realized it was a person, which raised the hackles on her neck. She couldn't explain why, but seeing that it was a person made her nervous. She caught a glimpse of what looked like a very faded flannel shirt. The figure looked like a man, and it looked as if he was wearing coveralls or overalls that were faded almost to white. She could tell they had been brown or tan at an earlier time. He looked to her as if he could have stepped out of a picture from the Great Depression. She never saw his face, and he quickly blended into the trees again and was gone. He had a swaying, awkward way of moving through the woods like a breeze.

Carla wondered what he could be doing there because she knew Mason has his land posted and, as Steve had told her, is very particular about who comes on his land.

Just then, a loud *crack* came out of the woods from the direction in which she had last seen the trespasser going. It sounded like a sizeable branch of a tree had broken off, and it made her jump in her tracks. The goose bumps rose all over her body, and for the first time, she felt the beginnings of fear. She tried to convince herself that she had nothing to be afraid of from some smelly old man who didn't see her and wasn't even coming in her direction.

Then another more distant noise of a branch being snapped came from the woods.

That was it for Stella; it was all she could take. She raced off into the woods toward the sound of the breaking branches and the stranger.

"Stella!" Carla hissed loudly but not so loud that the intruder might hear her.

The dog did not respond but kept bounding away off into the woods toward the unknown outsider. Nick reared back as if to take off after Stella, and Carla snapped at him, "Nick! Don't even think about it! Sit down!"

He sat right in place but kept focused on Stella as she ran off into the woods.

Overcoming her own fear of the situation, Carla shouted, "Stella, get back here!"

The dog did not slow her pace. Carla knew she must have heard the command, but she paid absolutely no attention and just kept running deeper into the woods. It was so unlike her to disobey, especially when given loud commands. She was always quick to please and so well-behaved. It was as if the dog had gone deaf or was in a trance.

"Stella, come here!"

Carla simultaneously ordered and pleaded. But Stella didn't stop and even seemed to be moving more quickly. Now Carla was afraid. She did not know what she was scared of, but she wasn't going to go running off into the woods to get lost forever and have her carcass discovered with a dog skeleton lying next to it by some hunter.

The strange man in the woods didn't look like any clear threat, but Carla was in a strange environment and frightened. She did not want to attract his attention. Was she afraid of being raped, abducted, or, worse, murdered? She didn't think so. Her fear seemed to be much deeper than that, almost primal. The mysterious sense of fear was growing within her and making her more alarmed by the second. She couldn't explain it, and she didn't like the anxiety she was feeling in the pit of her stomach. Her intuition was telling her to not draw any extra attention to herself out there. But why?

The only thing she knew with certainty was that her dog was not listening, and she felt very small in the vast woods of northern Maine. She just wanted to get her dog to listen and come back. Then she would hustle and get Steve to come out and see what the hell was going on. She wanted to find out who he was and what he was doing here.

Her last attempt at verbally retrieving the dog was a shrill frantic scream.

"Stel-la!"

It went completely unnoticed by the racing Rottweiler. The last thing Carla saw of the dog was Stella leaping over a sizeable blown-down tree. She was gone.

GOING AFTER STELLA

Steve had just hopped down from putting the ring back up on its nail. While he was hanging it, he had thoroughly inspected the nail the ring was hanging on. It did not seem to need replacing. It was a stout and sturdy spike that was driven well into the log of the eave under the gable of the cabin and was anchored well. He knew that because he hung most of his weight from the spike, and it didn't budge. It was sticking out of the log at least four inches, which was more than enough to support the ring, and was hammered in upward at a forty-five-degree angle. By all accounts, the damn ring shouldn't be falling off, although the little hurricane the night before was strong enough to have blown the walls down. The bottom half might need to be secured, but Steve was not going to do that without first consulting Mason, who was particular about such things.

If he didn't like it that way, Steve thought, *Mason would be a pissed off.*

As he was standing there looking up at the spike and ring, he heard Carla coming down the path crying.

Oh, shit! he thought and headed up the path toward his crying wife. He ran up the trail thinking, *Please, God, let her be all right!*

He rounded a bend and saw Carla jogging and crying, trying to wipe her eyes with both hands and holding them over her eyes, running blindly much of the time.

"What's the matter? Are you all right?" he called out to her.

She pulled her hands down at the sound of his voice and started to cry harder and run faster toward him.

"She's gone! She wouldn't listen! She just went running after him and wouldn't come back! I called her and called her, and she wouldn't come back." She continued weeping.

"Who's gone?" he said, tensely.

"Stella. She just took off into the woods after him, and she wouldn't come back."

"Him who? Who are you talking about?" Steve asked with an uneasy feeling in his stomach.

"There was some weird old guy out there in the woods. She just took off after him and never came back," she said, sobbing.

"Did this guy attack you or something? Did he come after you?"

"No. Nothing like that. I don't know if he even saw us. He was like eighty yards away in the woods when I saw him moving out in the distance. He never actually bothered us. He never looked at us. He didn't even run from us. I didn't see him for long, just a split second. But I got this disturbing feeling in the pit of my stomach. I just didn't like the way he moved. It was like he was gliding through the forest. The whole thing was unnerving, and I don't know why. All I know is that I have had enough of this place, and I want to go home."

Steve knew he needed to calm her down, help her think clearly, and ease her stress. He thought she just had a case of the "willies" from being in the woods alone. She bumped into someone she was not expecting, and that threw her into a panic. He wasn't about to try to get her to see it his way because of her highly agitated state. She would just insist on leaving. He wanted her to realize for herself, once she calmed down, how she was overreacting. Once she looked at it objectively, he thought, she would agree with his view without being embarrassed and defensive. The goings-on of the night before and the warning he gave her this morning probably primed her for this little breakdown.

He started by taking her into his arms and saying gently, "Eeeaassyy, easy, easy, easy. Just calm yourself. You know I would never let anything happen to you." He stroked her hair, and she started to calm down. Her sobbing slowed as she felt the protection of his arms. He started to wipe the hair and tears away from her face. Her eyes were bloodshot, and her tear ducts were inflamed. He was genuinely concerned for her—and for Stella.

I'll find her later, he thought with a sigh. *I hope she's all right. But if our unwanted guest did anything to hurt her, I'll bend his legs the wrong way.*

After a few minutes, Carla said more calmly, "I didn't know what to do. Stella just took off like a shot and would not listen or come when I called to her. She just took off into the woods after that man, and she never came back. I called and called and called for her, but she never came. I listened to see if I could hear her barking, but there was no sound. I hope she's all right. I didn't want to go into the woods and get lost like you warned me, but it was more than that. I was scared, very scared, and I don't know why. That old man completely spooked me, and I was so scared I almost couldn't move. I know it makes no sense, but I was, and now because of me, we might have lost Stella."

She grimaced as her eyes started to fill up again with tears.

"You did the right thing," he assured her. "Nothing would have been gained by you charging off into the woods. As for Stella, she's a big girl, and nothing in these woods is going to want to mess with her. She's a big dog, and not even a bear would want to mess with her if it didn't have to."

Carla was getting back to normal; he wanted more clarity about exactly what had happened in the woods with the strange man.

"So slowly tell me everything that happened step by step, from when I watched you walk up the path and until you returned. I want every detail you can remember, no matter how insignificant you might think it is. Don't skip a thing."

Five minutes later, she had gone through every detail she could remember—the air, the smells, the noises, her reactions, the dog's reactions, her unexplainable fear, everything. Once she heard herself telling the entire story in minute detail, she began to realize how illogical she must sound to him. She started to feel embarrassed, and Steve sensed her apprehension. He let her finish and responded in a way to let her know everything was all right. He gave her a big hug and kissed her on the lips.

"After everything that has happened in the last eighteen hours, I would say you had a natural reaction to all of the weird stuff going on around here. You go for a walk to clear your head and put all of that creepy stuff behind you. You go off in an area you are unfamiliar with, in the big woods where you have no experience, nervous from the warning I gave you. Then you bump into some peculiar old man who doesn't belong there in the first place and your dog takes off. That sounds like enough crap to get a good case of the heebie-jeebies. Don't you think?"

"I guess you're right."

She didn't seem to be feeling embarrassed and seemed to see that her fear of the old man in the woods was mostly unfounded. Still, they had to go find Stella and see if they could find the stranger. Steve would have called Mason about the old man, but there was no cell-phone reception out here. He didn't feel like traveling back into town twenty minutes both ways to find out something he was sure had very little impact on their current situation of having a lost dog.

"Do you mind walking me back to the area where Stella took off? She's probably just sniffing around somewhere close by there."

"I'll take you there, but I'm going to be right next to you when you look for her. I'm not staying out on the trail alone. I don't want to feel like some worm on a hook with some sinister, strange old guy lurking around out in those woods."

"That's fine," Steve replied with a chortle.

Carla retraced her steps along the logging trails. It wasn't too difficult. If she became unsure of where she was, Steve could pick up her tracks and send her in the correct direction.

"We're here," Carla blurted tensely. She was surprised they were already there, but this spot was unmistakable in her mind. She saw the blowdown that Stella leaped over and the woods that the trespasser had melted into. This was definitely the spot.

She recounted the story to Steve in a highlighted fashion. She pointed to the woods where she first saw the movement and the glimpses of the old man. She pointed out where Stella and Nick were standing when Stella took off. She stood in the same spot where she was frozen in place just an hour ago. Her hackles rose again at the back of her neck. She didn't want to feed into her fear or tell Steve and feel embarrassed again. *Why does this place give me the willies so much?* she thought.

Steve surveyed the area, trying to get his bearings and make heads or tails of the landscape. To the best of his understanding of the layout of Mason's land, Steve thought they were well within the boundaries of the property. They were somewhere in the southwest corner of the land, but the closest property line still had to be four hundred to five hundred yards away to the south. The main road that leads to Mason's camp was down that way. It was all swamp—huge webs of thorns, brambles, and every type of nasty foliage he could imagine in the woods. The swamp had some deep holes and was impassable. He knew that because he had tried to hunt in this area in the past, but it was so miserable in there that it motivated him to leave and never go back in. It was a tough swamp that forced Steve out in less than a half hour. He made at least ten attempts to get in or around that area. At best, he penetrated fifty yards deep before running into some form of waterlogged, thorn-infested impasse.

"You're telling me some old man just slinked into those woods over there like he was skipping down the road? That is the most hellish swamp I have ever dealt with in all my time in the woods. I couldn't get more than fifty yards into it, struggling all the way, and some old salt just glided in and out of it. I'm impressed. Mason doesn't even try to go in there anymore because he has had such bad luck trying to navigate it. This old-timer must be from the area or from one of the other camps way up the road and is very familiar with this entire place."

"It looked like he just kind of evaporated into the woods. One second he was there, the next, he was gone. I told you it was eerie. He just kind of drifted through the trees and was gone," she recalled.

"I'm going to go over there and see what I can see. Do you want to come?" Steve said.

"You're damn right! I'm not staying here alone. I told you I was going everywhere you went. Right on your hip! That's as far as I want to be from you," she replied.

As they stepped off of the path and into the brush, Steve could tell that Nick had picked up what was probably Stella's scent trail. The scent was heading in the direction of the blown-down tree. He hoped to himself that it would be a little easier if Nick could stay on Stella's trail.

Nick reached the blowdown before Carla and Steve, stopped on this side of the tree, and sniffed into the air. As Steve got over to him, he realized how big the blow-down was. It was over his head, and he was six foot two.

"You're telling me Stella jumped over this tree in a single bound? Are you sure this is the right place?"

"Yes! I'm sure!" Carla said impatiently.

"All right. Don't get upset. I asked a simple question. I just didn't know she had it in her. I know she can run like the wind, but I didn't know she had such rise."

"It looked like she was running as fast as she could by the time she reached this spot." Carla pointed to the top of the blow-down.

Steve looked down in the mud and saw distinct dog prints, running dog prints. He followed them back from the tree at least ten yards. They were coming straight from where they had been standing and headed directly to where Carla said the dog went. Steve followed them back to the tree again. The last tracks he could see were bounding tracks, with a characteristic pattern he had seen many time before while in the woods. The feet were wide, and the toes were splayed wide open. He knew that it's what an animal does when it's trying to grip the earth and get leverage. The tracks were deep, and the mud was almost thrown out of them, indicating great speed and effort. It was obvious this was the place where Stella had soared over the tree.

He couldn't see around the tree to the other side. Carla also was trying to peer around it, but to no avail. Steve saw a place where he could force his way through. He grabbed a branch from the spot he came through and swung himself up onto the main body of the blowdown. When he got up on the fallen tree, he saw something that puzzled him. For as far as he could see, it was swamp—a deep, sepulchral area of swamp—with dark black pools, waterlogged rotting stumps, and soggy holes. He half-expected to see Swamp Thing. There didn't seem to be any dry ground in the boggy quagmire to provide footing for anyone. The trees were mostly dead. The trunks of the ones that were alive, the swamp maples and such, went straight down into the water and muck. Directly on the other side of the blowdown was a deep murky pool of swamp water that was twenty feet wide and probably eighty feet long.

Landing in that fetid water should have snapped Stella right out of it, he thought. *And what the hell was this guy walking on out there? He must have been wading through the water for some reason. It would explain his strange, lurching gait.*

"What can you see?" Carla asked anxiously. "Can you see any signs of Stella?"

Steve broke off a branch that was about eight feet long from the blown-down tree.

"Well?" Carla pressed, annoyed.

"Just hold on a minute!" Steve was starting to get irritated with the entire situation. None of it made any sense to him. He took the branch and stuck it down into the murky water. The branch reached down at least five feet before he started to feel the mud on the bottom. He was lying on his belly on the main body of the blowdown with about a foot of the branch left in his hand when it finally got lodged in the mud enough to stand on its own. Granted he stuck the branch into the rank pool at an angle, but that was at least seven feet. If the branch was standing upright, it would mean that the black water was at least five feet deep, and that was before the two feet or so of muck at the bottom, he realized.

He wondered how in the hell the guy got around in there. Did he have a canoe or something?

Steve stood up and brushed himself off. He did not want to alarm Carla. As he jumped down from the tree, he shared with her his assessment of the situation, the optimistic version and not the version he felt in his gut.

"As far as I can see, it's pretty much a boggy woods swamp in there. I can't see any sign of Stella, but that doesn't mean anything. She could already be waiting at the camp for us when we get back. It does look like pretty hard going in there with swamp and thorn bushes everywhere. It would be a lot easier for an animal to move around in that mire, much easier than a man who doesn't know the layout of the interior of the swamp. I'd rather skirt the swamp and call for her than try to trudge through it. I'll be able to hear her if she's in distress and go in after her if I need to."

"The old creep moved around in there like he was on a path or something," Carla said, her stress evident in her voice.

"He must be from the area and be very familiar with this swamp. Let's start heading back to the camp, and we'll call for Stella. If she's not already back at the camp, she'll probably come running out of the woods like nothing ever happened. In the meantime, I'll leave my shirt here on the ground. It's covered in my scent. She'll probably come right to this spot and be lying on it in the morning. It's an old rabbit-hunting trick that works for beagles that take off after rabbits or on deer trails and don't come back," he assured her.

"Stella is no little beagle, and the thought of her spending the night out here in the woods just breaks my heart."

"Again, she'll probably be back at the camp by now, and if she isn't—well, think about it—she always lies all over our dirty clothes at home. Besides, she's a big girl, and she can take care of herself. Remember what we talked about earlier? Nothing's going to want to mess with her out here. She's too dangerous. I promise you, if she smells this shirt, she'll be right here tomorrow morning. We'll find her safe and sound eventually."

———————◆———————

"Stel-la! Come here, girl!"

They worked their way back to camp, calling the entire time. They were looking for any sign of the lost dog, but to no avail. By the time they got back to camp, it was a little before noon. Carla was weary and ragged from the events of the morning.

"Why don't we have some lunch, and I'll go out and look for her after," Steve said. "She probably will show up here on her own, and I'm sure if she smells a couple of hamburgers being grilled, she'll come running, knowing her. I think that's the dog's one true motivation—food and how to get more of it." He was trying to break up the melancholy mood that was settling over the camp. "It's only noon. There are about eight hours of sunlight left. Chances are she'll show up on her own."

"I'm not all that hungry," Carla said drearily. "I just want to take a nap, and we'll go out and look for her after. I only need about a half hour, and then we can go."

"Honey, why don't you just take a nap, and I'll go look for her on my own for a while," he said as he got up and went over to Mason's supply closet. "I can cover a lot more ground if I'm on my own, and it would be good to have someone here in case she returns, or I should say, when she returns."

"Absolutely not! There's no way you're going to leave me here while Stella is lost out in those woods. Especially while Mister Mcfriggin' creepy is somewhere out there doing God only knows what!"

"I'll leave Nick with you, and you know he would tear apart anything that would try to come across that doorway." He paused for a moment as he looked through the supply closet. "Just what I'm looking for!" He held up two radios. In the closet, he saw that Mason had left behind a twenty-pack of AA batteries that were specifically for the radios. "Mason sure does come prepared. These are perfect. They're two-way radios that have a five-mile range. We'll be able to keep in constant contact on the entire property with these. So if anything happens that you don't like, if you need me for anything, or if Stella comes back, you can call me, and I can be back here in a moment."

"How long of a moment?" she replied warily.

"A quick moment. The property is a hundred acres, but I could get across it in a couple minutes. It's not that large."

"If I hear one cricket chirp I don't like, I'm going to be calling you to get back here. I'm overtired, and this place has my nerves shot."

"You'll be fine. It's broad daylight. Lock the door, and get some rest. Nick will be here with you, and if you need me, just give me a call. I don't think old man creepy will come a knocking because if he is so familiar with the property, he must have seen Mason's No Trespassing signs, and I'm sure he knows there are people here. Why else would he stick to that miserable old swamp where he knows no one in his right mind would travel? He was trying to go about his business without being detected," Steve reasoned.

"It's 'his business' out there that has me concerned."

"He might have some old distillery out there, or maybe he was poaching. These people out here in these woods hunt all year round in order to feed their families. I have no problem with that. We'll just leave him alone, and he'll leave us alone." At least, that's what Steve hoped.

"All right, but I want you back well before dark. Do you understand? I don't want to be in this ramshackle old shack with you lost in the woods. I would freak out! Get it?"

"I get it!" he responded.

With that, Steve packed the backpack he always brought with him into the woods. It had everything he would need and then some.

"Hopefully, this won't take me too long, but I like to be prepared," he told her. He saw she was wondering why he would need all of that gear. "Prepare for the worst and hope for the best, I always say."

He threw the backpack over his shoulder, stuffed the radio in the front thigh pocket of his olive drab cargo shorts, put his Red Sox cap on, gave Carla a kiss, and headed out the door.

"Please be careful," she pleaded. She knew he was very competent in the woods. As a matter of fact he was the Tarzan, minus the loincloth, who had always taken good care of her. He always made her feel protected. She knew his capabilities, but something was still making her feel uncomfortable about the whole situation, and she couldn't help it.

"I will be, and don't worry. If you want to call me on the radio every once in a while just to check up, I'll let you know my progress. If I find her, I'll call you immediately and let you know. Okay?" he said, trying to reassure her.

As Steve headed down the path toward the entrance and the gate, he knew she should be watching him with anticipation. As he reached the gate, he turned toward the camp, and sure enough, she was standing in the door with her arms crossed in front of her for security. They were about 150 yards apart. He reached into his pocket and got the radio.

"How's it working so far?" he said into the radio. He saw her turn around and go inside to grab the radio.

After a moment, her voice came over the radio clear and strong. "Pretty good for now. Your voice is actually clearer than I would have expected."

"Okay," he responded. As he faced the cabin looking at her come back to the doorway, he pointed to his left up the road, which was west, and said, "I'm going to go up along the road to see if I can find her tracks in the dirt. Then once I reach Mason's border with the road, I'm going to head north back up into the property. I plan to circumvent the swamp and end up back at the camp before dusk. If I cut her tracks or see anything, I'll give you a call and let you know of any developments."

"All right, honey," she said into the radio.

He put the radio back in his pocket, gave her a wave, and headed west up the dirt road that led the five miles back into the woods to Route 77 and civilization.

He had been scouting up the road for about ten minutes when Carla called on the radio for a progress report.

"Seen anything yet?" she asked.

"No, nothing yet, but you made it about nine minutes longer than I would have expected," he jibed. "How is it back at camp?"

"Pretty slow. Nick's asleep. I ate some cheese and crackers, had a soda, and now I'm starting to feel a little weary. I think I'm going to lie down and take a nap."

"I think that's a fine idea. Just get some rest, and I'll give you a call if anything changes. Nick will be your ears if Stella comes back."

"I will. Ten-four or whatever it is you're supposed to say when you sign off of one of these things," she wisecracked.

"Just say, 'See you later.' That would work just fine for me."

"See you later," she said into the radio. She put the contraption down on the table, shuffled over to the bed, got under the covers, and was asleep before the sheets were settled.

Steve went back to trying to track down Stella. The only tracks he saw were from their tire marks from the day before. He didn't see any dog tracks or any human tracks; in fact, he didn't see any animal tracks at all—not even the track of a mouse crossing the road. He thought that odd.

Up ahead, he saw the pink surveyor's tape tied around every fifth tree or so that marked the boundary of Mason's property. The taped trees eventually disappeared as he looked north. In between the taped trees, posted signs warned against trespassing on the land. On each sign, Mason had handwritten his name and address. Steve knew those signs encircled the property. He thought that must have been quite an undertaking.

As he reached the southwestern border of the property, he knew the swamp was north, northeast of his current position.

One good thing, he thought, was Stella had not crossed the road. *At least she hasn't crossed this road and is still north of here. That removes one border I don't have to worry about.*

He left the road and started to head north along the posted signs and surveyors tape to see if he could get around the swamp and get his bearings. The farther away from the road he went, the thicker and darker the woods became.

After following his current course for about ten minutes, all the while checking for tracks or sign of the missing dog, something off in the woods caught his attention east-northeast of him. He wasn't sure what it was—movement, an animal, Stella? He knew he saw something. He froze in place and observed. Then he saw it. It was just a flash, but he saw it plain as day. It was the old trespasser that Carla had seen before.

He caught just a glimpse of the man and couldn't tell if he was old, but he was just as Carla had described—tattered, old flannel shirt, completely faded work coveralls. As best as Steve could make out, the man was tall and lanky, probably looking for dead trees to cut up to heat his cabin. The woodsman probably realized that no one would come in there looking for heating wood or for any other reason and bother him. He'd probably been doing it for years. Steve did note that it seemed like the old codger just glided through the trees.

He was about one hundred yards away when Steve saw him for that brief moment. He believed he had not been detected by the woodsman and stayed in place for a minute or so to see if he could catch another glimpse of him or get some idea of what the old guy was up to. After not seeing anymore of him, Steve cautiously and quietly worked his way over to where he had last seen the old man. When he finally arrived to where he thought that was, he settled down for a moment by the stump of a tree and assessed the situation. He knew he was in the right spot because in his mind, he had marked the tree he was now leaning against.

He looked around in the dirt and mud for tracks but couldn't find any. Much more to his dismay, he realized he was at the edge of the swamp. He was on the southern border now, unlike earlier that day, when he was on the northern border. Thorny green vines formed a barrier that was impenetrable to any human without getting cut to ribbons, anyway. The viny thorn barrier looked almost like a cloud in the sunlight because of the size of the mass and the angle of the sunlight. It must have gone on for forty to fifty yards in either direction and was eight to ten feet tall the entire way. He saw blowdowns and trees entangled in the mass of barbed hell.

Where the Christ did this guy go? Steve wondered. Eventually, he got back up.

Fuck it! What am I worried about? Then he hollered, "Hello! If you are out this way and can hear me, I could use your help."

No reply. He tried again.

"I saw you a moment ago. I know you can hear my voice. I would just like some help finding my dog. I promise you are not in trouble. I could just use some help finding her."

Still nothing. "Son of a bitch!" Steve spat to himself.

He realized his attempt to enlist the aid of the old woodsman was in vain. With just so many hours of sunlight to look for

Stella, he didn't want to waste them caterwauling into the woods to the deaf ears of some weird old hermit. He decided to move on, and if he saw the old bastard again, he would close in on him and get some answers.

After a short while longer, Steve ambled back to camp disenchanted and fatigued from the day's efforts. *Carla would surely be bummed out by Stella's absence from the cabin that night. Hopefully, she's all right and will show up tomorrow,* he thought. *If not, maybe we can stay until Monday.*

Aside from his fleeting encounter with the woodsman, the day's efforts and the search for Stella had turned out to be a confounding lesson in futility.

THE BAD NIGHT

The remnants of the evening were glum back at the camp. Steve knew Carla felt responsible for Stella taking off.

"It wasn't your fault, you know," he said to break the melancholy silence of the small cabin. "Stella is a big girl, and she knows better than to run off. As we talked about earlier, nothing is going to want to mess with her in those woods tonight."

Carla replied with a quivering lip and building tears lining the bottom rims of her eyes, "If anything happens to her, I will never forgive myself."

"It's not your fault, babe. She'll probably show up tonight out of pure hunger, and if not, I'm sure we'll find her tomorrow," he said, even though he had no idea where to look next. "Let's turn in and get some sleep. We'll get an early start looking for her tomorrow, if she doesn't show up tonight."

Morosely, Carla replied, "Okay, but I want to get looking for her at first light. I probably won't sleep much, so I'll be looking to get moving in the morning."

As her husband settled the camp and lit the wood burning stove, Carla got undressed and into bed. Steve went out to the small front porch, which was packed with coolers and a grill, to check once more for Stella before he closed and locked the door for the long night. The evening was beautiful, clear, and silent. He heard a twig snap way out in the woods.

"Stella?" he said without yelling. There was no response from the dark timber, just a gentle breeze. He stood there for a moment listening. Nothing.

He turned around, went back inside, and twisted the dead-bolt shut.

After stripping off his clothes, he slid into bed with Carla. His wife was out cold. The stress and commotion of the day had caught up with her. He was glad. She needed the rest. He kissed her on the forehead and whispered to her, "Good night, sweet-heart. You'll see. Things will be better in the morning."

Whimper. Scratch, scratch. Scratch, scratch.

Steve was jerked bolt upright out of his sleep by what he thought he had just heard. He heard it again—whimpering fol-lowed by double scratches at the door. He was briefly disoriented. In the orange glow of the wood burning stove, he remembered he was at Mason's camp. He looked down at his watch and saw it was two fifteen. The noise he heard was Stella's usual request to be let back into the house. He heard the dog padding back and forth on the front porch, whining to be let in. Steve swept back the covers and shot out of bed toward the door. He was relieved he could hear her as plain as day on the other side of the door.

"I'm coming, girly," he said with a smile he wasn't even aware of. He unbolted the door, swung it open, and—nothing.

Stella didn't come bolting through the door as he was expect-ing. Steve jerked his head out the door and—nothing. Stella should have been right there in front of him. Perplexed, he stepped out naked onto the porch and called out, "Stella?"

There was nothing. No sound.

"Where are you, girl?" The only thing he heard was still the icy silence. He went to the edge of the porch and peered out into the night.

Kawang! An explosion of metallic sound erupted next to him.

Steve jumped out of his skin. The rusted oval that was hang-ing above him had guillotined down onto the granite steps of the porch and rolled out to the same place in the front yard. *How the hell does it do that every time?* he wondered.

Stella never came. He yelled her name a few times, but there was no response from the dark woods.

Unnerved from the fallen oval and Stella's vanishing, Steve slipped back into the cabin, distracted. He closed and locked it in one motion. He started to say, "I thought for sure—"

He stopped. Something wasn't right.

Carla was standing naked at the foot of the bed, trembling.

"Something's the matter," she said worriedly.

"What, honey?" Steve replied.

"Something is wrong."

He moved toward Carla, but she fended him back with a hand out in front of her like a traffic cop.

"What, what is it? I thought I heard Stella and went out to investigate and—"

Carla cut him off. "It's not that. It's something else!" she snapped at him uncharacteristically. "I'm being drawn."

"What the hell are you talking about, Carla? What do you mean, you're 'being drawn'?" Steve replied tensely.

"I feel like I'm being drawn."

Unsure and starting to feel nervous because his wife was not acting like herself, Steve said in an irritated voice, "What the hell do you mean 'being drawn'? What does that mean?"

"Look," she said in a detached tone. She looked up and, with one hand, grabbed the small toboggan that was in the rough-hewn rafters above the floor of the bed. She dropped it on the wood floor in front of her. With a blank look on her face, she swayed onto the sled with heavy feet.

At that moment, Steve saw something neither physics nor any law of nature could explain. The old toboggan his naked wife was standing on started to move. It slowly jerked along the floor in the direction he was standing. He was confused about what he was seeing and stood motionless, his mouth agape. Every hair and hackle on his exposed body stood on end as he observed the unexplained phenomena.

Carla looked at him with a concerned yet subtly vacant expression on her face and said the last word he would be hearing from her for a while. She looked him in the eye while on the inexplicably moving sled and said in a plaintive voice, "Honey?"

That snapped Steve into action. He tromped across the floor and grabbed her off of the shifting toboggan. Her head fell back with her eyes closed as her body went limp. He tried to shake her back to consciousness.

"Honey? Honey?" he said shrilly as he shook her.

Then Carla snapped her head up and opened her eyes. He had her in a bear-hug embrace. They were four inches apart when she opened her eyes to him, and he saw something that he never ever wanted to see in his life again. He could actually see the whites of her eyes become bloodshot in a pattern that could only be described as cauliflower-like. He saw it happen right in front of him and felt a wave of heat flush through her body. She felt like she was 120 degrees. But the thing that left the mark on his soul was what happened next.

With a deviant smile and in a gravelly voice that was nothing like her own, Carla said to him, "She's with me now."

Steve's world crashed at that moment. He swooped up his wife and plowed through the dead-bolted door with her in his arms. The door gave way with a shattering smash as they stumbled onto the coolers and grill out on the deck, scattering them everywhere.

The staggering couple flopped over the coolers and grill down the granite steps onto the cool front lawn. With all of the commotion, Nick was standing at the door, barking toward the night. The cold earth brought Steve back to reality for a moment.

He lifted Carla off of the cool grass and carried her to the truck. He opened the driver door and stuffed her in as far as he could. He called Nick, who was now out on the front grass barking directly at the oval on the ground.

"Come on, Nick. We're getting the fuck out of this place!"

The dog hopped up in the truck and stepped on Carla as he climbed into the back seat. Steve started up the big truck with the keys he had left in the ignition and spun the rig around, with his foot pinning the gas pedal to the floor. Throwing grass, dirt, and gravel into the air, Steve sped the truck up the driveway of the camp and drove straight through the crossbar of Mason's rough gate.

Never taking his foot off of the gas, he jerked the truck to the right and headed westward up the dirt road toward civilization and rationality. As he was pulling away from the camp, he said to himself, "Good luck, Stella. You're on your own now. Be safe."

As Steve was careening up the rough road, he tried repeatedly to wake Carla from her unconscious state. "Honey! Carla!"

He shook his unresponsive wife. He had a few very close calls while he was ripping up Long Shadows Road, almost sliding off of the road or barely avoiding hitting trees several times because he was so distracted with concern for his wife.

Steve never slowed down as he approached Route 77. Just before the truck reached the intersection, Carla mumbled something he couldn't make out. Then he distinctly heard her say in her own voice, "With me now." He was so relieved to hear her normal voice that he was completely distracted and looking at her when everything around him exploded.

HOSPITAL

Breaking glass. Screeching tires. Screaming women. Pain. Flames. Brutality. Torment. Eternal bondage. Steve jerked from a fugue state into consciousness, a consciousness of bright lights. antiseptic smells, buzzing and beeping of electronic machines and pain, an all-body total pain. He was sore from head to toe and groggy. As the sensory overload of his burgeoning consciousness overpowered the memories of his sleep state, Steve tried to make sense of his current surroundings. He was thoroughly disoriented and could barely open his eyes. When he did, the glaring lights were painful. He tried to sit up but was restrained by his wrists, and he felt hands gently press him back down against what he assumed to be a bed.

"Easy, Mr. Babin," a strange, gentle voice said. "You're safe here and all right. Your wife is also here and resting comfortably. You two shared a miracle to live through that accident. You've been unconscious for some time now, but aside from that, you seem to be fine. A little roughed up, but fine.

"My name is Nurse Irene. You're in the ICU of St. Bartholomew's Regional Hospital in Derry, Maine. You and your wife were in a terrible accident. You both were very lucky. As a matter of fact, I heard your dog even made it through the accident unscathed, and he wouldn't let anybody near you two to receive treatment. A bunch of police and paramedics had to tackle him with a blanket and take him off to the Maine Society for the Prevention of Cruelty to Animals—the MSPCA. I guess he put up quite a fight, so he'll be waiting for you there when you get out of here."

"How long have I been here?" Steve asked.

"The ambulance brought you in about four. It's now about seven forty-five in the morning, and you already have a very concerned guest waiting to see you. A Mr. Macfarlane. He was very concerned when he arrived."

"Can I see him now?"

"Not yet, dear. Dr. Toomey still wants to come in and talk with you. If he says you're well enough to see visitors, then I'll let him in to see you."

Nurse Irene was the gentlest version of firm Steve had ever encountered. She was no Nurse Ratched, but Steve sensed that he did not want to mess with her, especially considering his current state.

"Can you at least remove the wrist restraints? I'm not under arrest or anything, am I?" Steve pleaded.

"Oh no, dear. You're not under arrest. You were fidgeting in your sleep, and we didn't want you to pull out the IV hydration tubes that were in your wrist. I think the police have some questions for you, but I don't think you're in any big trouble at this point." She removed the Velcro restraints from his wrists, and his eyes cleared to see the pleasant face that belonged to the pleasant voice. "You just rest now, dear, and Dr. Toomey will be in, in a minute." She gently stroked his hair out of his eyes and left the room.

Steve thought it was just like having his auntie look after him when he was a kid, a pleasant thought that occurred to him just as he dozed off again.

He was reawakened when Dr. Toomey entered the room and looked at his chart.

The doctor felt Steve was looking at him and said without looking up from the chart, "You do know that it's a miracle that you, your wife, and even your dog, from what I have been told, are alive and in such good condition. Do you remember what happened to you? What caused you to be brought here to St. Bart's?"

It all came back to Steve like a tidal wave. He had memory flashes of Carla standing in the room, sliding on the toboggan, going into the trance or whatever it was, and saying, "She's with me now." All of the memories cascaded over him and flooded his memory. He remembered flying up the dirt road in the truck while trying to wake Carla. Then the explosion of glass and noise. Then blackness.

"What exactly happened?" Steve asked the doctor. "Is Carla alright? Where is she? What happened?"

"Relax, son. Your wife is just in the other room. You had a horrendous accident with a logging truck. From what I understand, the trucker broadsided your vehicle as you drove out onto Route 77. It's amazing the two of you are in as good a shape as you are because I understand you were not wearing your seat belts, and I hate to admit it, but that might be exactly what saved your lives. The front half of the cab of your truck was crushed, and you two were thrown into the backseat. It obviously was not your day to die, not from lack of trying anyway. The question I have for you is, why were you two naked in the truck? The paramedics brought you in with no clothes on. Did something happen where you were staying?"

Steve pondered that last question and realized he probably should not mention Carla's behavior.

He quickly responded, "We sleep naked together. I had woke up in the middle of the night to go the bathroom, and when I returned, Carla had taken some form of a fit or a seizure. She has no medical history or family history of such things. She was unresponsive, and then it looked like she was having difficulty breathing, so I just swept her up in my arms and ran out to the truck as is.

"My wife comes first to me. I love her more than life itself, so if that means that I have to carry her naked into a hospital to save her, I don't give a good shit. As we sped up the dirt road, she was unresponsive, but just as we reached the intersection, she said something that distracted me, and the rest is history. I never saw the truck coming and didn't even know we were in an accident until you told me about it.

"How's the driver of the truck? Was anybody hurt or worse?" he asked with dread.

"The driver was fine. As a matter of fact, he didn't get a scratch from the whole ordeal. There was no one else involved in the accident. The police were on the scene almost instantly because that is a heavily traveled road, and regrettably, you are not the first person we have had here from issues on Route 77.

"However, what concerns me is your wife," the gray-haired doctor went on. "She seems to be in some form of light coma, but the injuries she received in the accident were minimal, really just superficial, to be quite frank. She has just one long scratch on her, and that is only on her forearm. We have run diagnostic tests on her and a CAT scan on her head and neck, checked her abdominals, reflexes, toxicology—everything. There were just trace amounts of alcohol in her system and none in yours.

"What's confounding me is that her cardiac sinus rhythm is fine, and she is responsive to external stimuli. Her neurological exam checked out fine, with no signs of trauma or internal hemorrhaging, so she's not quite in a coma. That's why we say she's resting. Maybe she had some form of shock or psychological trauma from the accident or the seizure beforehand, but she's just sleeping comfortably for now in the next room. We're going to give her some time and then reevaluate her this evening to see if things haven't changed—provided, of course, that she doesn't just wake up on her own, which is very possible, considering her condition."

Steve had a sinking feeling that wasn't the case, but he was optimistic about her prognosis.

"What happens next, Doc? I am a little sore"—he lied—"but I don't feel bad"—he lied again—"I would like to get up and see my wife, if that's okay."

"You can go see her, but take it easy. You have a friend here also, who wants to see you. He can come in, but just for a few minutes. I want you to build your strength and relax."

Steve sat up in his bed, an action that made him a little woozy.

Dr. Toomey observed Steve's dizziness and said, "Why don't we wait until later to see your wife? She's just in the other room and isn't going anywhere. Would you still like to see your friend? Maybe he'll raise your spirits a little."

"Yeah, please. If you could send him in, I'd appreciate it."

The doctor left the room, and a few moments later, a very concerned Mason Macfarlane walked into the room. As soon as he saw Steve sitting up in bed, he was relieved.

"You sure know how to make a dramatic exit from a place, don't ya?" Mason said in a slightly flustered tone.

"I'm all right. It's Carla I'm concerned about. Mason, please don't think I'm crazy or was hit on the head, but something happened out at that camp that I can't explain. It's how all of this started."

"What are you talking about, Steve? What happened out there? Did a bear attack you? Or was it some kids? Was someone bothering you and Carla or the camp?"

"No. It was nothing like that. Please don't think I'm nuts, but I think your camp's got something the matter with it."

"Steve, what the hell are you talking about? Just slow down, and tell me what happened."

Steve told him everything that had occurred the night before, exactly as it had happened. He could see the storm clouds of frustration and doubt come over Mason's furrowed brow. Then Mason did the worst thing possible: he spoke to Steve as if he were talking to some crazy old fool.

"Steve, now you just take it easy, and I'll go make sure everything is all right at camp while you rest up a bit."

"Mason, don't you dare talk to me like I'm fucking crazy! I know what the fuck I saw!"

"What do you want me to tell you, Steve? I bought that camp the day Ken was born. I have owned it for thirty-six years and have never ever had a problem like what you're talking about. The place is so quiet that it's boring, and that's what I like about it.

I drove up this morning and come to find my place destroyed, and my guests have been in a hideous accident. Now I'm hearing some far-fetched ghost story, and to boot, not even all that much wood had been split. Don't think I didn't notice. I don't know what you two were up to out there, but it all doesn't look very good from my perspective at all!"

"Trust me on this, then. The place has changed. And stay the hell out of there! I don't know how else to tell you, Mason." Steve felt a little piqued and woozy.

"What are you telling me, Steve? To never go back to my camp? You realize how ridiculous that sounds, don't you?"

Steve was fading fast, but he was trying to get his point across to his friend. "Mason, I'm telling you, something's going on out there that isn't any good, and if you want to do yourself and your family a favor, you'll never go back. You'll just burn the place to the—" His advising of his friend abruptly ended as Steve passed out and slumped back down into his bed.

Mason was more ticked off than alarmed. He knew Steve must have got pretty tossed around in that accident, and it obviously shook something loose in Steve's brain. After some rest, he'd probably be back to normal. All Mason knew was that he would have to get back to camp and get it back in working order. Most of the day was left, and he was sure he would need all of it to set things right at his Long Shadows camp.

Once Mason got on the road back to camp, he started to cool down and think more clearly. He gave his son, Ken, a call. He knew he was on duty, but he just wanted to hear his son's voice after all of the goings-on of the morning.

Before being connected to Ken, who was out in his police cruiser, Mason thought about Steve and Carla. He hoped they would be all right and especially that Steve would shake himself out of it before he talked crazy to the wrong person and ended up with the rest of the nuts as a guest of the psyche ward in Denton at the state hospital.

MASON GOES TO
CAMP–FIRST ENCOUNTER

By 5:45 a.m., Mason had made good time. It was a beautiful Sunday morning, and he was already halfway to his camp. At this pace, he would arrive around 6:30 a.m. with some coffee and danish for all of them to sit and chat over.

He hoped he would not be too early and would not wake them up. But knowing Steve, he's probably putting the wood to Carla, as opposed to putting the wood in the shed, he thought, bemused and somewhat embarrassed.

He hadn't slept much the night before because of his looking forward to "supervising" with Carla and Steve. He just plain liked them and was looking forward to spending some time visiting.

His wife, Sarah, had kicked him out of bed at five that morning because he wouldn't stop tossing and turning.

"You might as well get up and get moving. You've kept me up with your restlessness half the night, and I can still salvage the morning's sleep if you get out of here," she had said to him in a feigned dour tone. "You're fooling no one with your wanting to 'supervise Steve while he cuts the wood' bit. I'm onto your game. Now get out of here, so I can get some rest!"

How did she know? Mason wondered. *I thought I was pretty convincing.*

That was how his morning began, and it was the only excuse he needed to get showered and on the road.

———◆———

By 6:15 a.m., Mason had reached the turn off Route 77 north onto Long Shadows Road. As he was turning onto the dirt road, he noticed hellacious skid marks on the tar and small pieces of what he assumed to be headlights and larger pieces of vehicle about the size of playing cards that had been swept to the side of the road.

This is an awful corner, he thought as he turned onto the road. As he was driving toward his camp on Long Shadows, another thought came into his mind. I hope that wasn't from Steve and Carla. It couldn't be. Steve has been up and down that road probably fifty times, and Carla drives very cautiously, he assured himself.

On the five-mile stretch of dirt road to Mason's cabin, six other camps lined the south side of the road. Mason's was the only camp on what was the old farm on the northern side of the road. There wasn't another camp in the last three miles to his cabin.

Mason knew that on weekends, local kids went down this road in order to go drinking or parking, but his camp was never bothered. He remembered hearing that several kids riding in a car were killed on a weekend night quite a few years back. They came roaring out of this road onto Route 77, and a logging truck hit them too. All of the kids in the car were killed instantly except one girl, who was still up at the State Mental Hospital. The word was she was never the same after the accident; in fact, she went quite mad, as he recalled. "Poor thing," Mason murmured aloud to himself in the car. What a waste of young lives, snuffed out before they even had a chance to start living, he thought.

As Mason pulled up to the dooryard that led to his camp, he noticed the crossbar wasn't up. He saw it sticking out of the sage and raspberry bushes on the other side of the road, as if it had been carelessly tossed there. This annoyed him because he was very particular about such things, and Steve knew that and knew that Mason always wanted the bar up. It was not Steve's style to do something like this. Even if he was going in and out of the dooryard quite a bit, at least he could have placed the crossbar neatly next to the entrance, instead of flinging it into the brush. When Mason stopped his truck and got out to retrieve the crossbar, he looked down the road to the camp and saw that something was not right.

Instead of retrieving the bar, he got back into the truck and drove down to the camp. The first thing he noticed was that the front door to the cabin was destroyed. It was half-open, hanging from one hinge at an awkward angle. The glass had been smashed out, but the pane was intact, and the old curtain on the door was lightly blowing in the morning breeze. A cooler, most likely Steve's, was open on the grass with all of its contents strewn throughout the front yard: wrapped steaks, sandwich meats, bread, mustard, a broken mayo jar, cookies, and snacks all over the grass. The grill was knocked over and on the grass next to the steps, along with the oval ring. Mason thought it must have been a huge crash or something to create so much havoc. It looked like a bear had broken in, which was quite common in the woods of Maine. He just hoped that if that was what happened, Carla and Steve were not harmed.

Then he realized all of the contents of the cooler were undisturbed and still there. If a bear had broken in, it would have eaten the meats and snacks at least. If it had been run off, it would have returned to collect the food items. Unless, of course, he drove up while it was happening, and the bear was still inside the cabin. Blindly and without fear, Mason ran toward the cabin and hopped the steps in a single bound that carried him directly into the dwelling in order to face the potentially marauding bear. He was a born and raised Mainer, and he sure as hell wasn't afraid of a goddamn bear if it was in his place hurting his friends. There was nothing. No one. No bear. The cabin was pretty much in order, except for the unmade bed and the toboggan, which was in the middle of the floor. He knew something was wrong, but he couldn't tell what.

"Carla. Steve? Are you folks in here?"

No reply.

What the hell happened here? he wondered.

The clothes they had been wearing were laid out on the bottom bunk, and their bag of clothes was on the upper bunk. There were still residual coals in the wood stove, and heat was coming from it, so they hadn't been gone too long, but it was obvious they had left in a hurry.

Then with dread, he remembered the skid marks and broken headlight glass out on Route 77.

He gasped, "Oh, no! No no no no!" and started to head for the door.

When Mason left the dooryard, he didn't bother to stop to put up the crossbar, either. He turned right and headed up the road west, back toward Route 77.

He was about six hundred yards up the road when he looked back just in time to see what looked like a woodsman dressed in dilapidated tan overalls and an old, tattered plaid shirt slip into the woods on the side of the road Mason's camp was on.

Mason slammed on the brakes, thinking, *Maybe he knows what happened, and if not, what the hell is he doing on my property?* He jerked the truck into reverse and backed up about one hundred yards to where he thought he saw the old man enter the land. Mason got out and hollered, "Hello! Hello!"

There was no reply. Then way off, a little more than 150 yards through the trees north of him, he saw movement. He yelled again, "Hello. You there. Woodsman!"

Again, no reply. Without hesitation, Mason headed into the woods in the direction he had last seen movement. When he arrived in his intended location, where he had last seen the trespasser, it dawned on him that he was standing on an old, overgrown trail he had never seen before. The trail was overgrown with laurel and briars that had mostly reclaimed it, but he could still make out a distinct old pathway. As he looked up the trail, he saw the movement of a man going deeper into the woods. He made his way up the trail northward, and the farther he went, the thicker the thorns and briars became. It seemed to him that every thorn and briar in the woods was sticking to him and pulling on his clothes. It was as if the woods were in some weird way trying to prevent him from going up the path.

"Damned thorns, for Christ's sake!" Mason growled to himself as he wrenched himself forward up the path through briars that were raking scores of thin lines of blood on his forearms and hands.

The path ended abruptly at an eight-to-ten-foot growth of thorns and briars. It was an entanglement of vines, long thorns, and razor-sharp briars the likes of which Mason had never encountered before. It was almost like a wall of pure thorn bushes that he couldn't even see through. By now, he was good and aggravated.

"I'm sure as hell not going to be turned around by a god forsaken thorn bush!" he seethed loudly to the bush and anyone who might be listening out in the woods.

Mason backtracked until he found some six- to eight-foot sections of manageable blowdowns or dead logs. When he dropped the first log on the wall of briars, it barely moved, but after about eight logs, he had cleaved a path through the wall of thorns and could see something low to the ground on the other side. It was the remains of some sort of old building with collapsed roof and walls. Mason had never seen it before in all of his thirty-some years of owning the camp because this section of the property was so swampy and overgrown with thorns that he rarely came out here.

He voiced his growing irritation, "I am coming back here with a weed-whacker, machete, axe, and a friggin' flame thrower, if I have to, and take back this section of my land! The friggin' thorn bushes don't pay the taxes on this place. I do!" He glowered.

He peered through the gap he had made through the thorn escarpment and saw that the collapsed outbuilding looked to have been only about ten feet by fourteen feet in size. The area smelled of rotten wood. *It must have been one of the original buildings of the farm*, he thought.

Then his mind snapped back to Carla and Steve.

I don't have time for this, nor do I want to clamber over those logs and take a peek at that now. I'm going to have to save that for another day, he said to himself in his head.

"When I come back and cut down all of these fucking thorns!" He said this aloud so that the thorns and briars could hear him. On that, he turned and headed back to his truck, which he had left idling with the door open in the middle of Long Shadows Road.

KEN'S LAST CONVERSATION

Veteran Officer Kenneth Macfarlane of the Aranville Maine Police Department had just got back into his cruiser. He had just resuscitated a four-year-old boy who had choked on bacon while eating Sunday breakfast at Denny's with his family. Luckily, he had been right in front of the restaurant, at a stoplight when the 911 call came over the radio of his vehicle. He had been the first on the scene.

The scene in the restaurant had been utter chaos when Ken arrived. By the time he reached the child, he was mostly unconscious and turning blue from lack of oxygen. The father was pounding on the boy's back with an open hand and screaming the boy's name. The mother was desperate and shrieking at the top of her lungs.

Ken took the boy out of the father's hands and put the boy on the ground without asking. He knew time was of the essence. He took his Mini Maglite and shined it down the boy's throat. He could just see the end of the obstruction. Ken grabbed his Leatherman from his belt and opened it up to the needle-nose-pliers setting. He knew he had only one chance to clear the obstruction because time was running out for the kid. Ken put the Mini Maglite in his teeth, then pulled the boy's tongue out as far as he could and reached far down into the unconscious boy's throat until he was able to grasp onto something. It was either a clump of food or one of the kid's tonsils. He gently pulled on the slippery object with the grip of the pliers.

To his relief, he saw a large glob of chewed bacon dislodge from the boy's throat. As soon as he cleared the bacon, Ken gave the boy two shallow breaths of mouth-to-mouth resuscitation, and all of the boy's color returned to normal. Then Ken heard the best noise he had heard in a long time. The kid let out a wail like he was having his toes plucked off and screamed for his mother.

The restaurant exploded in applause. The frantic mother swept her son off of the ground into her arms and sat in her seat, crying and kissing the boy repeatedly.

Before Ken could stand up, the father lifted him to his feet like he was made out of feathers, which was no easy task because Ken was six feet tall and weighed about 265 pounds. The father was an enormous woodcutter or lumberjack. He was a full six inches taller and at least fifty pounds heavier than Ken. With tears in his eyes, he bear-hugged Ken so tightly that it squeezed the air out of Ken's lungs and locked his arms down by his sides. In a thick French-Canadian accent, with tears streaming down his cheeks, he held Ken by the shoulders, looked him in the eye, and thanked him heartily.

Ken said it was his duty and pleasure. He checked the boy one more time as the paramedics arrived, briefed them on the situation, and headed toward the exit. The entire way to the exit, people were clapping and congratulating him with huge smiles on their faces. Patrons and employees patted him on the back; he even got a few kisses on the cheek before he reached the exit. He felt like a million bucks. He felt like a hero.

As he sat down in his vehicle, the dispatcher said over the radio, "Officer Macfarlane, your father is on the phone and wants to talk with you. Are you available?"

"Yes, but tell him I'll call him on his cell phone, and also tell him to press the green button when he hears it ring. Thanks."

He pulled his phone out of his pocket and called his father. The first few times, Mason kept pressing the green button and disconnected. Ken was getting frustrated and said aloud, "When the hell is he going to join the twenty-first century? It's a cell phone, for Christ's sake, not a rocket ship!" This was one of the many things Ken loved about his dad. He was an old-fashioned Mainer and was going to end his days as one. Just to get his father to accept the phone was a feat, but to get him to use it was an entire other ball of wax.

The fourth attempt was the charm. Mason picked up on the other end, obviously frustrated as well from the previous snafus.

"Kenneth. Kenneth. Are you there, son?"

Mason was the only person in the world who called him Kenneth.

"Yeah, I'm here, Dad. How are you? This isn't the norm, you calling me on a Sunday morning. Is everything okay?"

"It's funny you should ask that, son, because no, everything is not all right."

"What's the matter? Is Mom all right?" Ken asked with alarm in his voice.

"Everyone in your family is safe and well. Don't be alarmed about that."

"What is it, then?"

"Steve and Carla came up to do some work at the camp this weekend and had a terrible accident."

Upon hearing that, Ken rolled his eyes because he never really liked Steve. He didn't like Steve's non-Mainer ways. He didn't care for Steve's loud and quick manner of speaking. He didn't like how Steve could have a conversation on just about anything and be comfortable in almost any situation. He didn't like that he and Steve were almost the same age, yet he always felt like the youngest person in the room. He didn't like Steve's laugh or sense of humor. In fact, the only thing he liked about Steve was when Steve left, and camp settled down again. The thing Ken especially didn't like about Steve was how he weaseled in on Ken's parents, charming them and endearing himself to them. He always heard about Steve, Steve, Steve, and his lovely wife, Carla. Didn't Steve have his own parents? If Ken never saw Steve Babin again, it would be altogether too soon.

Ken never told his father about his dislike of Steve. Mason really liked him, and it would only create tension.

"Kenneth, are you still there?"

"Yeah, Dad. I just lost you there for a moment. So what happened with Steve and Carla?"

Mason told him what had happened, even his conversation with Steve in the hospital. Ken did not like what he heard at all. It sounded to him like Steve and Carla were doing drugs or something weird out at the camp. Whatever they were doing must have caught up to them. It also sounded to him like they were trying to come up with some lame excuse, and it backfired on them.

"Dad, I'll be down in about two hours and help you sort through things. Maybe we'll be able to make heads or tails of the whole thing if we put our minds together. You know, for future reference, do you really need these outside hassles in your life, just for being generous to people?"

"What do you mean, Kenneth? They've never been an issue before on any level. As a matter of fact, they've been quite delightful and excellent friends."

"I understand that, Dad, but are they so delightful right now, or are they more of a pain in the ass at this point? I'm just saying, think about it. All right?"

"Okay. I will. I'll see you in a couple of hours or so?"

"Yeah, probably a little less. I had an excellent day at work today, and no one will mind if I take a little hiatus. I'll tell you about it when I get there."

"All right. I'm looking forward to it. I'm just pulling up to Long Shadows Road now. Kenneth, I'm very proud of you, and I love you."

"I know, Dad. Are you all right?"

"Yes, I'm fine. But this whole accident they were in reminded me of how quickly life can vanish, and it's important to me that you know I love you."

"I do, Dad. I love you too."

"Good. I'll see you when you get here, son."

"I'll talk to you then, Dad."

MASON'S RETURN TO
CAMP - SECOND ENCOUNTER

After his disturbing conversation with Steve at the hospital, Mason returned to the camp to put the place back in order and try to figure out exactly what had happened there. He was relieved they were both all right physically, but he was deeply troubled by Steve's description of what had happened, and he was concerned about Carla's coma-like state. He just could not believe what Steve had told him. It just wasn't like him. Steve always kept his cool and had his head screwed on straight. That was one of the things about him that appealed to Mason. Steve always kept his composure under any circumstances. He was known for his coolness in handling immense pressure at work. Yet that man was the furthest thing from the man Mason spoke to in the hospital.

Mason slowly shook his head in disbelief, thinking, *I've spent scores of nights here alone. I've had over thirty or forty guests here over the years and have never had a problem. None of them have ever mentioned a problem or an issue, ever! Granted, I can't remember a lot of women coming to camp—any, for that matter—but I still have never seen or heard anything along those lines. That wreck probably took more out of Steve than he realized.*

He could not accept what he heard from the young man he had come to enjoy and respect so much over the years. "Ghost stories," the old Mainer spat to himself. "I mean, what the hell is that?" He was starting to get irritated again. He felt his blood pressure rising. It just didn't make any sense. *Maybe they were up here drinking or doing drugs*, he thought. It would explain a lot.

But Mason knew Steve was never into drugs. He had grown up in the city down in Massachusetts and had seen many of his friends lost to drugs. Mason knew that because he and Steve had many long conversations about almost everything.

He also knew that Steve was not afraid of a drink. But the more Steve drank, the happier and mellower he became. Even on bourbon, which tends to make some men more aggressive or angry, Steve's smile would just get a little wider and he would laugh a little more.

"It just doesn't make any sense," Mason said, sighing, as he walked across the front yard of the camp.

He walked up onto the steps and assessed the situation. The place was a wreck. Whatever happened there was violent and intense. He took hold of the mostly unhinged door. Two of the three hinges had been torn out of the frame and were still embedded in the door. The bolt of the lock coming from the side of the door was still sticking out straight as if it were still engaged.

It must have been one hell of an impact to do this, Mason thought.

After restoring the door to working order—not to his liking, but it would do for now—he patched up the window with some Plexiglas and duct tape. It looked awful, but it was functional enough and pretty damned sturdy, Mason thought. "I'm like a damned surgeon," he said, amusing himself.

Next he turned on his heels, headed back across the yard to his old shed, and grabbed a ladder from inside. As he walked back across the yard to the front, he again wondered what the hell had happened here.

Having already stood the ladder against the front eave of the cabin, Mason bent over and grabbed off the ground the old, tarnished metal oval that he had hung off the front of the cabin since he owned the place.

This piece of crap is never falling off again, he thought. *Right after I get back from hacking down all of those friggin' thorns, I am going to come back and weld this bastard to the side of the camp!*

He climbed up the ladder, and just as he placed the cold steel oval on the nail it hung from, he saw movement off to his left. From up on the ladder, he looked to the western side of the property. To his irritated surprise, he spied the same woodsman he had seen earlier that day, moving directly away from him, heading northwest. He could also see he had a dog with him this time, a fairly large black dog that was trotting along beside him.

"That's it!" Mason hissed to himself through gritted teeth.

Without a second thought, he hopped down from the ladder and instantly started to pursue the woodsman and his dog companion.

Those are open woods out that way for a little while before it gets swampy. He won't be able to slip away from me this time. I'll be able to see him from three hundred yards out, he thought as he picked up his pace to a light jog.

This time in his pursuit of the decrepit woodsman, Mason did not call out to him. He wanted to catch up with the trespasser and confront him directly.

As Mason jogged, he saw the intruder off in the distance, and it seemed to him that he was gaining no ground on the lanky old man, who seemed to be walking at a regular pace. Mason stepped it up to a full jog. The figure he was pursuing took a hard left and headed south toward the briars and swamp. The man and the dog were heading toward the same location where Mason had seen the woodsman earlier that day.

"Oh, for the love of Pete! Don't go back in there," he said aloud, but only to himself.

Mason picked up his pace more, trying to close the gap between him and his quarry the best he could. He wanted to reach the trespasser and his dog before they got into the briary hell section of the swamp.

He was in excellent health for a man his age, but he couldn't remember the last time he had run this much, and it was starting to wear on him. He hammered his fists back and forth and pounded his feet in a vain attempt to reach the strangers on his land but never closed the gap by much.

With pure dismay, Mason watched as the woodsman and the dog slipped into the ocean of briars and thorns about two hundred yards ahead of him. As he reached where he thought the two had entered the hellish thorn area, Mason had to stop and take a breather. His heart and lungs were pounding. As his ribcage heaved trying to catch air he thought two things to himself. The first was what escaped his mouth between breaths, and that was, "It sucks getting old." The second was, "That old man has twenty years on me, and he made it look easy. I better start doing something if I want to last a few more years."

YOU HOLD ON

Shards of light. Damp darkness. The coppery scent of blood. Quiet death.

These images make no sense, and no logic to Steve, yet they seem familiar in a distant sort of way. Just whispers of his dreams that slipped away as Steve regained his consciousness for the second time that day in the recovery room of St. Bartholomew's Hospital. He had no idea how long he had been out this time, and then he remembered his conversation with Mason. It hadn't gone so well. Telling Mason the whole story of the night before, the look on Mason's face, Mason's appeasement of him like Steve was some old fool, and ultimately Mason's agitated response to Steve's outburst. It hadn't gone well at all.

A nurse walked into the room (not Nurse Irene) as Steve was recalling the conversation, interrupting his line of thinking. She hadn't noticed he was awake and went about reading the machines in his room and registering the recordings on a page attached to a clipboard.

"How long have I been out for this time?" Steve gravelly choked out.

With a start, the plump nurse spun around. "Whew! You got one up on me there! I thought you were still sleeping. You've only been resting for about forty-five minutes since your friend left. I was at the nurse's station as he walked by to leave. He said you had fallen back to sleep and that he would be back later this evening to check in on you. He must be a good friend."

"He is. I've known him for years. He didn't by chance say where he was going, did he?"

"No. He didn't. He just moved down the hall like a man with purpose. Is he married by the way? The reason I ask is because he is quite handsome and in pretty good shape. My mother would give him a run for his money."

Steve chuckled. "Sorry to report, but he is. Please break the news to your mother gently." He grinned as he thought, *If your mom is built anything like you, honey, he wouldn't stand a chance, I'm suspecting.*"

On that note of another lost opportunity for maternal matchmaking, the plump nurse with the massive thighs (which Steve had not noticed before) shot him a mischievous, warm smile and exited the room.

Oh, he wouldn't stand a chance at all if she is built anything like you, Steve mused.

Once the nurse left the room, he acknowledged to himself the dreadful deduction he would not face while he was talking with his stout caregiver.

As soon as she had mentioned during their brief conversation that Mason had "moved down the hall like a man with purpose," he knew Mason was headed directly back to camp, paying no heed to his warning about the place and the happenings of the previous evening.

Steve felt the old place had taken an irreversible step, a shift that had changed the place forever. For the first time since knowing Mason, Steve feared for his old friend at the camp where he had always found so much solace.

Why now? Why in all the years and all the times I've been there has nothing ever happened before? he wondered. *It just doesn't make any sense, but one thing I do know is I have to get out of here ASAP and get Mason the hell out of there before something happens to him. I don't care if I have to bind and gag him and stuff his cantankerous old ass in the car myself. He's leaving with me!*

On that note, Steve reached down and pulled the IV tubes and needles out of his arms. He slowly slid his traumatized body over to the edge of the hospital bed and swung his legs off as gently as possible. He could not believe the ocean of pain that these simple movements immersed him in. He lay there only for a moment, amazed at how much the pain from these simple actions took his breath away. He heard his father's voice pop into his head: "It doesn't matter how many times you get knocked down. It matters how many times you get back up. Get up on your feet, boy!"

He sat up in bed and refused to give in to the pain. From his previous conversations with Dr. Toomey, he knew his body was structurally sound, just beat up a bit. This knowledge gave him resolve. He knew the more he got moving, the more he would loosen up and the less intense the pain would be.

He put his feet on the floor, braced himself, and stood.

Another baptism of pain, and as an added benefit, a bout of wooziness accompanied these actions. He stood there for a moment and steadied himself.

Once the dizziness had passed, he opened his eyes and focused on making his aching body move. As he took his first cautious step, he believed he could feel each and every ligament, tendon, and muscle fiber in his legs and hips move as if they were all filled with beach sand. He shuffled another step out into the middle of the hospital room. In addition to the almost perfect pain he was experiencing, he also became aware of the cold air on his butt, which was hanging out of his hospital gown. Thankfully, his feet were wrapped in warm and very comfortable hospital socks.

He shuffled across the floor to the counter and cabinets on the other wall of his empty room. There in a glass-paned cabinet that was supposed to be locked, he found what he was looking for—pain killers and good ones at that, Oxycontin.

"Better living through chemistry," Steve said with an exquisitely pained look on his face as he swallowed two of the capsules without water. As he was doing this, he noticed his name on the prescription bottle.

Next, he knew he needed to do something about trading in his hospital gown for something he could wear in public without getting arrested. He spied a laundry cart in the hall. After looking up and down the hall to make sure it was clear, he pulled the cart into his room. He found hospital scrubs in the cart, some XLs that would fit him, tops and bottoms. In the other cabinet of the cart, he found a pair of rubberized clogs that fit him fairly well and slipped them on. When he inspected himself in the mirror after his change of clothing, he thought he looked like anyone who would be expected to be working in a hospital, except for the bruises and lacerations on his face.

Next, he had to find his wife and see her before he set off to extract his friend from whatever unknown menace they had experienced at the camp.

When Steve stuck his head out into the hallway, he saw that his was the last room before the back staircase. He slipped up the hallway to the next door and slid inside the room so as not to draw any attention, slowly closing the door as he backed into the room. He took a deep breath and turned around. There she was, the love of his life, lying there, quiet and still. She would have looked as if she was just peacefully sleeping if not for the long scratch on her forehead and the monitors all over the room. He stood there remembering the terrible, confusing events that led them to this place, and the anger started to well within him.

I can't give into that now, he thought. *I have to keep my head clear and think my way through this.*

He walked over to his unconscious beautiful wife and just stared at her from the bedside. He swept a few of her dark brown curls from her face and slid his finger ever so gently down her cheek.

"She's with me, you son of a bitch!" he spat out from between seething teeth. "I am going to find out what the hell is going on and kick your fucking ass! No one takes my wife from me!" He felt the rage boiling in his skin. "I don't know what is going on or who you are, but it won't stand!"

He spoke defiantly into the open air of the empty hospital room, standing there with his eyes tightly shut, grasping the railing of Carla's bed, and feeling the rage course through him.

Then he opened his eyes, bent over, and kissed his wife on the lips.

"I will get you back. You hold on and fight," he said to his unresponsive wife as he studied her face from less than an inch away.

Then he spun on his heels and headed to the door.

GODFORSAKEN PLACE

Stooped over, catching his breath, trying to justify not going back into the thorny hell, Mason wondered if maybe the man had lost his dog and was just trying to find it when he saw him earlier cut across the road onto his property.

He probably didn't want to get into a long conversation and just avoided me, Mason thought, trying to convince himself.

Just as he finished that thought, Mason heard the most agonizingly painful wail erupt from the thorn-enmeshed woods before him.

It was not human. Mason guessed it was the dog, but he wasn't sure. The wail was so high-pitched and languid that it made the hairs stand on the back of his neck. The horrific keen was a continuous flow of the most disturbing sound of anguish he had ever heard. Mason couldn't tell if the dog was stuck in the middle of a patch of thorns or if the strange woodsman had tried to kill the suffering animal and failed. Whatever was happening out in those woods, his woods, in front of him, he knew he had to put a stop to it, even if it meant going back into those claw-like webs of thorns.

As Mason entered the thorn and brambles that entangled the woods, he noticed it was a little easier this time to move around. He was approaching from the northeast instead of directly from the south as he did last time. He heard the hideous crying coming from not far away, probably only about thirty yards away, and he kept vigilantly moving in the direction of the tortured howls.

As he moved in closer to the commotion, he could barely see through the clumps of tenacious thorns. They were so thick all around him that it was like trying to peer through fog. As he moved forward, he found the thorns were not the wall they appeared to be. The thorny growths were almost like a mirage that evaporated as he moved toward them. Yet, if he reached out and grabbed a vine, he plainly felt its barbs. It was a visual effect he had never experienced in the woods. He could barely make out shapes in the growth. Then he suddenly realized he was looking at the collapsed outbuilding he had seen just a few hours earlier.

Mason moved with ease through the few remaining yards of briars and thorns and stood outside the remains of the old building. He could hear the dog whimpering under the pile of rubble inside the collapsed structure. Walking quickly around the remnants of the building and looking down between the large cracks in what must have been the boards of the roof and walls, he saw no sign of movement of the stranger or the dog. From where he stood, he could not tell whether they were both down there or just the dog. He could still plainly hear the dog, although it wasn't nearly as loud as it had been before. The tortured canine was maniacally whimpering at a feverish pace.

Mason bent over and moved a few of the moisture-rotten boards. Old growth and moss covered everything. He peered down into the opening he had made and caught a brief glimpse of movement about ten feet below. Much to his astonishment, he saw that a cellar that had been dug underneath this long-forgotten building, something that was unheard of in structures this old and of this size in this area. Sheds of this type were either built right on the ground or builders of the time put down a rough stone floor with no mortar or binder at all.

Building up his nerve, Mason spoke down into the cleared hole he made in the boards, "Is anybody down there?"

The dog never stopped its frantic whimpering.

No human voice replied to Mason's query.

He surveyed his surroundings one last time and said aloud, "What the hell is going on here?"

Grudgingly, he realized he was going to have to go down there, if only to rescue the dog.

He moved the rotten old boards once more and made the hole wider, making a rough opening into the cellar hole. As he inspected the rotting wood, he wondered how in the hell the dog had got down there. Aside from the entry Mason had made in the rotten pile, there wasn't a hole big enough for a squirrel to squeeze through, let alone the big black dog he had seen before— if that, indeed, was what was down there.

When Mason dropped down into the dark cellar hole, he landed on some more of the rotten old boards that probably had accumulated there during the decay of the old building. It took him a moment to get his bearings and for his eyes to get used to the sporadic light in the cellar. The only shards of light in the cellar came through the small gaps in the old boards overhead that had made up the walls and roof. He couldn't see well, but he could still clearly hear the tormented dog frenetically whimpering. In the dank and dreary cellar, all that Mason could smell was rotting wood, mold, mildew, and dampness. It was a place conducive to childhood nightmares.

As his eyes adjusted to the lack of light, he picked up movement and shape that looked like the dog in the far corner of the cellar, nervously whimpering and digging at the earthen floor. The dog didn't acknowledge his presence. As Mason moved toward the deranged animal, even in the scant sunlight that reached down into the musty cellar, he could see that the dog had torn off most of its claws in its furious digging at the floor. It was a surreal scene. The dog was in a frenzied state, tossing dirt and blood all over the far end of the cellar. Its mouth was frothing, and it was whimpering frantically. The walls of the cellar were streaked with slashes of blood and mud.

None of what Mason was seeing made any sense. The obsessed dog looked like it could be Steve's dog Stella. It had a cropped tail, and its back was all black. He caught a few glimpses of its head.

He had seen Steve's dogs on many occasions, and Stella was his favorite. She was a hundred-pound Rottweiler that just loved to be loved. When Mason first met the dogs at Steve and Carla's, he was amazed at how gentle she was for her breed, which had such a fierce reputation. Stella would climb up on his lap for hours when he would go and visit. He would make a fake fuss over her, but he secretly always enjoyed the time and would pet her as long as she would stay.

He would know this dog anywhere, but what was in front of him right then, maniacally consumed by whatever it was digging out of the floor, was not the dog he had come to know and enjoy so much. It looked just like her, but was acting like anything but her.

Bewildered, Mason said in a clear voice, "Stella? Is that you, girl?"

The dog never stopped its frantic digging.

He tried again to get the dog's attention, this time using a sharper tone. "Stella!"

The dog snapped its head up as if it was broken from a trance. From ten feet away, Mason could tell it was Stella. He opened his arms slightly in a welcoming gesture.

"Come here, girl. It's all right. Nobody's going to hurt you," he said while motioning her toward him with his fingers.

The dog turned toward Mason, and for a brief moment, he could see recognition in its eyes. Then slowly it drew back its lips and exposed all of its teeth in a savage, almost demonic, expression. It slowly let out a low, guttural, insidious growl. The sound was unlike anything Mason had ever heard come out of an animal, never mind Stella, who had always been the sweetest dog in the world.

"Stella, girl. It's okay. It's okay. I'm here to get you out of here."

Stella turned toward him and stood in a possessive manner directly over whatever she had been digging. She was crouched low with her hackles raised.

She lunged at Mason with her mouth of razor-sharp teeth opened wider than he thought possible. Before Mason could blink, she had sailed across the ten-foot span between them in a single lunge. In instinctive protective reaction, he managed to get his arm out across his body to ward off the fierce initial onslaught.

Just as he raised his arm, Stella was on him. Her first bite was powerful and brutal, and she sunk her rear teeth into Mason's forearm. The first bite severed the tendons and ligature of the last two fingers of his left hand, rendering them instantly useless. The attack also opened arteries and veins in his forearm, and his arm hemorrhaged like it had been caught in a bear trap. Instantly, both he and Stella were covered in the blood from his veins.

Stella stayed clamped onto Mason's arm like it was hers and writhed ferociously back and forth.

Mason let out an agonized bellow that had no effect on the malicious canine. He kicked the dog in the stomach with everything he had, and she released briefly.

Mason was not the type of man to get hurt, give in to pain, or get scared. He was the type who gets angry, murderously angry. He screamed, "Stella, what the fuck is the matter with you?"

Her response was another fierce bite to Mason's upper right thigh. He again let out a scream of pain, his fury and rage building. In agony, he punched the dog in the side of the head with his good right hand. The dog flew across the room and landed, dazed, on some of the rotten boards.

"That's the way it's gonna be, then bring it on, bitch!" the wounded man yelled.

Mason had turned a corner in his mind to a condition he hadn't been in since he had served in Vietnam—when the animal takes over and the rational man ceases to be, when one is truly ready to kill and looking forward to it. He picked up the firmest piece of board he could find and headed toward the dog.

Stella was struggling to get back to her feet just as Mason descended on her.

"Come on, you bitch!" he hissed. "Bring it !"

And she did. Stella lashed out at him again, and this time he was ready for her. He smashed the dog's head with a board. It sounded like hitting an oak tree with a wooden baseball bat.

Stella let out a scream. The force of the blow sent her flying and landed her squarely on her back. She popped up like it had never happened and attacked Mason, catching him completely by surprise. Her teeth looked like shards of bloodstained glass. In a flash, she was all over him, biting him everywhere, answering every punishing kick, punch, and shove of the desperate man with a furious bite.

In his waning attempts to defend himself from the feral onslaught, Mason fell against the wall of the dimly lit cellar. Ancient rusty farm tools that had been hanging on the wall fell all around him. He dove at what looked to be a completely rusted pitchfork, grabbed the old tool from the ground as he rolled to his feet, and squared off against the blood-soaked creature. He was bleeding so much from so many places that the relic of a tool was greasy in his hands. He and the dog were almost circling each other. He was keeping the dog at bay with the head of the pitchfork between them. The handle was soft and spongy in his hand, but it felt solid enough at its core to fend off an attack or deliver a blow.

The dog lashed out in a series of hellacious barks and bites on the tines of the rusty pitchfork. To his dismay, Mason saw the rusted tines disintegrate in the mad dog's teeth.

I better do something fast, or I'm screwed, he thought as the hellhound sprung at his face to deliver what Mason was sure was the deathblow. He jammed the crumbling pitchfork straight out, hoping it wouldn't fracture into a million pieces. With a cruel satisfaction, he watched as two of the three remaining tines on the pitchfork sunk into the dog's chest all the way to the hilt. He drove the dog to the ground with all of his remaining might, all the while screaming in a hysterical tone, "How does that feel, you little bitch! How does that feel!"

By the time Mason regained his composure, he was standing with the remnants of the pitchfork in his right hand. The handle had snapped twice during the fight, only half of one tine and about four inches of another tine were left. Blood from both the dog and from Mason was everywhere. He was slumped over at the shoulders, breathing hoarsely, above the dog, now writhing in the throes of dying. Blood was coming out of Stella's mouth, nose, and everywhere else.

Mason stood exhausted from the battle for his life and said out loud to the copper-scented crypt, "What the hell just happened here!" He tossed the remnants of the bloody pitchfork across the room in disgust.

The dying dog looked pitiful. She looked just like the Stella he had always known, not the insane mad dog that had just ravaged his torn body. She looked up at him in her fading life and let out a soft whimper almost as if to apologize to Mason. He reached down and stroked the fur on her head, and she died.

"What the fuck?" he said, sadly agitated.

He was bleeding badly, but he had to find out what she was defending so stalwartly. As he walked over to where Stella had been digging, he ripped off the torn remnants of his clothes and wrapped them around the areas of his worst bleeding in an attempt to stem or stop the flow.

In the broken shards of light coming in from overhead, it looked like she had unearthed a bunch of sticks, but looking more closely, he realized they were rib bones, probably from some unfortunate deer that had made the mistake of walking across the top of the collapsed pile of boards overhead, falling through and sealing its fate down here with no means of escape. They were about the size and width of deer ribs and about a foot long. The bones were old; some were broken. Mason couldn't understand why the dog had protected them so viciously. The meat that had been on those bones was long removed by the passage of time by insects and other smaller animals that had come down there to feed.

As he stood surveying the surroundings, he noticed something that didn't quite fit with the other components in the pile. He couldn't quite make out what it was, so he reached in with his good hand and took hold of something that was pliable and damp. It was some sort of muddy, wet cloth, like tattered burlap or denim. It had a greasy texture, and Mason could almost pick up the slightest scent of fuel.

He realized it was kerosene-soaked denim of some old, rugged weave. He remembered reading that in earlier times, some materials were soaked in kerosene in order to preserve them or weatherproof them, a common practice in the days before chemical treatments and waterproofing materials. He also remembered something about a circus tragedy in Hartford, Connecticut, back in the forties or fifties: a canvas big top that caught on fire because it had been soaked in kerosene. It went up like a roman candle. The kerosene on the piece of burlap he was holding was almost completely gone. He could barely pick up the scent of it.

Mason slowly pulled on the greasy material. As the old piece of cloth slowly emerged from the pile of earth, he realized with dread that the bones looked more human than animal. Something that looked like a hip girdle fell out of the material. He gripped further down the grimy fabric and kept drawing it out of the loose earth that Stella's incessant digging had created. He found the absolute proof he had a feeling was in there but did not want to see—a human skull. It was lodged in the bones caught in the material. The skull had a large crack above the empty left eye socket, which spoke to Mason of brutal trauma.

He decided to get the hell out of the cellar hole. Just as he twisted the top half of his body up out of the entry hole he had made in the rotten boards, he looked up with eyes that weren't adjusted to the glare of the sun and was startled to see the outline of the old woodsman he had been following earlier. He was standing there, right in front of him. His face was obscured because of the glaring light.

The presence of the unknown man startled Mason so that he flinched. The movement was enough to snap the board he had most of his weight on. He tumbled backward into the black cellar hole he had just clawed his way out of. As he fell, he spun around just in time to be impaled through the abdomen by the very pitchfork he used to fend off the ravenous dog. He actually felt the remnants of the tines protrude through his back. As he was drifting into shock, he wondered again what the hell was going on there then thought, *I don't want to die in this godforsaken place!*

PERFECTLY WRONG

Steve quietly walked down the hall to the back staircase. He slipped open the door and headed down the steps toward the ground floor. He was wracking his brain to figure out a way to get back to Mason's camp and get him out of there. He had no money, no ride, no idea where he was, and absolutely no idea what was going on at that camp. For all he didn't know, he knew what happened at the camp had something to do with Carla's current state of being. Of that much he was sure. But what the hell exactly did happen at the camp?

As he strode down the hall of the main floor of the hospital toward the back doors, he thought, *All right, I have a rough plan, but now I need to get my butt to Mason's camp. I have no one I can call. I don't really want to steal a car, but I will if I have to. Hopefully, I can bum a ride from someone without drawing too much attention to myself.*

As he exited through the back door of the hospital, he noticed the employees smoking area in the back parking lot. A small group of employees was lighting up and chatting away. About ten people were huddled under a clear fiberglass canopy, some sitting on long bench seats like the kind in any baseball dugout at any baseball field anywhere. He could tell from their different styles of dress that the people in the smoking area were employees from all levels of the hospital—a maintenance man, receptionists, security people, nurses in scrubs, and a couple of doctors in their white coats, with stethoscopes around their necks, and a priest. They were all chatting it up and chuckling. It reminded him of a costume party, except it was outside in the back parking lot of a hospital.

What amazed him, though, is that all of them should have known better than to smoke. He would have bet that all of them had interactions with people who died from smoking, from the maintenance man cleaning up their bodily fluids to the priest blessing them and sending them off into the next world. Steve was no preacher on the subject of smoking. He liked a good cigar once in a while and a corncob pipe at hunting and ice fishing camp. He was not opposed to an occasional smoke while having a drink or two, but he didn't work in a hospital. The scene caught him off guard, but it also gave him a place to see if he could hitch a ride.

As the doctors saw him coming, they snuffed out their cigarettes and headed off in a direction different from the one from which Steve was approaching. He could see in their faces their slight embarrassment and their awareness of their contradictory presence in the smoking area.

Everyone has his own dark little secrets, Steve thought, chuckling to himself as he saw first the doctors exiting and then the priest fast on their heels as he approached. The chatter subsided a bit as he walked into the enclosed area.

With a sheepish grin, Steve uncomfortably said, "Please don't stop on my account, folks. I was just coming up to bum a smoke if someone has an extra one."

"If you smoke menthols, I got one for you," a man said in a thick Maine accent. It was the maintenance man.

"Why, yes, I do, if you don't mind me mooching one from you. Thank you," Steve said with a smile as he walked toward the middle-aged man.

The maintenance man fished in the left breast pocket of his blue work uniform and pulled out a half-full pack of generic menthol cigarettes. "They ain't the fanciest, but I'm thinking after what you've been through, these should do for you what you're lookin' for," the man said in a quieter voice that only he and Steve could hear.

"Does everyone here know what I've been through?" Steve asked.

"Not yet, but they will soon enough. It's a small town, and word gets around fast. I was called up to the ER to help clean up the mess they made while patchin' you up. The cops say it's a miracle anyone lived through that wreck. I'll give a smoke to anyone that beats the odds. Name's Toby, Toby Arsenault. How's the missus doin'? Any change?"

"No, not really, Toby, but thanks for asking."

"How you doin'?" the janitor inquired.

As Steve was standing there talking with Toby, he realized exactly how large of a man he was. He stood at least six foot five and must have weighed close to three hundred pounds. Toby didn't seem to be just nosy; he seemed to Steve to be genuinely curious and of a good heart.

"I'm fair," Steve replied, "but I'm kind of stuck here. All of my and my wife's things are out at camp, and I have no way to get there. Is there a bus or something that goes out that way?"

"No. Why don't you ask the constabulary for a ride back to get your stuff?" he said with a smirk that let Steve know Toby had no true love for the representatives of the law.

"I'm full up with my experiences with law enforcement and would rather get back there on my own, thank you," Steve replied, hoping to appeal to the large-framed maintenance man.

"Well, then, you're in luck. I just finished my shift, and I'm going on vacation for two weeks down to Old Orchard beach. I just came by to have one last smoke with my fellow smokers before I left for vacay. You know we have to stick together, us smokers. We're a dying breed."

When he said that, the rest of the members of the smoking group let out a moan that let Steve know it was something Toby said too often.

"Would you use another punch line?" one of the group's members said. "Go on vacation already."

With a huge toothy grin, Toby said to Steve, "They hate when I say that. But deep down inside, they love me."

Steve smiled at the big man. "I love hazing people myself," he said. "I see we have something in common."

Toby motioned Steve to the car and said, "I have to drive right past your road to get home. I'll give you a hitch, but I ain't goin' down to that camp. That place gives me the creeps. I'll tell you more in the car. Do you need to go up to your room to get anything?"

"No," Steve replied. "They carried me and my wife in here naked. Everything I had with me was at the camp or in my truck."

"That must have been a sight," Toby observed, smirking.

Steve shook his head. "I couldn't tell you."

The ten-year-old F-150 was immaculate, except that the inside reeked with the smoky remnants of the thousands of menthol cigarettes that must have been smoked in it over the past decade, and both of its passengers were now adding to the pall of the interior. The truck was in perfect condition and ran like it was brand new. With the exception of the odor of the interior, the truck was enjoying the benefits of being owned by a man who makes his living maintaining things.

"She spins like a top, don't she?" Toby smiled with a sense of pride that was plainly evident. "She's my second love and sometimes my first when the old lady is actin' up."

"I can tell. The truck looks like it's brand new," Steve replied.

"She—the truck—I call her Carrie Anne because she doesn't 'carry on' like the other woman in my life. She'd skin me if she knew that's how I came up with the name, but it fits right for me." Toby chuckled.

"Amen to that, my brother! Amen to that! It's amazing how they can get going when they're upset." Steve said. His mind then snapped onto Carla in the hospital bed, and not realizing it, he went silent and just stared out the window, lost in his thoughts.

Reading the situation, Toby said, "From what I heard the doctors sayin' she wasn't too beat up at all in the accident, and they think she should snap out of it and pull through at any moment."

"I hope so," Steve said with a sigh. The thoughts of his wife in the hospital bed snapped him back to the task at hand. "Why does the camp I'm staying at give you the creeps?" he asked.

"It ain't just the camp. It's that whole set of woods that creep me out. And it ain't just me. No one from around here goes in them woods or up that road, really. Maybe kids on a dare, tryin' to be brave or just plain foolish, but them woods have gone sour. Long ago too. How long you been goin' there? Is this your first time?"

"No. I've been hunting up there for years. I've never had a problem ever," Steve replied.

"Have you ever seen another hunter while you been up in those woods? Ever?" Toby asked. "For that matter, have you ever seen an animal up in them woods?"

After a moment to think about it, Steve realized his superstitious companion was correct. He never really thought about it, but he had never seen even one squirrel or bird while out at the camp. He enjoyed the quiet, solitude, and companionship so much that he never really noticed the lack of wildlife around the camp.

"Actually, I would have to say no to both."

"That ain't a surprise. There was an accident years ago right where you had yours. In the same exact spot as yours. Four kids were killed and one kid, a girl named Denise Moynihan, ended up in the asylum in Denton. To this day, she's as crazy as a shithouse rat, screaming into the night like she's in agony, they say. I talk with the other maintenance folks at the union meetings, and you hear about her every once in a while. It's a shame because she was a pretty little thing. No one knows exactly what happened because all the young men in the car were killed. The cops found beer cans and weed in the wreckage of the car, and that's what they blamed it on.

"No one goes in there from around here. The only folks that go in there are not from the area. There're old bad stories about the place. A whole village of people disappeared back there almost 180 years ago. Both whites and Indians disappeared. There never was any explanation. There have been stories more recent than that—people missing, strange occurrences, stuff like that. The place sat vacant for years until some guy from Bangor bought it. I don't think that's you, is it?"

"No. He's a friend of mine. I stay up at his camp. He's owned the place for thirty-six years and has never ever had a problem. I was just talking with him today about that very issue. And now I'm worried for him, after hearing all of what you had to say."

Then Toby looked him straight in the eye and asked a question that caught Steve off guard. "Have you ever had any troubles up in them woods?"

"I don't want to say anything, except I think it's a very good idea for you and your friends to stay out of those woods. Make sure of it! And yes, the hunting does suck!" Steve answered earnestly. He looked around and recognized the area.

Just then, Toby spoke up to break the uncomfortable silence. "We're coming up on your road. You can see all of the skid marks and small pieces of vehicle on the road from your accident. Wow! It looks like it was a humdinger! Looks like you went off the road in the process. Man, you are lucky to be alive. I'll drive you down your road a ways, but I ain't goin' to the camp itself. I think I've done my fair share to help you."

Steve replied, "I can't thank you enough for all your help. However, there is one more thing you could do for me."

"What's that?" Toby asked with a raised eyebrow.

"Could I bum one last smoke from you before we get there?"

"Absolutely! Any man that can beat them odds and walk away from a wreck like that, I'd be pleased to give a smoke to."

Toby turned the truck onto Long Shadows Road as Steve lit up his smoke. The two men drove in relaxed silence for about five minutes.

"The camp's about a quarter-mile from here if you want to turn around," Steve said, breaking the silence.

"Yep, I do. I don't want to do anything that might jinx my vacation with the old lady."

"I completely understand," Steve replied. "By the way, what's your wife's name? I know your truck's name, but not your wife's."

With a huge toothy grin, Toby said, "It's Kerrie-Anne. They both require a lot of maintenance, and I like taking a ride on them both!" The big man winked as he closed the door to the truck with a big smile on his face.

"Thanks again for the help!" Steve said.

The big man turned the truck around, waved, then headed back to Route 77 and his vacation.

Steve faced east down the road toward the camp with a pit of dread in his gut. His last time here didn't go so well, as he recalled, and he was hoping for a more positive outcome on this trip here.

KEN'S ARRESTING RAGE

As Steve approached the camp dooryard, he saw the roughed-up but mended gate hanging in its spot at the entrance. The crossbar's presence at the gate told him Mason had indeed returned. As he reached the gate, he saw that some of the carnage from the night before had been picked up—not all of it, but most of it. He pondered for a moment on what exactly had happened here last night. Seeing the ladder leaned against the front porch of the cabin snapped him out of his wandering mind. Mason would never leave that there for very long.

He must be close, Steve thought. He saw Mason's truck on the left side of the dirt driveway.

He lifted the gate and set it aside. Steve was not planning to stay here long with Mason, even if it meant picking his stubborn butt up and jamming it in the back of his own pickup, hog-tied. They were leaving; Steve would try to make it up to him later.

"Mason! Are you here? Mason!" he called out as he approached the camp.

He passed Mason's truck and came upon a scene that was everything he did not want to see. On the ground lay his friend, ashen white and covered from head to toe in an enormous amount of blood, confirming Steve's worst fears.

He ran over to him, expecting him to be dead. Kneeling, he lifted Mason's upper body into his arms and off the ground. Steve saw a trail of blood leading back into the overgrowth of woods that spoke of massive blood loss. Suddenly Mason's eyes fluttered open, and he weakly gasped for breath. He was barely alive. He tried to speak but instead coughed out a spray of blood onto himself and onto Steve's face.

"Relax, old buddy," Steve said softly. "I've got you now. I'm going to get you out of here. Just relax and conserve your energy. Just keep breathing."

Steve was gravely concerned and starting to form a plan when Mason choked out, "Too late for that now...shut your mouth... listen—you were right"—he gasped—"something's wrong here"—another series of gasps—"bones in corner...cellar hole... woodsman...Stella..."

Mason lifted a weak, brutally injured left arm and pointed toward the bloody trail of his path out of the woods. He looked Steve in the eyes and tried to say something else. His lips were slightly moving as he passed on. He lay there, his eyes fixed on Steve's.

Just then, Steve heard a commotion and looked up to see Ken Macfarlane pull into the dooryard of the camp.

———————•—•———————

From inside his cruiser, Ken first noticed that the crossbar was not up on the gate.

"The old man is not going to be happy about that at all," he said to himself. Then he noticed the carnage of the door and the items from the front porch all over the yard.

"Oh, he's gonna be pissed!"

He was so distracted by the condition of the yard that he didn't notice Steve holding his father until he shut off the cruiser. He looked over and saw ten feet away the horrific scene of his father's bloody body in Steve's arms. Something so much deeper than rage instantly snapped inside him. It could more aptly be described as wrath, an evil, furious wrath that was instantly consumed in the white-hot flame of hate. Ken instantly slipped into a berserk rage as he left the cruiser.

"You motherfucker. Look at what you've done! What the fuck have you done?"

He drew his sidearm, pointed it at Steve, and pulled back the hammer. He was going to shoot him through the face for what he had done to his father but then realized Steve wouldn't suffer enough getting killed right away. Ken wanted him to suffer. In a flash, Ken ran over and kicked Steve in the face with his steel-toed police boots, violently knocking him away, and he grabbed his father.

"Dad! Dad! Speak to me! Please!"

Distraught, Ken spun and aimed his gun at Steve and screamed, "What have you done? What the fuck did you do to him?"

With pain pulsating from his freshly kicked face, Steve stammered, "I…I…didn't do anything. I just got here right before you and found him like this! I don't know what happened, either! All's I know is we should get him to a hospital as soon as possible." He tried not to pass out from the tornado of pain that was in his head.

"Shut the fuck up!" Ken growled in anguish.

Steve tried to summon the strength to gain his feet in order to help his old friend. Still reeling from Ken's enraged kick, he said. "Ken, I know you hate me right now, and you are confused, but we have got to get moving and get him to a hospital fast. There might still be time."

When he heard that, Ken got to his feet and moved toward Steve, pointing the gun at him as he approached. He swung his sidearm with all of his pent-up ferocity and slammed it on the side of Steve's head.

"I told you to shut the fuck up!"

Steve saw a flash of light and then fell back unconscious.

———◆———

He was disoriented, shaking, and bouncing around violently. There was a commotion and the sensation of movement. Over the sound of a racing engine, he heard frantic screaming, crying, rage. Steve realized he was coming to from Ken's rap to the side of his head, which was pounding with pain. Amidst all of the commotion and pain, he realized he must be in the back of Ken's police cruiser, and they were racing up the road to get Mason to the hospital. With a horrible dread, he also realized his hands were cuffed tightly behind him. He could feel only half of the fingers on both of his hands. He knew he was in a terrible situation but had no idea how much more terrible it was about to become.

Ken was shrieking and cursing wildly as tears raged down his face while he sped up Long Shadows Road. He looked more like some form of blotchy, enflamed ogre than the man Steve had known over the years. The only emotions Steve could read on the unhinged man's face in the reflection in the mirror were enraged anguish and fury. A pale white version of Mason was buckled into the seat next to Ken. His head was hanging back with his mouth wide open. He looked like he could be sleeping, except for how violently he was jerking back and forth from the way Ken was driving up the old dirt road.

At that moment, Ken looked into the rear view mirror and saw Steve observing him. He slammed on the brakes of the cruiser, forcing Steve to bounce, face first, off of the steel cage that separated the front interior from the back seat of the vehicle. As the cruiser skidded to a halt, Ken flung his door open and was at the back door next to Steve, even as dirt and rocks from the road were still flying through the air.

Ken ripped the door open and tore the still dazed Steve from the backseat by a fist full of his hair and flung him head-first into the rear side panel of the cruiser, causing a deep dent.

Ken's voice reflected his tortured frame of mind. It was a mix of hysterical shrieking and wailing with a squeal-like sonata.

"What the fuck have you done to my father? What the fuck have you done?"

As Steve collapsed onto the ground from having his head driven repeatedly into the quarter panel of the cruiser, Ken pulled out his Taser gun and shot the darts of the unit instantly into Steve's back. He pressed the button on the Taser and instantly delivered fifty thousand volts of electricity into the wilting man at his feet, delivering more pain than Steve had ever known. Ken held the button down, his mouth frothing in an evil glee of pure hate. The last thing Steve remembered was shrieking out squeals of torment he could not control, just as he could not control his bladder at that moment.

JUST WHITE

Agitated, angry voices, speaking quickly, penetrated Steve's fog as he realized he was coming out of it. Ken's was the more active and angry of the two voices; the other, he did not recognize. The voices were not directly in front of him. They sounded like they were coming from down a hall. Steve had the coppery metallic taste of blood in his mouth and quickly became aware of intense pain from every inch of his body. His head ached like his skull was three times too small for his brain. He could feel his right eye and cheek throbbing. They were sore without touching them. His entire body ached. He lay with his eyes shut, not knowing where he was, and tried to assess his pain and his situation.

He started to piece together the series of events that got him where he was, starting with Ken's rage, the brutality of the ride in the cruiser, and Ken repeatedly using the Taser on him.

Then he remembered with dread—Mason.

Why did you have to go to that goddamn place? I tried to warn you, he thought. *Why wouldn't you just listen, you stubborn Mainer son of a bitch? Why? Poor Sarah. She's going to be heartbroken.*

Steve's heart felt like it weighed twenty pounds and was sinking into his soul.

What the hell did he mean a woodsman with an axe? Who is this guy, and what the hell is he doing on Mason's land? Is he responsible for Mason's death? Can he explain what happened if he didn't kill him?

I need to get out of here and exonerate myself. There is no way I will be able to get a fair trial around here! Or get any local police department to help me. Not with Ken running around poisoning them against me, telling them I killed his father. Mainers take care of Mainers, cops take care of cops. I'm screwed on both sides if I plan to look for any help. I need to figure this thing out to save my own neck.

First, I have got to get the hell out of here. Second, I have to get back to that camp and figure out what exactly is going on if I'm going to get Carla back. I have to do all of this and not get hung by a lynch mob of angry Maine cops.

An irate voice from down the hall intruded into Steve's thought stream.

"That motherfucker does not leave here or receive any medical help until I get a BCI team out there. Then I'll come and get some friggin' answers from him! No one in, no one out! I don't care if the president himself shows up at the door! That bastard sees no one until I get back and can get some time alone with him. He killed my father! I have to go back to the hospital where my father's body is and do a positive ID. Then I have to break the news to my mother, and that's going to suck. I'll only be a couple hours, and then I'll be back to get my answers."

Ken realized he had to calm down. *Thank God, this guy is an old school part-timer,* he thought about the officer on duty in the jail. It's Sunday. *No one knows Babin is here.*

Steve slowly opened his eyes. He realized he was on the cot of a jail cell in some godforsaken podunk town. It was an old jail, with round steel bars reminiscent of jail cells in old Western movies. He was cuffed to the frame of the cot so tight that he could barely feel his fingers.

He heard footsteps coming down the hall and closed his eyes again, thinking it would be best if they didn't see he was awake. The footsteps stopped in front of his cell, and the door slid open with a loud metallic *klang.*

They're trying to wake me, he thought.

"Let's see if we can't get this bastard up before I go. I want to start getting some answers from him!"

Steve did not stir. He felt a kick to his feet.

"Come on. Get up," the unfamiliar voice said to him.

Steve lay there limp.

"He looks like you damn near killed him," the stranger said.

"Most of that was from the accident he had this morning, but some of that is from me," Ken retorted.

"I heard about the accident, but another one of the guys covered the scene," the stranger said. "That corner there is a bad spot. About thirty years ago, there was almost exactly the same type of accident at that very same spot. Some teenage kids were partying down in the woods, came ripping up the same dirt road your dad's camp is on. Whoever was driving just flew out onto Route 77 like it was some old cart path. It was busier then than it is now because the interstate wasn't in yet. Route 77 carried a lot of traffic and big trucks, mostly logging trucks. Well, those kids were packed into that car like sardines. There were seven of them, six boys and a girl. The moment they cut out onto the road, they were piled into by a logging truck. Six of those kids were instantly killed at that spot.

"The only one who survived, if you want to call it that, was the girl. Something inside of her died that moment with her friends. Since that night, she's lived in hospitals. She was in St. Bart's intensive care for a while after the accident, but when she came out of her coma, her mind was shattered. She would just shriek, and scream, mumble, and murmur. The only thing she would say was 'She's with me now.' She upset the other patients at the hospital, and they transferred her up to the asylum in Denton.

"It was a shame because she was pretty popular back in the day. Her name's Denise Moynihan. She's still up there to this day. She never got any better; she never got out. She just quieted down a little bit. She still has outbursts, as I'm told by some of the staff. She'll scream that she's being raped or she'll scream in agony as if she's being tortured, but she usually just sits around murmuring to herself or drawing big circles on the wall of her padded room. I guess what she keeps murmuring is some gibberish no one understands, but she also keeps saying, 'She's with me now.'"

Steve almost sat bolt upright when he heard the story about Denise Moynihan. For the sake of his own safety and in order to find out more, if he could, he persisted in his feigned unconsciousness.

That's something else to put on my list of things to do—get up there and find out what the connection with Denise Moynihan is, Steve thought

The stranger's voice almost had a quiver in it. "Those guys were my friends. We were all in the same class. I would have been in that car if it weren't for my parents dragging me off to some family function that I didn't want to be dragged to."

"I'm sorry to hear that. That must have been rough for a young guy to deal with," Ken replied before continuing coldly, "Back to business. The cheek and the side of his face is my work. If I killed him, he would have got off easy. What I have in store for him, believe me, he would rather be dead."

His voice simmered as he barely kept the lid on the hatred he was feeling for Steve, who, at that moment, felt a searing bolt of pain coming from his damaged cheek. Someone—probably Ken, Steve thought—was pushing with his thumb into his cheek. Steve mustered what strength he had to force himself to just lay there limp, not responding to the punishing thumb. With his eyes closed, all he could see was white, the perfect white of searing pain. He heard something lightly crunching and squishing around in his cheek. *Must be a bone chip in there*, he thought, just before he passed out again. He felt no more pain. Just white.

JAILBREAK

Coffee? Is that coffee? Steve thought he could smell it. His eyes were still closed, and his body still ached. His cheekbone was throbbing like it had just been punched. With dread, he realized he was still in the old jail cell. The painful cuff was still torqued down onto his wrist and attached on the other end to the cot.

He heard footsteps coming down the hall toward him and kept his eyes shut as he had before. The door to his cell slid open again, and he felt his feet get kicked again. The smell of coffee was stronger now. Steve didn't respond.

The deputy spoke to him as if he was awake, "My name is Deputy David Lynders, and I am personally going to make you wish you never laid a hand on Officer Macfarlane's father."

Lynders had the thickest Mainer accent that Steve had ever heard. He sounded like he was right from Aroostook County, and many of the folks from that area did not care for outsiders, especially outsiders accused of killing a Mainer cop's dad.

Lynders kept talking to Steve as if he knew Steve was listening.

"You must be some kind of prissy boy because you were brought here over a half hour ago, and you're still passed out. You look like a priss to me, all smoothed out and lookin' like the type of flatlander me and my boys liked to beat the shit out of during the summers back in high school. All the goddamn big money flatlander prissy boys would come up and strut their stuff until me and the boys would get a hold of 'em and put a stompin' on 'em they'd never forget."

The deputy's voice rose and got more vicious the more he talked.

"We would grab a pretty boy flatlander behind a bar or leavin' some back camp party and beat the smug, spoiled, entitled prissy looks off their prissy boy faces! I'd be willing to bet if I poured some of this red hot coffee right in your face, I bet that would change the arrogant, prissy, look right off your tough-guy mug. Wouldn't it?"

Steve felt the deputy's breath on his face and smelled the acrid scent coming from the man's mouth. He smelled the coffee in the cup in Lynders' hand and felt the heat from the lava-hot fluid and knew he had to make his move.

Lynders was so surprised when Steve popped his eyes open directly in front of him that he didn't see the clenched fist coming for his face. With his free left hand, Steve inadvertently punched the Styrofoam cup that the red-hot coffee was in before he hit the deputy. The scorching cup of fluid exploded onto the deputy's face as Steve's fist rocked him across the jaw. Lynders screamed in pain, more from the searing black coffee in his eyes than from the blow to his jaw.

Steve pounced on the blinded and battered jail keeper in a flash. He grabbed Lynders by the hair with his free hand and drove his head into the solid steel bars of the cell door. Blood squirted onto the hallway floor as the deputy's nose mashed into a shape that would accommodate one of the bars. Then Steve turned and smashed the groggy man's skull into the bolted steel frame of the cot. He felt Lynders go limp in his angry hands.

"Take that, you country bumpkin bastard! Who are you going to pour your coffee on now, bitch?" Steve roared triumphantly into the empty jailhouse.

As he collected himself, Steve reached down and checked the unconscious deputy to make sure he was alive. There was a pulse, but Lynders looked like he had been beaten with a ten-pound can opener. He was bleeding from everywhere on his face. The bridge of his nose was the concave shape of one of the bars on the cell door.

Steve looked down in disgust and realized he had a clump of the man's hair still in his hand. He threw it at the unmoving jailer. "That's for all of the prisses you and your spineless boys didn't have the guts to take on man to man," he snarled.

He knelt down beside Lynders and searched for keys. He found them on the back of the deputy's belt, fished them out, and released the vice-like cuff that had him shackled to the jail-cell cot. He was standing, rubbing the sensation back into his wrist, when he heard the deputy moan. Steve reached down and grabbed the Taser from the deputy's belt, clicked the button, and used it on him. The man lurched on the floor and was out again. Steve smashed the Taser unit on the floor next to the deputy. He was genuinely pissed off. From his experience of getting arrested by Ken, he hated the damned Taser and didn't want anything more to do with it.

Steve lifted Lynders up onto the cot and gave the man a taste of his own medicine. He used the pair of cuffs that were still on the cot to shackle both of the deputy's hands behind him and manacle him to the frame of the bed. He used Lynders' own cuffs and repeated the process with the man's ankles. Just before he left the cell, he made sure both sets of cuffs were on tight.

When he reached the front office of the jail, he used the keys to look around for clothes. He wanted to change out of the hospital scrubs he had swiped earlier. He also wanted to get out of there as soon as he could.

He found the deputies' room and went in. It was a small cramped room with lockers and a shower. The only locker door that had an open lock hanging from it was on Lynders' locker. From lifting and moving the unconscious jailer around earlier, Steve could tell the man was a little larger than he was but didn't think that would be a problem. Steve changed into a gray T-shirt, a flannel shirt, and tan jeans. The shoes were a little large, but he tied them up and headed out into the office.

Once there, Steve saw he had a key to the gun case.

"Probably best to stay away from those," he said aloud and walked down to check on the deputy. Lynders was still out, but he had spat out an alarming quantity of blood onto himself and the floor. Steve grimaced at the sight.

I'll be screwed if he dies. How can I get him medical attention without getting seen? he thought. *Then it hit him like a thunderbolt.*

He was outside in Lynders' car when the ambulances arrived. The paramedics hopped out and ran up the steps into the jailhouse. He hoped Lynders wasn't dead but had just had some sense knocked into his country-bumpkin head. Steve saw one of the paramedics come back out to the ambulance a minute later. The EMT talked into his radio as he dug medical supplies out of the back of the flashing orange and white van.

That was when Steve slid the deputy's car out of the parking lot of the Denny's, about three hundred yards up the road, where he had parked it in order to be able to observe and slip away without being noticed. A few minutes later, he was heading north on Route 77. Sheriff's department and state-police cars started to fly by sporadically.

Steve wondered if this was how Jesse James would have handled his first jailbreak.

BLOOD TRAIL

Steve knew if he was going to have time enough on Mason's land to try to figure out what the hell was happening, he had to leave no tracks or trace so as not to tip off the local police. He was sure they would be coming for him once they discovered the deputy. He had to ditch the deputy's car in the woods at the main road so he wouldn't leave any tire tracks on the dirt that would lead back to Mason's camp. That would be a dead giveaway to the police that he had returned to the area.

He hid the car in an abandoned barn about a half mile up the road and covered it with boards and other debris in the barn. The barn was set back from the road on the west side of Route 77. Once the car was inside the barn, it couldn't be seen.

Before he concealed the car, he searched around inside it and took inventory of anything that might be useful to him in his next desperate hours. There wasn't much—small rusted mechanics tools; electrical tape, which he pocketed; dirty clothes; fast-food trash; and a couple of law-enforcement magazines. But further digging under the seat produced one useful find—a police radio, something he had overlooked grabbing in his rush to get out of the jailhouse. The radio would help him monitor police activities and adjust his tactics as he was trying to figure this whole thing out. He clicked on the radio to see if it worked. A small green light came on, and a display screen lit up. It was a rechargeable unit, but it was low on power, with only about a quarter of a charge left. That meant he would have to travel with it off most of the time and periodically check to see if there was any police activity related to him.

Steve made sure there was no traffic on Route 77 and scurried across into the woods on the eastern side of the road. He would have to lie low and stay undetected if he planned to pull this off.

For the next hour and a half, he made his way the five miles back toward Mason's camp. He stopped from time to time to monitor the radio and check out the woods before him. Moving quickly but cautiously, he made sure to leave no tracks. He stayed off of the road and out of any mud or dirt along the way. During his trek back to the camp, he did not encounter anyone or anything, but he did see some things he had never seen on Mason's land—plenty of tracks, animal droppings, a few feathers—signs of normal woodland life. He realized he hadn't noticed how much of this was missing from the land Mason's camp sat on. He had just thought there wasn't a lot of wildlife in the area. To see the abundance of signs of life in the woods all along the way to Mason's land was refreshing. He was in his element, and a sense of well-being washed over him for the first time in a while.

He thought he might just get out of this thing with his skin still attached.

Not if Ken has anything to do with it, the dark side of his mind reminded him.

That thought brought a cloud of dread to his fleeting sense of hope and snapped him back to his reality. He was an escaped fugitive, who was wanted for the assault (most likely attempted murder by now) of an officer of the law and for the murder of Mason Macfarlane. Steve knew he had to focus on the job at hand—resolving this tempestuous state of affairs before it spiraled completely out of control and destroyed everything that he considered to be his life.

What he was undertaking was not just for him, but also for Carla, whose current state, he knew in his heart, was somehow related to all of this. He just had to figure out how. The camp held the answers, and it was up to him to find them.

With this newfound cheerless inspiration, he headed east again toward Mason's camp and, he hoped, some answers.

He arrived to an unsettling scene. The place was still in disarray. The front gate was thrown to the side. The coolers and their contents and the grill from the front porch were rent asunder all over the front yard. The fucking ring was in the same spot in the yard. One thing was different—the front door that he and Carla had plowed through had been fixed.

The most distressing aspect of the chaotic scene was the huge bloodstain in the soil and grass where Mason had been lying. Steve went over to the spot, looked down at the stain, and sighed with deep sadness.

"Dammit, Mason! Why couldn't you just listen to me?" he said aloud.

As much as he didn't want to, he knew where he had to start. He turned and went into the cabin to get his backpack. He would need it for wherever he was going and for the work that probably would need to be done.

Steve went back to the dark stain on the ground. The path from the west that Mason had taken back toward his camp with his grievous wound was clearly visible. He braced himself and started to follow the blood trail, which was so pronounced that Steve was able to walk at a quick pace without losing the trail.

After about ten minutes, Steve realized he was heading toward the border of the swamp. He also realized how tough and strong Mason was to have been able to go all that way back to the camp, having been run through the guts by who knows what, and how incredible it was that he had lived that long.

The blood loss had been substantial. It was still fluid in some leaves that were naturally cupped and seemed to cover everything for a five-foot-wide swath that led back toward the camp. Rounding a bend, he saw another wall of viny swamp thorns. The blood trail came straight from there.

What were you doing in there, Mason? Steve asked himself.

He saw some logs had been dropped down onto the thorny mesh, and a rough gap had been created in order to pass through the barrier.

Why didn't I think of that before? You were a pretty sharp old cuss there, Mason, Steve thought. *Then again, after seeing everything that happened to you, I'm glad I didn't.* He gulped, contemplating what might have happened to him when he was searching for Stella earlier.

At that moment, he saw something in the mud that made his soul squirm—a footprint he recognized as his own from his earlier search. He could tell this was the very spot where he had turned back and headed around the western border of the swamp.

Uncanny! he thought. *What are the chances?*

As he was looking down, he saw the blood trail and stepped onto the logs that cleaved the thorny mass, trying to avoid stepping in the blood. He wasn't sure why he was trying to avoid the blood, but he suspected it was out of respect for Mason.

He clambered over the bridge of piled logs into the open space on the other side of the wall of thorns and saw what looked like the debris of a collapsed old building ten feet away.

What do we have here? he wondered.

The crumpled pile of boards was covered and interwoven by long viny braids of green thorns. As he looked over the heap of boards, Steve saw that the trail of blood led back to the corner of the pile and to a hole he thought must be the cellar hole Mason had gasped about as he died.

He wondered if Mason had been walking across this ruin and had fallen in. *Impossible,* he thought. *Mason would have known better than that. He was a Maine outdoor guide, for Christ's sake. He would have been more careful than that.*

Steve staggered over to the hole and saw handprints of blood where Mason must have hefted his large mass out of the hole.

What a tough son of a bitch! It must have taken a Herculean effort to lift himself out of that hole in all of that pain. My god!

Kneeling, he peered into the hole. All he could make out was that it was deep—deeper than he suspected. It was about eight feet down, judging from the broken splinters of light that shone on the subterranean floor or the ancient structure.

He thought he ought to go down there and take a look but dreaded doing so. He really did not want to go down there. The thought of dropping himself down into some musty, old death-trap stirred considerable anxiety in him. But he realized he had to go down there, if for no other reason that that it might help him exonerate himself. If he could bring the authorities to this spot, maybe it would help.

In his mind, Steve heard his father's voice: "You and you alone are responsible for your life. It is up to you to keep yourself alive. I have done my job with you. I have protected, prepared, comforted, and kept you alive up to this point. You are a man now. I will always be here to help you with anything, but your life is up to you. If you ever have kids, it'll be on your shoulders to keep them alive until they become adults. For now, though, just worry about keeping your own skin on and making the right decisions."

His father had told him that on his eighteenth birthday. He knew his father had always loved him. His father also had imbued him with confidence enough to face anything, with common sense to deal with most things, with the strength to deal with adversity, and with a will to not accept what he did not see as right. It was his father who had showed Steve how to get around in the woods under any conditions. What mattered in the woods (and for most things in life) was to keep thinking clearly and to keep trying to solve the problems you were faced with, his father had taught him.

Remembering those lessons strengthened Steve's resolve, and he knew he could handle anything that might be down in that hellhole. First, though, he had to figure out how he could get down there safely. He assessed the situation, and an idea came to him. He got the strongest logs and branches that had been thrown on top of the thorn bushes, angled a few of them down into the dim cavity, and then laid the strongest ones across the top. Checking to see if the top logs were anchored and sturdy, he held onto them and swung his feet down into the void. He lowered himself and hung there for a moment to get his bearings. His eyes needed a moment to adjust to the darkness that was broken up by shards of light seeping through the boards and vines above. As he was dangling there, he felt some rotten old boards at his toes. He dropped down onto the boards and knelt there to give his eyes more time to adjust.

After a minute or two kneeling silently, listening for the slightest noise from his new surroundings or up above, his eyes began to adjust. Even with his diminished vision, he could make out large stones that were piled vertically to create the rough walls. Once his eyes fully adjusted, what he saw was a nightmare. It looked like Jackson Pollock had tossed sinuous strings of crimson everywhere. Steve had to take a moment and swallow so he could steady his nerves. The scene seemed more akin to a slaughterhouse than merely the product of one man's horrendously bad fortune.

How did it get all over the walls? Steve wondered. *Was something else happening that brought Mason down here to help? I didn't see any other blood trail or anything else. Is this all his? He couldn't believe one man could have left all of this.*

He leaned forward from where he was kneeling and put his hands out to steady himself. As soon as he put his hands down, he knew he had put them into something he did not want to touch. His hands were immersed in a pool of sickeningly sticky liquid that he realized was the beginning of Mason's blood trail.

STELLA

After getting over his displeasure about the unfortunate place-
ment of his hands, Steve moved carefully around on the rotting
pile of boards, searching in the sporadic light for what Mason
had tried to tell him about with his dying words. He found the
corner with freshly churned earth but did not see any bones. He
scrutinized the area where nothing seemed to be out of place,
except the fresh earth.

What were you talking about, Mason? Steve wondered. *I don't
see any bones down here. What were you doing in this corner?*

He toed the soft earth with his boot and felt something underneath the soil. Reaching down, he felt a greasy, rough cloth-like
material under the dirt. He pulled it up out of the earth and, with
dismay, found the first thing Mason had told him about while
struggling for breath.

It was the bones, wrapped in some old type of burlap that had
been soaked in a preservative. The material was old and weather-
beaten and infused with soil. Time and the elements had worn
holes through it but were not able to completely destroy the covering. He sniffed his fingers and detected the scent of kerosene,
which he remembered was used long ago to waterproof and preserve materials. Looking down at the intertwined pile of bones,
soil, and burlap, he wondered why Mason had taken the time to
rebury the bones. It made no sense to him.

He knelt down again and dug into the pile of bones. Removing
the mass of burlap and the rest of the skeleton, including a gray
and discolored skull, he realized he had never held a skull in his
hands. For that matter, he had never before held an actual human

bone before. As he cleared the hole of loose earth, he felt something else deeper in the ground. It felt like more material set in the earth. It did not pull out as easily and ripped in his hands. The earth around this bundle had not been disturbed and had been tamped down over time into a compressed semisolid.

Steve looked around for something to help him break up the soil and retrieve the soaked burlap parcel, which felt smaller than the first. He wanted to take out this one intact in order to inspect it more closely. He worked his way around the circumference of the muddy fabric with a piece of board that constantly splintered as he was digging. Finally, he unearthed the object enough to be able to get his hands underneath it and lift it out in its entirety. It was a little more than two feet long and looked like a large Indian papoose or giant muddy cocoon. It had been wrapped meticulously so that was all folded back into itself with no loose ends. He laid it on the ground and carefully unwrapped the shroud. Sure enough, it was another skeleton, much smaller than the other one, probably a child.

He wondered how this child had died until he found a very disturbing clue—a visible crack in the skull that ran from the top left forehead down across the top of the nose and into the right eye socket. Steve was no coroner, but this looked to him as an indication the child had died from a massive blow to the head and face. Out of curiosity, he turned around and picked up the other skull. Now that he was looking more closely at it, he saw a crack that ran across the top of this head. The crack went from side to side, almost from ear to ear, again indicating massive trauma.

As he was kneeling there examining the two skulls, Steve looked back down into the deeper section of the empty grave and thought he spied more burlap sticking into the void from the sidewall of the hole.

This burlap was only six inches down into the ground. It looked like a folded bottom corner as compared to the intact papoose he had lying in front of him. The newly discovered cloth was coming from the side of the hole where the skulls of the first two skeletons had been positioned. Steve reached down and grabbed a handful of the cloth object from beneath and lifted up in order to give the newly discovered object leverage to break through the compressed earth above it. This one was larger. He repositioned his hands and hefted the dirty bundle out of the ground. It was tied together in the same manner as the smaller papoose. He reached into the wrapping and pulled out the skull.

This skull disturbed him more than the others had for two reasons. First, remnants of patchy clumps of hair were still attached to the bone. Second, the hair changed the nature of his observations—from objective forensic observations to the realization this was a human being that had most likely been savagely murdered. The back of this skull was shattered. As he lifted it out of the death cloak, pieces fell to the ground and back into the pall.

With the epiphany that these were real people and not some archaeological dig, Steve's mood crystallized into a deeper concern, which was almost morosely incapacitating. He knew he could not afford to let this disturbing experience break his will. So he dug deeper into the reserves of his resolve and moved forward with what had to be done. For the next thirty minutes, he followed the wall line around the cellar hole. Kicking the old boards out of the way and quickly digging two feet away from the previous hole each time, he dug down a few inches and encountered one tattered burial mantle after another.

When he was finished, he had uncovered eleven papoose-cloaked skeletons. They were all prepared and folded up the same way. None had been buried with any clothing. They were all laid underground in a long, narrow circle along the wall, with the exception of those bodies that were buried in the corners. They were kitty-cornered from the others and not laid directly along the wall. All had been interred head to toe. All of the skulls showed signs of blunt trauma, and one of the skeletons looked like it had been burnt. It was charred to a black greasiness. The only difference among the skeletal remains was their variation in size, from large adults to small children—one even looked like an infant.

The layout of the shallow graves and the swathing process of the dead were reminiscent to him of the old Roman catacombs. He remembered there was religious significance attached to how the martyrs' bodies were laid out in certain areas beneath the Coliseum. The martyrs waiting to meet their fates in the arena above were very particular about the process prepared for the dead. It was done so they would be readily received by their Lord and Master in the afterlife.

Only one hole had two sets of remains. That was the first one he had found. He thought he should dig a little deeper in this hollow and see if there wasn't another burlap bundle down a little farther in the soil. With another board, he scraped down into the earth a little deeper. About two inches down, he hit something solid. At first, he thought it was a rock, but the board slid across the top of the object along a unified plane.

"What is this?" he wondered aloud. He removed clumps of loose earth with his hands to reveal a flat metallic surface, which he wiped off. With his fingers, Steve dug around the sides and edges of the top of the box-like thing to try to get an idea of what he was dealing with. It looked like it was about two and a half feet long and a foot and a half wide. The surface felt like it was made of lead—probably to resist the elements, Steve thought. If it wasn't a box, it was some sort of heavy lid that wasn't budging. He looked around for something to help him dig with, a bigger stick perhaps.

Feeling around in the half darkness, he grabbed what felt like a metal stick with grease on it. When he looked at it in the broken light, he noticed the grease wasn't grease. It was blood, and a lot of it, and the metal stick wasn't a stick but some sort of rusted metal rod that had been snapped off of whatever it had originally been a part of.

Blood was everywhere in the cellar, and Steve thought, *Goddammit, Mason, why did you have to come down here? What brought you here in the first place? Did you just fall, walking over this hellhole? How the hell did you not see the pile of boards? What the fuck are all of these bones? Who did this? Did you do this? If not you, then who? What the fuck is this box?*

Steve was getting frustrated and angry—a deep, scary anger, which was not healthy.

He was scared—scared for Carla. His emotions and frustrations began to snowball.

What was the matter with her? Why wasn't she coming out of it? Her wounds were not serious enough for her to be in a continuous coma. What the hell was that trance that started all of this? What was that she murmured—"She's with me now"—what the hell was that all about?

He was scared for Mason, even though he was dead.

He was scared of Ken, who wanted to put the worst hurt on him he could, using all of his police powers with as much personal vengeance as possible.

Why is he so angry? He knew I loved Mason.

What is the story with that girl in the mental hospital? I have got to find out what is going on up there, and how it ties into this entire shitstorm.

He was scared because he did not want to take the fall for all of this and end up in some Maine hellhole of a prison for something he did not do.

But most of all now, he was angry. And it was an anger that he could not let control him because he wouldn't be able to stay clearheaded and think his way through this terrible situation in which he currently found himself immersed.

He looked down at his hand and realized he was clenching, squeezing the bloody rod so tightly that his hand was white. He threw the bloody rod across the musty cellar hole in disgust with an arch of the rage that was trying to take him over. As he did so, he realized it could be from a pitchfork.

With eyes that had adjusted to the fractured light, he scanned the cellar for something else he could dig with. In another corner, under some of the boards he had kicked out of the way, he thought he saw some old tools. He went over and saw ancient tools, rotten and rusted from many years of nonuse. Many of the handles were spongy rotten and broke in his hands. On the others that had strong handles, the metal was rusted to a brittle uselessness. He kept looking until he came across something that looked like an old trowel. It seemed firm enough.

As he turned to go unearth whatever the lead-like thing was, he caught something out of the corner of his eye. It just didn't fit with everything else in the cellar hole of broken light. Whatever it was, it was a subtle reddish-tan something that was in a crack of sunlight under a pile of boards. It looked like the fur of an animal. *But what the hell is it? A badger, a rabid fox or coyote, a bear?*

He went over to it slowly because he did not want to be trapped in the blood-soaked cellar hole with whatever might be under those boards. He approached the fur armed with the trowel as a weapon in case the unknown thing lunged at him. He poked the woodpile just above the fur; nothing moved. He took a tentative step forward and flipped over a few boards to expose more of it.

Is it in some type of hibernation mode or something? Is it asleep? he wondered. As he peered into the larger space in the woodpile, he realized in a horrific flash that it was a leg and it had the same markings as a Rottweiler.

He tore back the rest of the pile to reveal Stella's carcass, soaked in blood, which gave the fur the reddish tinge he had noted, and covered with what seemed like a hundred puncture holes. She was limp in death. He grabbed her up in his arms and gagged out a cry he was trying to stifle. He flopped back onto the rotten boards and held the dog in his arms and cried. The cry was a release. It released him of all the stress, tension, and fear he had been carrying since all of this had started. He cried for Stella, for Mason, and for Carla. He cried until he could not cry anymore and slipped off right there into an oblivious sleep in the cellar hole with Stella in his arms.

CONTENTS OF THE COFFER

Women screaming, tormented souls searching for exodus in a realm devoid of egress.

Steve woke with a start from tortured dreams in the cellar hole and realized he was still clutching Stella's lifeless body. The fractured sunlight still shone from up above. He looked at his watch.

Good, he thought. *I was out for only fifteen minutes.*

He looked down at the dead dog, gave her one last hug and said aloud, "Stella, as I am the man that I am, once I catch up to the son of a bitch that got you into this mess, I'm going to ruin his entire friggin' world. That I promise you, little girl."

He then set the dog's carcass near the entrance of the cellar hole. When he left this miserable little crypt later, he sure as hell was not going to leave her down here.

He didn't know why, but he was sure this place had something to do with Carla's trance and, ultimately, Mason's death. He could not see a direct correlation, but in his gut, he knew there must have been some relationship. He had a feeling the answer lies in this cellar hole, this catacomb.

Going back to the spot where he woke up with Stella, he found the trowel and went back to exhuming the leaden object out of the floor of the tomb. After about five minutes, he had loosened enough soil to get a grip on it. It was heavy, but he was able to get enough leverage to grind the container up out of the ground. As he was lifting it, he felt some things shifting inside, and he thought he heard a metallic *thunk*. He set the coffer on the ground next to the original hole and wiped off as much of the earth and debris he could with his sleeve-covered hand. It was about eighteen to twenty inches high, with heavy hinges on the backside and an internal lock. The keyhole in front was filled with dirt. Steve thought it must weigh at least eighty pounds. It resembled a pirate's treasure chest, as depicted in movies, except that the top lid was flat instead of being rounded.

Now to get the damn thing open and see what's inside, he thought.

Steve scurried over and grabbed his pack, which was on the ground next to Stella. He rummaged through the contents, took out the headlamp, put it on, and got his Leatherman Multi-Tool. There was some flex in the old box, and he wanted to use that to his advantage to pry the old thing open. If he could exert enough pressure between the lid and the bottom half, he figured he could pop the lock. He pried the trowel under the lid up to the lip of the beveled edge on one side of the lock and did the same with the stout blade on the Multi-Tool directly on the other side of the catch. Slowly prying them both upward at the same time, he felt the lead bending and his hands rising. Then he heard a *twang* from inside the mechanism, the top flopped open, and the whole thing almost flopped onto its back.

He caught the box and steadied it. Clicking on his headlamp, he peered inside. Again, burlap covered the contents inside the coffer, but this burlap was untreated and was in excellent shape. The inside was completely dry; it didn't smell musty or mildewy.

Steve gently removed the burlap to reveal the contents. They consisted of two books, one that was bound in intricately etched silver. Along with the intricate designs on the cover and the binding, there was a series of craters or pockmarks sunk in the covers and bindings. Steve guessed the craters were from large jewels that had been removed. The other book was leather-bound and had old-looking handwriting on it. At first glance, it looked like a diary or personal journal.

The coffer also contained an ornately etched silver chalice. It also had empty craters on it. It reminded Steve of the cup that he received communion wine from in church as a kid. The last item in the chest was a thin pearl-handled dagger that was still in its sheath. Looking more closely, he saw it had a double-edged blade that was still razor sharp after years hidden under the earth.

As best Steve could tell from a quick inspection of it under the headlamp, the metal-bound book was a copy of the Bible, a very large ancient copy. He thought it was handwritten in Latin. *This Bible would be worth a fortune in itself,* he thought. *What a find!*

Suddenly with horror, Steve realized this discovery would give Ken what he was looking for to hang him—a motive. He knew he had to get out of there fast with his newfound booty. He had completely lost track of time, and he knew that the incapacitated deputy back at the jail would motivate the police to get moving. It was not going to be fun lugging an eighty-pound chest of priceless antiquities around the woods while trying to evade the police. If he was caught sneaking around out here with the chest, he was done for. He knew it. It dawned on him that he had just buried himself deeper in his personal shit pit by making his inadvertent discovery of the coffer and its contents.

Steve turned the radio on to see if he could find out on the police channel if anything had changed. To his personal horror, he heard Ken's voice, loud and clear: "I just arrived back at the camp. I will see if I can locate any evidence and will investigate the area thoroughly. At first glance, I have not seen the fugitive or any trace of his presence. I will contact if I need reinforcement. How long until you're able to set up the roadblock on Route 77?"

An official voice replied on the radio, "Not for at least an hour. We need to wait for the reinforcements from Bangor to arrive and get situated. There are some troopers in transit that should be arriving soon. They'll be dispatched to your position as soon as they are briefed on the situation."

"I'll be here waiting for the bastard when he tries to sneak back and collect his stuff," Ken replied. "How's the deputy doing? Has he snapped out of it yet or is he still pretty groggy?"

"He's still groggy, but he's coming to. They have him up to the ER. He has a pretty good crack to the noggin', but it looks like he should pull through."

"This idiot sure knows how to dig his own grave," Ken sneered. "First, he kills the father of a cop, then he tries to kill a deputy, and then he has the balls to escape from custody. That sounds like three strikes to me."

"Just be careful out there and call if you see anything suspicious. This guy can be pretty vicious. He beat poor Dave half to death, put a gag in his mouth, and then horrendously shackled him to the steel cot. Now he's on the run. He's probably feeling very desperate, and as we know, he's capable of anything. I'm sorry to hear about your father. Are you sure you're all right to carry on?" the official voice said with a stoic compassion.

"Yes," Ken replied. "I have to see this through and make sure this son of a bitch gets a taste of Maine justice."

At that moment, after hearing that conversation, Steve felt like a man on the gallows awaiting execution, just before the bottom dropped out beneath him.

SUBTLE MESSAGE

After hearing the exchange on the police radio, Steve knew he had to get moving and fast. He also knew he could not leave the unearthed coffer behind as evidence that Ken could use in court to finally hang him. He had to put it where it would not be found. He could never get out of the woods with an eighty-pound leaden box before the police closed the dragnet and caught themselves a murderer who would then be subjected to "a taste of Maine justice," whatever the hell that was. Steve was sure he did not want to find out. He had to move. The first thing he had to do was get the box out of the cellar.

First, he grabbed the journal out of the box because it might supply some insights about what happened to Carla. He stuffed it into his backpack, then grabbed the pearl-handled dagger and slipped it into a side pocket of his backpack with the handle sticking out. The scabbard of the knife was wedged firmly into the pocket. He then dragged Stella's body to a resting place near the wall.

"I'm sorry I have to leave you down here, girl, but maybe you can help me save my skin by staying down in this shithole a little longer," Steve said, cheerlessly.

Next, he gathered up all of the decaying blood-soaked boards and began piling them under the hole that Mason had originally made to get down into the cellar. He piled them against the wall until he thought it was high enough for what he thought he needed. He went back to the coffer and slammed the lid down in order to try to reengage what was left of the old lock. It worked; the compromised lock held. He then hoisted up the box in his hands like he was carrying a baby and struggled up the loose pile of rotten boards until he could reach the entrance. It was a precarious setup. He kept losing his footing and almost fell a couple of times, but he managed to get to the top of the pile, where he was able, using a military press maneuver like a weightlifter, to raise the coffer up and out of the cellar hole through the opening in the boards. The coffer tumbled out of his hands and landed on the moist earth with a *thud*.

Exhausted, Steve jumped down and grabbed his backpack. He looked at Stella's limp body, again, and then down at Mason's bloodstain and said aloud, as if the two dead souls were sitting there listening to him, "Guys, I'm going to make this right." Then he climbed out of the cellar hole.

When he got up into the afternoon sun, he realized with revulsion how hideous he must look. He was covered in blood from head to toe. It looked like he was war-painted in it. He was repulsed, but he didn't have time to fool around. He needed to keep moving and get the damn box hidden. But where? He looked around, and then, it hit him—the swamp.

He knew he could make his way through almost any woods, but that bastard of a swamp had turned him back a couple of times. If he could get in there three hundred to four hundred yards, no one would be able to track him. No dog could follow a scent back there. Getting in that far would require him to do some swimming, but he was sure he could find a small swamp island and cover up the chest so no one could find it.

He was moving again, his mind alert, and he wasn't wasting any time. First, he hid his pack under a thick thorn bush fifty yards away from the blood trail and cellar hole. Then he carried the chest over to the edge of the swamp pool. He chose a spot and waded into the black water until he was chest deep. He felt his feet sinking into the mucky ooze beneath him. The smell being released from the bottom of the swamp into the murky water was almost unbearable. It reeked like a hundred years of compounded decay and rotten eggs. Just as he was getting a little concerned about the depth of the water, he felt the coffer start to float in his hands, much to his relief. He made sure the water was not above the seal on the floating container.

Although he could not see three inches down into the black pitch in which he was enveloped, he felt some soggy branches on the bottom that weren't completely stable, but he was able to get some footing on them. He moved on in this manner, heading west into the swamp, pushing the leaden vessel in front of him.

After about twenty minutes, he found what he thought would be the perfect spot. It was a small island in the middle of the swamp, about ten feet in diameter, roughly circular, with tall saggy swamp grass all around it. Dead trees had fallen across it, forming something of a teepee. He waded over and hefted the coffer onto the island, making sure not to tread on or crush any of the grass. He wanted the setting to look as pristine as possible. Taking time to conceal the coffer in the thickest and tallest part of the little island, he repositioned some branches and fluffed up the sage.

He jumped back into the murk to examine his work, trudging around the circumference of the island. The coffer was completely concealed. Even if someone went directly onto the land, he would not see the coffer unless he stepped on it. He noted the island's location and headed back.

As he made his way back toward his point of entry into the swamp, Steve waded the last fifty yards to the shore with extreme caution, retracing his path in so as to not disturb the swamp anymore than necessary. Earlier, on his way out, sliding shoulder-deep through the black water, he had stuck to what he could determine were the deepest pools in order to minimize any scent or trace of his presence. As he got onto the branches on the bottom that he had encountered when he first entered the swamp, he submerged himself under the filthy scum to wash away as much scent as possible and any blood that remained on him. He would rather stink of swamp than his good friend's blood. As he was submerged, scrubbing away at the remaining blood in his hair and skin, he felt one of the branches he was standing on break free and float up alongside his body.

When he reemerged from his disgusting bath and wiped the grime away from his face and eyes, he found himself staring directly into the opaque eyes of a rotting corpse.

He breathed in so quickly that he sucked in some of the rotting water surrounding the putrefying flesh and instantly gagged and vomited. Lurching back out of the water, all the time uncontrollably retching, he scrambled over the briars onto the shore. He stayed there for a moment gagging and catching his breath. Once everything had been wrung out of his system, he wiped his mouth with the back of his hand and looked into the contaminated water with disbelief.

"Is there any place on this land that doesn't have a fucking body on it, for Christ's sake?" he spat aloud.

As he was looking at the rotting cadaver, another body floated up directly beneath the first corpse. The arms of this one came up out of the water on each side of the body above it and suspended in the air in an open-arm embrace like a store mannequin. He stared in disbelief at the grotesque embrace and couldn't help thinking this display looked like a hideous conga line one might see in the River Styx.

The corpses seemed to be two women, one of whom had on a headlamp similar to his own. He noticed they were wearing high-tech hiking jackets made of polar fleece and wondered if they had been down in the cellar hole.

They must have died at night, he thought. There had been a warm snap for the past week or so during the days, but he remembered that the temperature drops in the evening around there.

He wanted to know more about the rancid bodies, but the process of decay had started. The faces of the women were covered in massive weeping blisters that concealed any clues about them. From the mottled texture and greenish hue of the two cadavers' festering skin, he figured they had been dead for at least a few days.

Questions about who they were and how they happened to end up in the swamp flooded his troubled mind, but Steve knew he could not afford the time to stick around and play Dick Tracy. He had to re-sink the bodies and get out of there fast.

Back into the swamp, he went and grabbed the bodies. He unzipped the fleeces, then pushed the bodies around an impenetrable patch of thorns thirty yards away, where the water was deep and black. He returned to the briar shore, searched around, and grabbed two heavy rocks. Returning to the cadavers, he placed a rock gently on each of the torsos and re-zipped the fleeces. He laid the bodies near each other at the bottom of the inky pitch.

He added the ballast to the bodies to keep them submerged and undetected; he did not want to end up being charged for three homicides. He was acting like a guilty man, he realized, covering up so many crimes that he hadn't committed, and he was annoyed that Ken had him acting and thinking like a criminal on the run.

Steve checked the area before he left, taking care to cover up any tracks that didn't jibe with the story he wanted to leave behind on the trail if he was followed. He swept the area using a leafy branch, an old Indian trick his father had taught him. The tracks left behind looked like someone might have fallen into the swamp, stumbled out, rolled around, and barfed a couple of times. He hoped it would work. He disposed of the branch and went to his pack to take a quick inventory of what he had and to change out of the disgusting swamp-soaked deputy's shirt he had been wearing since his jailbreak.

As he was kneeling beside his pack, he felt something touch the base of the back of his skull and heard a voice he had hoped to never hear again.

"If you blink, I will blow your head off your body. I've been watching your dumbass for the last two minutes, wondering how to kill you and get away with it."

Ken was looking for an excuse to execute him right there, Steve knew. He also knew he would probably be dead in the next ten seconds no matter what he did. His anger began to swell at the thought of how wrong it was that Ken had him in this horrible situation when he hadn't done a fucking thing wrong.

With lightning-like quickness, Steve spun on Ken with his lead arm up to fend off the Glock that had been pointed at his head. The gun went off next to his head, the noise deafening, but the bullet missed its mark. In his other hand, Steve held the pearl-handled dagger that had been sticking out of an exterior pocket on his pack and, with it, slashed deeply across the back of Ken's gun hand.

Ken let out a scream, dropped his Glock, and grabbed his hand. In the next nanosecond, Steve followed up on the surprise assault by coming back around with a crushing blow with his fist to the side of Ken's meaty jaw as he held his hemorrhaging hand in terror. Ken dropped like he was poleaxed. Instantly, he was on the ground out cold, snoring like he had been asleep for hours.

It took every shred of self-restraint he had for Steve to not continue beating the hell out of the prostrate cop. Steve's jaw was clenched like a vice; he was bearing his teeth like an animal. He had to walk away to calm himself. As he regained his composure, he surveyed his cataleptic enemy. Ken's hand was still hemorrhaging. Although he felt he ought to just let the jerk bleed to death, Steve knew for Mason's sake he could not let his friend's only son die.

First, he secured Ken with his own cuffs, cuffing him by his good hand to a narrow ten-foot tree and tossing the keys into the swamp. He torqued down the cuffs so that when Ken woke up, he would feel the same discomfort Steve had felt earlier at the jail. Next, he dug the emergency kit out of his pack, stopped the bleeding from Ken's hand, and inspected the wound. The slice ran along the back of the hand and wrist. He could see the tendons in the wound, but it didn't look to him like any had been cut. Then he cleaned out the wound with a packet of antiseptic, wrapped it in a gauze bandage, and tied it off. It was wrapped tightly, but not too tight.

Then Steve did something he thought was pretty smart. Comparing the radio he was carrying to Ken's, he noticed they were identical models, so he just switched the batteries. That way, the police would still never know he had one of their radios and could monitor their every move and Steve's radio would have a new battery with plenty of power.

Ken started to moan and move around slowly, clearly regaining consciousness. Steve responded by kicking him viciously on the other side of the jaw.

"Back to la-la land for you, dickhead. You're lucky that's all you're going to get," Steve growled uncharacteristically. He wrote off his unusual aggression to Ken's not having been exactly nice to him for the past few hours.

After sending Ken back into his imposed slumber, Steve performed another old Indian trick he had learned from his dad. He walked along a trail that he wanted any tracking dogs to follow, urinating as he walked. Then as he walked along that same path, he scuffed his boots in his urine. He tried to avoid the swamp as much as he could and walked in a northwest direction away from it, heading off into the woods. He turned around and followed the same path back to where Ken lay.

Just before setting out for Route 77, Steve picked up Ken's gun and walked toward the downed officer shackled to the tree. For those who were going to be pursuing him, Steve planned to leave a subtle message.

DOGTOOTH

His journey out of the woods had taken him much longer than he had expected, and it was dark by the time he reached Route 77. He had taken a different path out, in a northwesterly direction, so as to avoid anyone who might have been following his previous trails and to throw off anyone who might be tracking him westward from the camp. He came to the edge of the woods about three miles north of the road that led to Mason's camp. Perfect. He wanted to draw any trackers as far away as possible from that swamp for obvious reasons. The objects he had left in that swamp could be used to suggest a motive for his alleged crimes, not to mention the female bodies at the bottom of the hellish bayou, which could raise other questions.

On the way, he had been formulating a plan. The next logical step, he thought, would be to try to get to the asylum unnoticed and see Denise Moynihan. He also wanted to review the journal in his backpack to see if it had any answers about how he could help Carla. He could not go back and get the deputy's car because if it had been discovered, the police would be staking it out to see if he was stupid enough to return.

The first thing he did was to change out of his swampy shirt and pants. As best he could, he washed himself with a small bottle of rubbing alcohol he had in his survival kit. He put on a fresh shirt, a fleece sweatshirt, some new socks, and a pair of lightweight nylon cargo shorts he always kept rolled up in the bottom of his pack. When he had finished, he buried the swamp clothes under a rotten-out log. Aside from the soggy shoes, he looked like any other hiker who had just stepped out of the woods reeking of rubbing alcohol.

"Sometimes," his father used to tell him, "it's best just to hide in the wide open while you're out there in the woods hunting. Sometimes, the animals are so much expecting something to come charging out of all the bushes or all the nooks and crannies that they don't pay attention to the wide open. If you blend in enough with an open area, you can pretty much move around undetected. They never think a predator would be so blatant."

With that thought in mind, Steve walked out into the open road. After a few minutes, he saw a vehicle approaching. He stuck his thumb out, and the vehicle started to slow down to pick him up. Of course, it was a logging truck.

He hopped up into the truck, which started to roll before he got completely in the door, and said without looking, "I'm heading to the asylum down in Denton. Not too far away. Only about twenty miles or so."

Only then did he look around at the interior of the truck. The décor coincided with the demeanor and the tattoos of the driver. He was a hulk of a man in his mid-forties, although his lifestyle seemed to have worn him well beyond his years. He had long blond pin-straight hair, a huge handlebar mustache, and monstrous arms that were covered in ink, and he was wearing wraparound sunglasses, even though it was so dusky that it was nearly night. Every shred of the man's being screamed that he was a biker, and from the tattoos on his arms and the colors on his truck, Steve could tell the trucker's allegiance was to one of the most notorious renegade gangs. He was exactly the sort of man Steve and his riding buddies tried to avoid while they were out rolling on their motorcycles.

"Name's Dogtooth," the trucker said.

Before Steve could respond, Dogtooth continued, showing he thought it best to get right to the point. "Why is a guy who just got done hikin' headin' to the asylum twenty miles down road at this time of night? And why is that same fuckin' guy stinkin' up my truck with rubbin' alcohol after just gettin' out of the fuckin' woods? And here's the biggest question I got, why does the guy that I just picked up off the fuckin' road look like the same guy the police have been describin' on the scanner all day? Could you tell me that, Mr. Rubbin' Alcohol Asylum Hiker?"

Steve damn near died. He didn't dare show any fear, and he sure as hell didn't want to scrap with Dogtooth. He had no other options, so he simply said, "Because I'm the guy they're looking for, and I need a place to hide until I can figure this fucking thing out."

The biker scoffed and smiled. "Your secret's safe with me, Steve. I been hearing your name all day over the police scanner. Word is you killed a cop's father, and then you beat the fuck out of another cop to escape from the local hoosegow. Any man that can do that shit and still have his own hide is welcome to ride in my rig any day. I hate the fuckin' cops. I been fightin' 'em my entire life. They can all kiss my ass."

Steve felt great relief to know he had a safe haven for the time being. "Truth be known, I didn't kill the cop's father. The man who died was a very good friend of mine. I found him dying and his asshole of a son tried to frame me for his murder. The son is a cop from Aranville," he explained.

"Figures the asshole son is a fuckin' cop," Dogtooth replied.

"But I did beat that deputy's ass," Steve continued, reveling in sharing his exploits with the renegade biker. Steve realized he had only one chance to appeal to Dogtooth on his level or he would be in deeper trouble than if the police caught him. "That motherfucker was going to pour piping hot coffee on my face, so I convinced him not to by mashing his face into the cell bars and educated him to the error of his ways. I didn't care if he lived or died. I hogtied him to the metal frame of the cell cot. That son of a bitch will never forget me, I'm pretty sure of that."

Dogtooth was growing fond of his new riding companion. A man who had such little regard for authority or the law was all right in his book. He could tell that Steve believed in old-fashioned justice as he did, and he liked that about the guy sitting in the shotgun seat next to him.

"I beat the shit out of the asshole cop, my dead buddy's son," Steve added. "I clubbed him to the ground about an hour ago. I left him cuffed to a tree after I knocked him out twice. He had it coming. He had a gun against the back of my head. I had no other options."

Steve was surprised how good it felt to have someone he could talk to who could enjoy the punishment he had meted out to the lawmen. It was not his style.

That sealed it for Dogtooth. This guy was a keeper. He wiped out two armed cops in one day and a jailbreak! Steve was close to being the modern-day Viking that Dogtooth saw himself as. He never liked anyone this much this quickly. This guy had balls and the sense to not get caught. Steve was Dogtooth's sort of people. He could see that immediately.

"We're coming up on the roadblock they've put up for you," Dogtooth blurted. "Get in the back. There's a hidden compartment under the back of the cab. Just climb in there. I'll handle the rest. Don't worry, I ain't lettin' anything happen to you."

As Steve climbed down into the hidden compartment, he saw he would be sharing it with two kilos of cocaine, tightly wrapped in plastic. He got in as the truck slowed down, and the exhaust stacks chugged out the backpressure as the truck's speed diminished.

From his hiding place, he heard the conversation between Dogtooth and the state trooper.

"What's going on, Trooper? There an accident or something?" Dogtooth asked.

"No. We're looking for a fugitive that escaped this morning from the sheriff's department."

Steve felt movement in the chassis of the truck, which could mean only that the trooper had climbed up to take a look in the cab.

Once the trooper shined his light into the cab of the truck and saw the tattoos on Dogtooth's arms, his demeanor and tone changed for the worse. It was clear from his tone that he knew Dogtooth was a renegade biker. If he had not had the responsibilities of this dragnet, and if every available cop hadn't been tied up in looking for the fugitive, he would have searched every inch of the truck for drugs or illegal guns. But tonight wasn't the night. The trooper's hands were tied, and he knew it.

"Get the hell out of here, and don't pick up any hitchhikers," the trooper commanded. "You just got your free pass dirtbag!"

"You have yourself a good day," Dogtooth chided with a big gap-toothed grin.

As the wheels started to roll again, Steve started to breathe more easily.

"You can come out now. Those assholes won't be bothering us anymore," Dogtooth said into the back of the cab.

Steve popped out of the compartment and climbed into the front passenger seat. He was feeling upbeat, considering he was a wanted fugitive who was riding in a truck with a lawless drug smuggler and two kilos of coke.

"I hope you don't mind, but I used those plastic pillows in the compartment to take a nap while you were chatting back there at the roadblock with your newfound buddy," he said with a grin.

"Fuck you," Dogtooth said with a bigger grin. "Man cannot live on bread alone."

The more time Dogtooth spent with Steve, the more he liked him.

As they drove south, they heard police chatter about Steve. It sounded like every available cop in the state was involved or getting involved.

"This is gonna be an old-fashioned witch hunt, you know," Dogtooth warned. "If they catch you, they're most likely gonna kill you."

"Yeah, I know," Steve replied. "But I've got to keep pressing on until I can clear my name for the murder. Then maybe all of the other problems will go away."

"Keep hopin', my man, keep hopin'," Dogtooth said.

Over the police scanner came the news that Steve was dreading. From what he and Dogtooth could make out, no one could make contact with or raise Ken on the radio. So they were sending K-9 units and a search party to look for him. Steve felt gutpunched. With a bit of luck, the dogs wouldn't notice his swamp trail, and they would just follow his old track to Route 77. The two men, both outlaws now, just rode south in silence, listening to the scanner.

Dogtooth pulled the rig into a truck stop—to fill up, Steve thought. He was wrong. The big rig pulled up to the rear of the truck stop along the back tree line, and Dogtooth kicked on the emergency break.

He leaned over toward Steve and pointed out of the passenger window up a hill blackened by lack of sunlight.

"Make your way up that hill right there, hiker boy, and don't get seen. On the other side of the hill is the back side of the asylum. The place is an old piece of shit and the security sucks, especially in the back. You can sneak in a window or something out back. Me and a couple of my bros I ride with bust into that place and steal drugs from the pharmacy when my regular route slows down. No one ever reports it because half of the staff are stoned and steal the shit themselves. There're no cameras. No one has ever seen us come or go. It's like stealin' candy from a baby. Only once has there ever been an article in the paper, and some orderly took the fall for all of the crap that we took."

Dogtooth chuckled.

"If I ever go nuts, don't put me in that fuckin' place. Put a bullet in my head—you'll be doin' me a favor, brother. Now if you run into trouble, just get the fuck out of there and head off into the woods. It looks to me by your gear and that you came out of that last piece untouched, you can handle yourself in the big woods. Good. Believe it or not, I can too. Before all this riding shit, I was in a ranger platoon in Grenada."

That surprised Steve, and it must have shown on his face because the trucker went on, "Yeah, no shit. I was in the service. Anyway, if you run into a scrap where you need somewhere to turn, and you haven't been caught, call me at this number. I'll come in and get you out. I like a good fight, and you don't have a lot of friends. If you get caught, you eat this number and we never met. You got me there, hiker boy?"

"Loud and clear. Thanks for this," Steve said, looking the man straight in his eyes as he extended his hand.

The big blond outlaw grasped his extended hand roughly, biker style, and said, "You hang in there, Steve, and clear this shit up."

Steve slid out of the truck, grabbing his pack on the way. He closed the door quietly and slid into the woods behind the parking lot.

Once Steve was in the woods, Dogtooth admitted to himself, "That kid is fucked, but I sure like him." He then flipped off the e-brake, threw the rig into gear, and rumbled out of there.

Steve knelt on the hillside in the darkness of the trees, rummaging in a compartment of his backpack for his smaller LED flashlight that shone red. He wanted this particular light because the subdued red light did not draw as much attention in the pitch-black night forest as a glaring white light did. He was trying to use as much stealth as possible in order to go undetected. He zipped up his pack, threw it on his shoulders, and pressed on up the hill, stopping for a moment to watch the red taillights of the outlaw rig he just hopped out of disappear in the night.

He smirked and thought, *It's a relief to finally have an ally. Better than that, I have a guardian angel. Jimmy Stewart's guardian angel in* It's a Wonderful Life *was Clarence. My guardian angel's name is Dogtooth.*

TROJAN HORSE

Twenty-seven miles away, while Steve was sneaking his way up the hill behind the truck stop, two police K-9 units—one local, one state—took a right off of Route 77 and sped down the dirt road to Mason's camp. What they saw when they arrived was a chaotic scene. The two lawmen hopped out of their vehicles with sidearms drawn. The local officer advanced into the area illuminated by the vehicles' headlights and saw the obvious signs of some kind of struggle.

"Kenneth—Officer Ken Macfarlane, are you anywhere on the premises?" the Maine state trooper said into the handset of the loudspeaker on his vehicle.

He got no response. After a quick visual inspection, the officers saw Ken's police cruiser car parked off to the side of the driveway of the small building in front of them. They also saw some overturned ice coolers whose contents were scattered all over the front lawn and a grill that appeared to have been cast out onto the grass.

As the local officer moved toward the granite steps at the front porch of the cabin, he stepped on something in the grass that tweaked his ankle. It was a large rusty steel oval that could not be seen from the angle of the police vehicles' headlights.

"Goddammit! I just twisted my ankle on that thing," he said as he limped toward the granite steps.

"You all right?" the state trooper asked.

"Yeah, I'll be fine. It looks like there was a hell of a tussle here, though," the local officer replied.

As he climbed the two granite steps onto the porch, his limping diminished. His flashlight was out and turned on, its beam and the barrel of his weapon aimed toward the cabin. He had his hands crossed in front of him, his gun hand on top of the flashlight hand as he moved forward to check the door. The glass was shattered in a pattern like a spider web but was still holding. The door was locked, but he could tell from the large cracks in the door jam that it had been repaired recently.

The trooper made a sweep around the west side of the cabin with his hands in the same tactical position as the local officer, who left the steps and made a sweep around the east side. In the process, both shone their lights into the cabin, checking out the interior and exterior of the building. They met at the back of the cabin and nodded silently to each other.

In the edge of the trooper's flashlight beam, they caught a glimpse of another structure that looked to be a typical, one-person outhouse, about twenty feet away. They nodded to each other again and moved cautiously toward the vertical structure to check it out. They were about three feet apart when they heard something.

"Trojan horse," the trooper whispered to the other officer as he pointed towards the outhouse.

It was a shuffling sound, like a living being of some kind shifting its weight inside the dark outhouse. So as to not to startle the occupant into an attempted fast break, the officers pointed their flashlights to the ground, and the local officer shut his light off completely. They heard another shuffling noise inside the wooden restroom.

The two lawmen moved silently together, like a well-oiled machine. Each went around an opposite side of the outhouse. They ended up at the only door to the structure, and the trooper reached out for the door handle. He paused and turned to his companion, who had switched on his flashlight and had it pointed at the ground. The trooper strategically knelt before the entrance, silently motioned with his fingers—one, two, three—and wrenched the door open.

In the glaring beams of the Maglite, now pointed directly into the outhouse, a huge raccoon screamed at the surprise intrusion and launched itself directly toward the blinding lights.

"Jesus Christ!" the local officer shrieked as the terrified raccoon brushed by him in midair.

In the mayhem and confusion, the state trooper discharged his firearm and blew a perfect .40-caliber hole through the back wall of the Trojan horse.

INSANE ASYLUM

Steve crept slowly as he got to the top of the wooded hill. Behind him, he could see the top of the truck stop and the traffic on Route 77. The light from behind and below could not penetrate the wooded hillside, but moving through the tall red pines would be easy going. He clicked off his light and peered over to the other side of the hill, where he saw the old asylum, right where Dogtooth had said it would be.

From what Steve could see, the place was huge, seeming more like a citadel than an asylum. A massive courtyard about two hundred to three hundred yards long stretched from the back exits to the foot of the hill. It was neo-Gothic in architectural style, looking nothing like the sterile institution he had envisioned. Even in the dark, he could tell it was very old. He thought it might be one of those nineteenth-century sanitariums that people went to in order to get out of the polluted cities of the industrial revolution and cure their lumbago and such in the clean mountain air. It was nothing like the institution in *One Flew over the Cuckoo's Nest*, and Steve was pretty sure that Nurse Ratched would be a vampire in the edifice he saw before him. He shook himself and headed down the hill toward the eerie asylum of lost souls.

No high wall or fence barred his way as he cut across the expansive and poorly lit rear courtyard at the bottom of the hill. Half of the few old light posts lacked working bulbs. He made his way to the back of the main building and assessed the situation. The main doors were locked, so he slid east along the wall, quietly checking every window to see if it would open. As he was walking along, he slid his hand along the old limestone wall to guide himself as he looked at the windows, and at almost every seam, a little bit of mortar flaked off in his hand. He hoped the building wouldn't come crumbling down upon him.

The next-to-last window was open. Steve shined his red light into the dark room, which seemed to be an office, unoccupied at the moment. The window swung outward and upward, and he gingerly opened it as wide as it would go. First, he pushed his pack up into the open window and into the room to the top left side of a large wooden desk that was under the window. Then he slid his torso up at an angle between the glass and the exterior wall of the building. It was snug, but he fit. He had to move some books out of the way so as not to knock them over and draw attention to his intrusion. He leaned out over the large wooden desk and moved like an inchworm, with the red flashlight in his teeth, until he was completely in the office. As soon as he was in, he swung his legs over onto the floor and shut the window gently. He turned on the red flashlight and surveyed his surroundings.

It looked like a doctor's office, with medical textbooks, framed degrees from various institutions, patients' charts, file cabinets, a desktop computer that looked out of place, and an overstuffed swivel chair. Most important, on the coat rack in the corner was a white lab coat with an ID necklace hanging from it. Steve knew he would need that in order to see Denise Moynihan.

After he fished his compass clock out of his backpack, he was pleased to see it was only nine. He knew he would need all of the time he could get. But he needed rest most right now. He set the alarm on his battery-powered clock for ten and crawled under the large desk to avoid detection if anyone entered the office. He was pleased to be able to spread out completely and stretch his legs under the oaken desk. He crossed his arms over his chest and used his pack as a pillow, which was surprisingly comfortable. *I love this backpack*, he thought, and he was out. He hadn't known when he had dozed off the previous night at Mason's camp that he would get better sleep on the hard floor of a decrepit nineteenth-century insane asylum.

INQUISITOR'S JOURNAL:
CIFRAS DE GRACIA

Women wailing. Painful screaming. Wavering red-orange light, like nondescript flame.

Steve's alarm beeped in his ear, dispelling the troubling images of his dream. He woke quietly so as not to draw the attention of the phantom from his dream of anguish and torment and took stock of his situation as the dimly lit surroundings became more familiar. He was in a dark room, lit only by light that was coming from the space under the door. As his mini alarm softly beeped in his ear, he remembered he was lying on the floor of a doctor's office, under a large wooden desk in an old asylum, and was there to read the journal in his bag and to see Denise Moynihan.

He shut off the alarm, shimmied out from his unorthodox sleeping alcove, and sat up, feeling refreshed after only an hour's sleep. As he sat up and leaned against the wooden desk, the last demons of his perturbed sleep faded away to the point that he couldn't remember dreaming.

With the red flashlight he fished out of his pocket, he assessed the dark room. He stood up, stretched, went over to the door, and slowly dead-bolted it from the inside. He also quietly slid an inside slide bolt the room's owner must have had installed to ensure against unwanted company. Moving to the window he had entered the office through, he locked it and closed the curtains. He went back to the large desk and sat in the overstuffed chair. The desktop had a large fluorescent light on one side and a small reading lamp on the other. He opted for the reading lamp and clicked it on.

On the computer in the center of the impressive desk, a lava-lamp screensaver with changing colors was rolling around on the face of the screen. Out of curiosity, Steve tapped the space par on the keyboard. The screen fluttered and blinked on. The doctor who occupied the office had left while still logged on. Steve was sure he wasn't expecting a wanted fugitive who had assaulted two different lawmen and escaped from jail to break into his office and make himself at home.

Steve pushed the keyboard back to make space on top of the roomy desk. From his backpack, he retrieved the aged journal, gently placed the leather-bound volume on the surface before him under the lamplight, and examined it.

For how old the book obviously was, it appeared fairly new. The leather was in remarkable condition. It felt almost like velvet and was not dried out or cracked. It still felt supple to the touch and fit perfectly around the volume. Steve had never before seen leather with the pimply texture this leather had, and he thought it would make a great pair of boots. The cover and spine bore no text.

He opened it to the first scribed page. The text was Spanish—Medieval Spanish from the looks of the handwritten font. Although he knew his Spanish was a little rusty, he felt he would be able to read it.

The Inquisitor's Journal was the simple title on the first page.

"This is the journal of Inquisitor General Dante Perechine De Torquemada, regent of Catalonia, last direct descendant of Grand Inquisitor Tomas De Torquemada," the text read.

"It is the Lord's year 1693. I have just ascended to the post of inquisitor general for the region of Catalonia. This is where my story shall begin."

Steve paused in his reading to wonder what in the hell an inquisitor general's journal was doing in a lead box buried in the dirt of a cellar surrounded with bodies—out in the middle of the Maine woods.

"This oughta be good," he said with raised eyebrows.

The journal told of the writer's early years and his path to a position on the inquisitorial tribunal. Dante Torquemada clearly disagreed with the lenient approaches of some of his peers. He was not inclined to let people off lightly with a flogging or two. He also believed that women were the root of all evil and should be "purified."

"He might have something there," Steve observed aloud and chuckled in the empty room.

Ultimately, Dante Torquemada outperformed or outlasted his competition for the inquisitor general's post. For the people of Catalonia, nothing could have been worse.

First, he built his own Palace of Purification with funds secured from assets seized by tribunals under his jurisdiction. All of the seized assets were supposed to be sent to King Charles II's coffers in Madrid, but Dante knew that what he appropriated for his own use would not be missed because the king was so disabled and powerless.

Steve remembered from his studies in Spain that Charles II was far from the glory days of his reign at that point. He was the end product of the extreme inbreeding in which monarchies engaged in order to maintain the purity of the lines of succession for their dynasties. Keeping the lines too pure, however, produced poor creatures like Charles II, who was more of a monstrosity than a monarch. He was born deformed, with an enormous tongue and the worst recorded case of Hapsburg jaw in any royal dynasty. Unable to chew, he drooled and was unable to speak. He was mentally deficient, bald, blind, deaf, lame, and toothless. During his thirty-nine-year reign, Spain's economy and its control of the provinces declined, and the Catholic Church regained much of the power that it had lost earlier in the days of King Ferdinand.

Dante knew he had free reign to run his provincial tribunals however he wanted to, without regard to the accepted norms of the Catholic Church, the Inquisition, secular rule, and the monarchy.

For the work of the "greater glory of God," he custom-designed the palace to his precise desires. He had a great hall for the auto-da-fe rituals of accusation and public penance of condemned heretics and apostates that were carried out with much pomp and splendor. Members of the inquisitorial tribunal presided on a raised balcony, with Dante seated in the middle. His throne was higher than the other inquisitors to mark his station above the rest. Judgment and sentences were handed out swiftly. An accused could attain *limpieza de sangre* (cleanliness of blood) in only one way—death. Once the doors closed behind the accused person in Dante's Palace of Purification, death was the only one way out. The obdurate suffered horribly. For the accommodating, the end was swift. For both, the end came in "release" from their mortal bonds.

Dante staffed the palace with his own force of Dominican friars, who were Albigensians, members of a secret sect branded as heretics and persecuted by the Vatican. Dante was one of them. They believed that the principles of good and evil continuously opposed each other in the world. They opposed marriage, bearing children (because they thought bringing life into the world to be a sin), and eating meat. They advocated suicide, especially by starvation, so that when they died, they would have little taint on them and be free of earthly desires. During the Albigensian Crusades from 1209 to 1229, they were hunted down and slaughtered, and the scattered remnants of the sect went into hiding. After a century, the church erroneously thought every remaining Albigensian had been found and eliminated. The last remnants of the sect were executed by burning in 1321 at Fort Queribus, or so it was thought.

By the early fifteenth century, however, after they had gone underground, they reorganized and readopted many of their original beliefs, including their original name, *Cathars*. They implemented a more aggressive and clandestine approach in order to survive. A strong leader rose amongst them, one who would be able to conceal their existence, increase their ranks, and provide a power base that would be necessary for them to regain their power and influence and impose their beliefs upon the world. The leader had the support of a king and the ability to fend off the Vatican in Rome. The year of their clandestine resurrection was 1421. The king was Ferdinand of Spain. The leader was the original inquisitor, General Tomas de Torquemada.

Underneath his palace, Dante had a large multichambered dungeon built because, according to him, "the secular authorities are too inept, untrustworthy, and clumsy. The civil authority could not carry out an imposed sentence on a street rat correctly, never mind an infidel heretic." Because none of Dante's sentences were carried out by the secular authorities, none were catalogued or documented. No one knew for sure how many people were released by Dante's tribunal.

The construction of the Palace of Purification was completed in record time, and Inquisitor General Dante Perechine De Torquemada, regent of Catalonia, last direct descendant of Grand Inquisitor Tomas De Torquemada, went to work enthusiastically as soon as it was finished.

He cleansed and purified blasphemers, heretics, and infidels with a zeal never before seen. His power and wealth grew exponentially. The monarchy was powerless to stop him and seemed content to let him have his way, placated perhaps by his sharing of some of the seized assets. Rome knew it was being left out and did not care for his methods of procurement, which he didn't give a damn about because he knew the Vatican was powerless inside the borders of Spain.

In actuality, though, the power and money were not Dante's primary motivation; they were secondary benefits to his true magnum impetus, which was "purification." It was obvious this was the fire that drove his engines.

———•———

Steve wasn't sure he knew what purification meant. He expected it would be explained later in the book and, he hoped, would give him some idea about how he could help Carla.

Hearing someone walking up the hallway, he turned off the light, grabbed his bag, and put it on the desk next to the journal. Then he unlocked the window, just in case. As the footsteps on the other side of the door neared, he heard something being wheeled along and someone whistling. As the whistler was just about to pass by the door to the office, Steve tensed.

Suddenly there was a noisy clatter that ended with a heavy thud, followed by a very loud "Son of a bitch!" that echoed down the hallway. Steve heard a huge splash, and a copious amount of unknown fluid came racing in under the door. It soaked into the round cable rug that took up most of the floor. He was getting ready to get out of there when he heard the worst thing possible—keys at the lock. The deadbolt clicked back into the unlocked position. The door lock clicked unlocked a second later. He was frozen in place by the fear of his possible detection. The door rattled in its frame. The interior slide bolt was holding, but the door was loose.

"The drunk-ass has got the slide bolt up again!" Steve heard the fluid spiller say to himself. Between the amount of fluid that rushed under the door, the keys to the different locks, and the understanding of the unissued lock on the inside of the door, Steve concluded that the man on the other side must be the janitor and that he had unwillingly been locked out of this room before.

"The bum must be at the bottle early tonight, sleeping in his own piss, which I'm going to have to clean again!" the disgruntled janitor growled. "Fuck it. I'll clean both the floor and his piss tomorrow when he wakes up."

Hearing the irritated man right the spilled bucket, mop up what he could, and move along, Steve let out a long, calming breath and returned to the overstuffed chair and sat down. He opened up the drawers of the big desk one at a time and gave each one a quick going-through with his flashlight until he found what he was looking for in the bottom right drawer—a bottle of decent bourbon, half empty.

"Man, I need this!" he said as he retrieved a glass from a corner of the drawer. He filled the dirty glass halfway up with an unsteady hand. Then he raised the glass in a toast. "Here's to you, Dr. Piss-your-pants. You have really come through for me tonight! Thank you, sir!" He downed the sizeable shot of bourbon. It was heaven sent.

Once the booze kicked in, and Steve's nerves started to settle, he started to page through the journal to where he had left off.

Many of the pages told of the same horrible activities. Dante documented every "purification" and "release." After a while of skimming through the pages, Steve discerned a pattern. Most men were just severely flogged and then released—killed. The women truly suffered as they were purified. The ways the inquisitor general devised to brutalize the women and keep them alive were nauseating to read about. He committed unspeakable acts upon them in the name of God. He fed women their own flesh until they choked. He mangled their bones until they "moved as if they were filled with sand."

Most of the time, Dante carried on his torturous purifications for days. Probably most disturbing to Steve was that Dante always got a confession, in the first hour or two, at the most. Then he continued to do the most unspeakable thing to the women solely for his perverse pleasure and enjoyment. He hid his motivation and pleasure behind the "greater glory of God" credo. *The Inquisitor's Journal* was truly the most disgusting and disturbing account Steve had ever read in his life. Horrendous acts were committed on actual women, page after page after page. It was all the same—brutality, torture, amputation, strangling, and horror. It got to the point where it all started to look the same.

Steve flipped through page after page in amazement, recognizing phrases such as "cleansing incantations" and the personal euphemisms Dante used for the hideous acts. Doing this reading was not why Steve had minored in Spanish or studied in Spain. At this point, he wished he had never been able to understand the language.

While flipping through the pages, he started to notice a different notation time and time again in various records of purifications: *cifras de gracia*. As he translated the verse, he couldn't grasp the meaning. *Basin of grace? What the hell does that mean?* He paused for a moment and searched his mind for some religious significance or some other translation.

As he was scanning his memory, he realized he was looking right at the screensaver of the computer directly in front of him. He grabbed the keyboard and found the computer was still online. He typed "Google" in the address bar and pressed Enter. In the Google search subject line, he typed "Spanish–English dictionary." He ended up at Freedict.com and was automatically set in the Spanish-to-English Web page. He typed "cifras de gracia" into the search line, and in a blink, he got the translation: "basin or bowl of grace."

He went back to the first entry for cifras de gracia in the journal and was even more disturbed by what he read in the next entries than he had been by all of the entries he had previously read.

What he read of the inquisitor general truly spoke to him of the man's insanity. As far as he could determine, when the women were reaching the end of their hellacious "purification" rituals, Dante had some of their veins opened. He didn't have arteries severed because he wanted the women to be conscious during this final process of purifying. While they slowly bled to death in front of him, he had the cifras slipped underneath their hemorrhaging bodies to catch the runoff of their blood. He then excused the guard from his duties so that he could be left alone with the ruined women.

As they slowly drifted off to their death, he bathed his hands with their blood in the cifras de gracia. All the while spouting incantations and cleansing the impure contents of the sacred basin with his God-like essence from his own veins from a small slice on his wrist. He then drank some of the contents of the cifras in a communion-like manner to preserve the women's souls. His final step in the process was to "share the communion with the passing women." After first drinking from it himself, he made them drink a mix of their own blood and his just as they were dying. He did this for them in the name of God and the preservation of their souls.

Steve could not believe he had read what he had just read. *This inquisitor general, Dante Torquemada, was completely out of his friggin' mind*, he thought, as the hair on the back of his neck stood up.

He felt very alone.

FINDING OFFICER
MACFARLANE

The two silent lawmen walked back to their vehicles, looking at each other sheepishly and feeling like buffoons.

The local officer spoke up first, "I won't tell if you won't tell."

"Deal," the embarrassed trooper replied as he let a German shepherd out of the back door of his vehicle. He also grabbed his small medical kit. The trooper's K9, Shultz, was trained for not only police work, but also for search and rescue work (SAR).

The local officer reached into the back of his vehicle and attached a leash to his K9. He had a large male Rottweiler named Rex that was Schutzen-trained for police and attack work. Rex looked like he could chew open an Abrams battle tank if he wanted to.

"What are you expecting to run into out here? Look at the size of that thing! It's got to weigh 170 pounds!" the trooper exclaimed.

"You just never know what's out here in these woods." The local officer grinned as he patted Rex on his sizeable posterior. "All I know is that Rex here could drop a rabid moose if he had to."

The trooper went to Officer Macfarlane's police cruiser, opened up the driver's side door, and gave the order, "Scent!"

Shultz hopped up into the vehicle and started sniffing everywhere around the driver's seat. He sniffed the steering wheel, the foot well, the radio, the handset, and the inside door handle, inspecting everywhere Macfarlane would have touched regularly in his day-to-day activities.

"Mark!" was the trooper's next command.

The dog stopped all activities and just looked at the trooper for his next command.

"Heel!"

Shultz hopped out of the car, went directly to the trooper's left side, and sat. The trooper knelt and grabbed the leash he had released as the dog scoured the inside of the car. He then grabbed a worn pair of leather driving gloves that were on the front dashboard of the missing officer's cruiser. They were obviously Macfarlane's. He stuck them in a Ziploc bag he retrieved from his breast pocket and stuffed the bag in his back pants pocket.

"Track!" was his next order.

The dog put his nose to the ground and trotted, with the trooper holding the long leash, right up to the front door of the cabin. He sniffed around a moment, came back down the steps, and proceeded across the lawn, heading westward.

"Stop!" the trooper ordered the well-trained Shultz.

The dog froze in his tracks and pulled his head up. He looked to the trooper for the next command.

The trooper turned to the local officer and said, "We should call this in. The dog obviously has the scent trail of Officer Macfarlane. The trail is heading off into the woods in a westerly direction back toward Route 77. I'm going to call ahead to the roadblock and let them know to keep their eyes peeled for anything, especially this Steve Babin character."

"Sounds like a plan to me. Rex is a police dog. He hasn't been trained for SAR work. We'll follow behind you. If we bump into Babin, we can loose Rex on him. Your shepherd there has done all of the heavy lifting so far. We'll let Rex handle anything from there if we have to," the local officer said with an evil little grin.

"This search is nothing. All the scent is fairly fresh. A couple of weeks ago, Shultz and I were looking for a couple lady hikers who never checked in at one of their waypoints along the Appalachian Trail. We were just a couple of miles south of here.

We had no previous fresh scent to go on. It was all five months old from their belongings at home. Shultz worked for days. We never found anything. They still haven't surfaced yet. It's like they just disappeared."

After calling in the message, the men and dogs resumed their search, with Shultz in the lead. At the western edge of the front yard, Shultz stopped in his tracks with his nose to the ground. The annoyed trooper was about to reprimand the dog for pausing when he pointed his flashlight down at what the German shepherd was so feverishly inspecting. The trooper froze in his tracks; he instantly recognized what the dog was sniffing so zealously.

The town officer came up with Rex. "You got something?"

Instantly, Rex's nose hit the ground and excitedly inhaled. The officer shined his light next to the trooper's and saw plainly what had captivated both of the K9s—a large blotch of dried-up blood.

The trooper sprung into action with his dog. "Stop, Shultz! Strike! Strike, Shultz! Heel!"

The dog broke contact with the dried blood, went over to the trooper's left side, and sat down, awaiting the next command.

"Stay!" the trooper commanded.

It wasn't as easy for Rex to let go of the intoxicating blood scent. "Heel. Heel, Rex!"

The dog disregarded the order.

"Dammit Rex! Heel!"

With a mighty kick to the Rottweiler's ribcage, the officer caught the dog's attention, and the dog begrudgingly obeyed. Rex's mouth was frothing. His eyes were distant, and he was about a half second away from a full-blown wild-dog bloodlust. Rex and the officer took a quick walk to his vehicle to get some water and refocus.

The trooper went to his vehicle, retrieved a clean rag, soaked it with some bottled water, and then cleaned the blood-covered muzzle of his well-trained dog.

The officer returned with Rex, who had a renewed sense of obedience after getting his hide "refocused," which is a component of Schutzen training.

"What does the 'strike' command mean for your dog?" the local officer asked.

"It means to disregard the new scent he picked up that distracted him. Now I'm going to refocus the dog with this." The trooper retrieved from his back pocket the sealed plastic bag with the leather driving gloves. He unsealed the Ziploc, put the bag with the gloves right up to the Shultz's nose, and commanded, "Mark. Mark, Shultz!"

The dog snuffled feverishly in the bag. After the dog had given it his uninterrupted attention for a moment, the trooper ordered, "Stop!" The dog raised his head and froze. The trooper then resealed the bag and put it back in his pocket. "Track, Shultzie. Track!"

The German shepherd completely disregarded the dried-up blood and started pulling on the leash in a direction parallel to the blood trail that led away from where the blood had dried.

After about twenty minutes, Shultz ended up at the feet of a sprawled semiconscious Officer Macfarlane. He was cuffed by his left hand to a small tree and had two large welts on each side of his jaw. His hand was field-dressed in a gauze bandage, but a small amount of blood had soaked through.

"We found him," the trooper yelled over his shoulder to the local officer. "Macfarlane is right here in front of me. He's pretty beat up, but he's alive."

The local officer jerked Rex away from something that had caught the dog's attention about ten feet from where Ken was lying. He hurried over to assist.

The trooper reached into his medical pack for a vial of smelling salts. To the local officer, he said, "Can you call for medical rescue? I don't know what type of shape he may be in, and someone's going to have to take a look at him."

"Three-eight to control," the local officer said into the radio. "Be advised we have located Officer Macfarlane. He is injured. He is semiconscious and breathing. Send rescue to Long Shadows Road. Approximately five miles east to the old hunting camp. And tell them to step on it! He's not looking so good!"

The trooper snapped the vial under Ken's nose, and he instantly started to grimace and shake his head. His eyelids fluttered and opened. He was disoriented, and the flashlights in his face did not help. He sat bolt upright and tried to stand up.

"Easy, Officer Macfarlane. You're all right. I'm state police Sergeant Erdody, and this is Officer Phil Doris from Beldon. You're safe. We found you a moment ago. Try to relax for a minute and catch your bearings."

Ken flopped back down after the cuff to the bottom of the tree reached its maximum length. In a confused voice, he said, "Why do you have me cuffed to a tree?"

"We don't. We found you this way. Just relax, and we'll get the cuffs off you."

At that moment, Ken became aware of how much his jaw hurt. He could tell it wasn't broken, but it felt that way. He had one hell of a headache too. When he reached up to rub the sides of his jaw, he saw the gauze bandage wrapped around his free hand. *What the hell is this from?* he wondered. Then it all came back to him in a flash—following his father's trail of blood, seeing Steve cross the trail in front of him, sneaking up on Steve to execute him, Steve slicing him with the knife. Then it all went blank. He couldn't remember anything else.

"What went on here, Officer Macfarlane? How did you end up in this situation?" Erdody asked, as he released Ken from the cuffs with his own key.

"I was staking out this area, waiting for a BCI team to arrive and to see if the fugitive, Steve Babin, would return. Some noises came from out in the woods. I followed the trail of my father's blood back here. I was ambushed and attacked by Babin. That's where it all goes blurry. I can't remember a thing after he viciously attacked me with a knife."

"Why did he attack you?" Doris asked.

"I don't know. Why did he kill my father? He was half-insane and covered in my dad's blood when I took him into custody this morning."

"Did he attack you then?" Erdody asked.

"No. He was so out of it. He was easy to cuff and stuff into my cruiser. He offered very little resistance." There was an awkward pause. "By the way, thanks for bandaging my wrist. It feels like a solid dressing."

The sergeant peered at Ken through skeptical eyes and asked, "Then why was Babin in such bad shape when he reached the sheriff's department? The deputy, who looks ten times worse than you do, said Babin was unconscious and looked like he had been put through a meat grinder by the time you brought him to the jail."

"I have no idea. He was covered in blood, my father's blood, and I couldn't tell at the moment I took him into custody what the extent of his injuries were. Is this a friggin' inquisition or something? I mean, for Christ's sake, I was the one you found unconscious."

Ken got to his feet and took an inventory of himself. His jaw and head hurt like hell, and his wrist was sliced and bandaged. Worse, his police sidearm and both of his fifteen-round high-capacity magazines were gone.

"If Babin is such a victim, like you are implying, then why did he take off with my firearm?"

"He didn't," Doris said.

The two men walked over to the local officer, who was about ten feet away. He was shining his light down at the ground where Rex was sniffing something cautiously.

In his flashlight beam were Ken's two magazines, which were emptied of all of their bullets. They were laid on the ground, in neat rows of fifteen, directly next to each empty magazine.

Ken's department-issued .40-caliber Glock was about six inches away. The slide of the Glock had been removed from the top of the gun, rendering it useless until it was reassembled. One bullet lay next to the disassembled gun—the extra bullet Ken carried in his chamber. The entire setup on the ground looked like an exploded view of a gun and gun components that would come in any decent set of assembly instructions. It looked like each part and piece of Ken's gun and magazines had been catalogued.

The sergeant reached down and grabbed the lone bullet next to the disassembled gun. "These bullets are issued by your department? They look like armor-piercing rounds to me."

"What the fuck are you getting at, Sarge? What's your point?" Ken snapped uncharacteristically. "I'm getting sick of your shit and your accusatory questions."

"I'll tell you exactly what my point is, Officer Macfarlane," Erdody said, staring directly into Ken's eyes, squaring his shoulders before the overly aggressive and defensive officer. "What we have so far is a man that has been accused of murder with no witness except the deceased's son—you! Who actually didn't even witness the crime. The fugitive is running for his life from a cop whose judgment has been clouded by a personal tragedy. A cop who has been trying to railroad that man, Babin, who might be innocent because the cop never took the time to question him correctly and find out!

"In all actuality, you shouldn't even be working the goddamn case in the first place! Instead, though, you have been calling every police station and state trooper barracks that would listen to you spew venom against Babin. If he is ever caught, he might be executed on the spot!" Erdody's voice kept rising.

"We have a deputy that broke almost every policy, procedure, and law regarding handling of prisoners. The deputy, by the way, by trying to honor the code of the 'thin blue line,' got himself hospitalized, out of a job, and I'm sure will have himself brought up on charges. The capper to it all is now we have every free cop in the upper half of the state working on your personal little vendetta for a man who's probably not guilty of anything more than protecting himself! Because you made him too afraid to trust the law-enforcement community!

Do you know why I feel that this might be the case? Because I checked the guy out. Babin's record is absolutely clean! He has a better record than my mother! I don't know if the guy ever got a son of a bitchin' speeding ticket.

My favorite part to your whole little statewide pity party you're having for yourself is this: why would a guy who's supposed to be this murderous, violent criminal leave a deputy alive and call in an emergency distress message for that deputy while he escapes from jail? He then keeps your sorry ass alive, taking the time to bandage your wound, which he inflicted himself, because we sure as hell didn't. Most of all, why in the world would he not touch the weapons he had free access to at the jail and then leave your sidearm here with every bullet accounted for? Why would Babin do that if he is *sooo* murderous and dangerous? Can you tell me that, mister persecuted, pity party, country bumpkin, dumbass?"

Erdody tossed the illegal bullet in Ken's face. "Would you mind fleshing that one out for me a little bit? By the way, what type of asshole cop uses armor-piercing rounds in the woods of Maine?"

Ken stood in infuriated silence. He wanted to strangle the sergeant with his bare hands, and he would have tried if Doris had not been there.

Ken screamed, seething with anger, his eyes flaming with hate. "What the fuck do you know for shit!?"

"Let's throttle back a little bit, boys," Doris interceded. "We're all on the same team here, and there's no need for this."

"I'm not on this shithead's team!" Erdody spat as he pointed at Ken. Then he got eye to eye with Ken and spoke in a stoic tone.

"Know this, dickhead. I'm calling in twice as many troopers than we already have working on this case. I'm getting the best SAR team we have out here tonight to find this guy before anyone else does! I'm getting involved in this one personally. We are going to collect Babin, the sorry, scared bastard. We'll get the whole story out of him, and then I'm going to hang you out to dry for what you are—an asshole of a cop that used the resources of his position to try carry out a personal vendetta. An inaccurate one at that."

Ken shoved the trooper's chest with all of his might. "Good luck, dickhead! Stay out of my way!"

Shultz went to attack Ken, but Erdody called him off.

"I want to let the dog loose on you, but I'd prefer to see you in prison with all of the big bubbas that will love you. You're everything I hate about this job." Erdody walked off into the night toward the camp and his waiting vehicle.

Ken bent down and retrieved the pieces of his gun from the ground. He reassembled the Glock and reloaded the magazines with his special bullets, then reloaded and holstered his sidearm. He put the other magazine back in his duty belt. Once he was finished with that, he turned to Doris and said, "What's up that guy's ass?"

"I'm staying out of this one," Doris replied, and the two men walked back to the camp in silence.

INQUISITOR'S JOURNAL:
MISTRESS OF BONDAGE —
VESSEL OF THE ORDAINED

The title of this entry in the journal drew Steve's attention like a moth into a flame. After he finished reading it, he felt like the moth.

———•———

The Mistress of Bondage became the most difficult, longest, most continual effort of Dante's Christian life of servitude, yet she ultimately yielded his greatest reward from God.

It took him months of constant cleansing for him to purify her soul and get her to repent.

For her unwillingness to see the light of the Lord and, more importantly, the brilliance and kindness of the grand inquisitor, she was left in her bindings, suspended from the floor. She was gagged with a knot of leather stuffed in her mouth, and her head was secured by a binding that was tied off in the back. She lived in the darkness of her own room in the palace, there for the inquisitor to continue her purification nightly. Her bondage was of her own doing. If she had ceased to struggle against the inquisitor's purification and the bonds that suspended her there, he would have released her long ago. If she had repented her previous ways, accepted the Lord, and, more importantly, the inquisitor's guidance, she would have been free of her mortal cares.

After months of great effort, the inquisitor began to notice a difference in the mistress. Even through her constraints, he could see she was starting to change. She wore no covering except the leather bindings that traversed and spread her body open, revealing her "lock," which the inquisitor opened nightly with his ordained "key." But she was different now. It seemed as if her bosom was increasing in size, and her body was getting fuller. He could not understand how that could be because he doled out her meager sustenance himself. He kept her very lean in order to maintain the efforts he had poured into her. He did not want her regressing to the previous godless ways of overindulgence that had originally brought her to his attention.

Even though her bonds had sunk into her skin months previously, he saw that she was slightly fuller in areas of her body. He wondered if this had anything to do with her lock not seeping her lifeblood like it had almost precisely the same time in every moon's passing. (He never used the basin to collect this essence because it was not of his doing, as far as he could tell.) Being a man of God, he had very little experience or interest in such things as the changing of the female anatomy. Nor would it have been proper for him to ask anyone about such things. Some would consider this breach in his knowledge a weakness, and word would spread of his ignorance. That was unacceptable to him. God would lead the righteous down the path and decide all matters of man. Whatever would become would become. The inquisitor cleared his mind of it. However, her lock had not bled in quite some time.

Eventually, her abdomen had become completely distended and her bosom looked like it would burst. Throughout all of her transformation, the purifications continued. The inquisitor made it a point to never touch the mistress directly with his own hands or skin. He held the bindings for leverage. He ranted at her in Latin the entire time, cursing her soul. The only point of contact was his divinely unadulterated key and her lock. It was his gift that he provided to her by the power of God to capture her soul and cleanse it. Then he felt the power of God release from within him. He baptized the inside of her body and, ultimately, her soul with his precious life force. That done, he returned the key to its place beneath his smock. Then he said to her, as he had every time before, leaving her to another night of darkness in the dungeon, "You are safe now, child. You are with me now." And he returned to the sanctity of the upper floors of the palace.

One night, he woke with a start, awakened by a monk's knocking on the door of his personal chamber.

"What is it?" the inquisitor hissed.

"There is an issue down in the chamber that we are not allowed to enter, my lord, and we believe it will require your personal attention," the monk said nervously to the closed door.

Upon hearing this, the agitated inquisitor scrambled out of his bed and went to the door. Only two rooms in the palace were off limits to everyone. The first was his personal chamber, which no one could enter except in his presence. The other was the chamber of the mistress, which no one but prisoners could enter.

Only one prisoner at a time would be sent in under his direct guidance and in his presence. By the time they were forced into the chamber of the mistress, they had been so tortured and brutalized they had no desire or energy for any form of vengeance or insurrection against the inquisitor. They were broken souls, and they did exactly as they were told.

He had them clean the chamber. They removed the feces and filth from the floor directly beneath the mistress. They scrubbed the floor clean to the best of their abilities. Then he had them check and secure any bonds that might have slipped or loosened on the wretched woman who was suspended from the ceiling and walls by her constraints. After they had removed the feces and filth in a bucket, the inquisitor inspected the work they had done. If it did not meet his approval, he had them do the work again until it was accomplished to his satisfaction.

Once he was satisfied with their work, he would walk the prisoners to the door of the chamber, he would approach them from behind and reward them with a quick and painless death from a thin pearl-handled dagger that he kept up the sleeve of his cloak at all times. Dante would sink the dagger into the base of their skulls, instantly killing them and leaving no mess in the room. The maligned inquisitor would then summon his monk-guards, and they dragged the carcass out of the doorway, along with the bucket, for disposal in some unknown place.

The inquisitor had become very proficient at this process of cleaning out the mistress's chamber. He viewed sacrificing the prisoners as a gift he was giving them. It was—in that it released them from the lives of torment that were all they knew. Now their spirits could move on to a better place, having died serving the will of God.

As the inquisitor entered the forbidden chamber, he led with a torch, as he had always done before, and slammed the great wooden and steel door behind him. What he saw next was beyond his comprehension. Lying there in the filth, surrounded by a puddle of blood and unknown bodily fluids, was a crying baby. The mistress was breathing heavily and was unconscious. The infant had some form of huge vein that was attached to a bag of fleshy material that the inquisitor had never seen the likes of before in all of the purifications he had witnessed. The baby was covered in some form of blood, film, and greasy fluid. He didn't dare touch the child. He was repulsed by it in its current state. He had no idea what to do.

"Get me a surgeon now!" he ordered toward the door. "Bring me a surgeon now, and be quick about it!" He heard the Dominican guards clatter off up the stairs.

After about a half hour, the inquisitor heard a commotion, over the wailing of the infant, coming down the stairs. The door was partially pushed open. A very flustered and disheveled man was shoved into the torch-lit chamber. He peered toward the inquisitor, who was still kneeling down by the plaintive baby. The disoriented man was trying to let his eyes adjust to the light and figure out what he was looking at when he said timidly, "I am the surgeon, Your Eminence. How...how may I be of assistance to you?"

"You can start by coming over here and speaking in a more subtle tone," the priest said with an air of authority. "Discretion is mandated of your presence in this most sanctified of spaces."

The surgeon moved toward the genuflecting inquisitor. With a horror that swept across his face and one he could not conceal, he realized exactly what he was looking at that was draped from the top of the chamber. A new scream from the baby snapped the surgeon's head back toward the ground.

Past the inquisitor on the ground was a child. It was lying in excrement and filth. The umbilicus was still attached, the blood and fluid of birth had dried to its skin, and upon its head was a caul. Not a good omen.

"Can you help this child?" the inquisitor questioned the shaken surgeon.

"I believe so, Your Grace, but I will need some provisions. Water, clean rags, blankets, a knife, some thread and swaddling," the surgeon said, reading off his mental checklist. "If I could have a small table, it would help. How long has the baby been here in this situation?" the surgeon stammered, trying to figure out the chances for the baby's survival.

"Less than an hour. Now there will be no more questions. I want you to focus your efforts and skills on the child. Use all of your knowledge to ensure the baby's survival—and your own."

The inquisitor gave the order for the supplies and hissed at them that he wanted these things "immediately!"

In the time it took the surgeon to pick the baby off of the floor and start to wipe away some of the filth that covered it, all of the supplies he had requested were delivered. The surgeon wrapped the baby boy (along with the still connected afterbirth) in his tunic and gently laid him on the ground. The newborn had started to calm down. The surgeon set up the table with a few blankets spread out on top of it. He put the bucket of water down next to the table and laid out the rest of his supplies.

The grave inquisitor sat on a stool in a corner of the room, his hands folded over his crossed legs, and observed the process without a word.

The surgeon started by cleaning off the baby with the water and the rags. The child started screaming again because the water was cold. The surgeon bound the umbilicus tightly, directly in front of the child's abdomen, with the thread he had requested. With a swift move of the knife, he cut the cord that attached the baby to the placenta. Blood squirted out, displeasing the inquisitor.

The surgeon noted his disapproval and quickly assured him, "That was not from the baby. That was from the cord and is routine for this process."

The inquisitor settled back in his seat.

The surgeon then swaddled the screaming baby and walked over to the inquisitor with the baby in his arms. "This child needs to be fed," he said. "Would you like me to give him his first feeding? It will quiet the child down."

The inquisitor just raised his eyebrows, his look changing from a frown to one of apathy. Seeing that, the surgeon walked over to the mistress, found one of her exposed nipples, held out the screaming baby, and pressed him to the woman's breast. The baby instantly quieted and began to feed. These were the only moments that the mother and child would ever share.

The baby latched on and fed well from his cataleptic mother. The surgeon's arms were starting to get tired from holding the baby out in front of him. At that moment, the baby released himself from the mother and began to cry again. He had drained the first breast and needed more.

"This is a good sign of the baby's health, Your Lordship. The child is hungry and strong."

The other breast was not so exposed; the surgeon had to look around for it among the bindings. Absentmindedly, he reached out and moved one of the constraints to reveal the nipple. He pulled the breast out of the straps.

This blind move infuriated the inquisitor. If the inquisitor was unsure before of what to do with the surgeon, he had absolutely no doubts about the nervous man's fate now. The surgeon had just defiled the mistress with a simple touch. It had taken the priest months to cleanse her body and soul. In the inquisitor's twisted mind, with a simple, inadvertent touch, that was all destroyed.

After the child latched on to the mother's other breast, the surgeon was able to prop the baby up on the woman, anchoring him in among the bonds without fear of the child falling.

"You will have to employ a wet nurse to feed the child," the surgeon recommended. "Unless, of course, you would prefer to come down here to feed the baby every couple of hours."

The inquisitor summoned the surgeon to him. "I am going to release you from your duties to the church. Remember that your discretion is paramount."

"Yes, Your Eminence," the surgeon supplicated, looking down at the floor.

"Good, then I will show you to the door," the Inquisitor said as he guided the man by the arm.

The surgeon slowly breathed a sigh of relief to himself.

The inquisitor opened the door and shoved the surgeon into the arms of the guards who were waiting on the other side. Coldly and without emotion, he said, "Execute him immediately for blasphemy against the church. Let me know when you are finished. Then burn his body and throw the remnants into the sewer below the palace."

As the inquisitor heard the horrified man being dragged off to his imminent demise, he spun on his heels and headed in the direction of the mistress. The baby was asleep on the oblivious mother's bosom. The nipple was still in his mouth. The inquisitor snatched up the baby, taking care to make no contact with the comatose mistress. He opened the door to the chamber, grabbed the torch, closed and locked the door behind him, and ascended the stairs undetected by anyone.

A few minutes after the inquisitor arrived in his chambers, there was a knock at the door.

"Enter."

"My lord, the heretic surgeon has been executed," the monk-guard said stolidly.

"How?"

"Beheaded. Now his remnants are being burned. After that, we will toss them in the sewer as you ordered," the monk replied.

"You have done good work. There is another thing I am going to need for you to do for me. I am going to need a wet nurse here tomorrow morning by the time I awake. Do you understand?"

"Yes, Your Holiness."

"Good! You may now leave."

The monk-guard opened the door and slid out of the room.

———◆———

That was how their lives together as father and son began.

In his eyes, the inquisitor's son was an ordained gift from God. His son was a gift given to him for his efforts to cleanse and save the souls of lost women, especially the mistress, who was the vessel of the ordained.

UNHEEDED DECREE

Steve skimmed quickly through chapters of the journal when he did not see anything new or relevant to his interests.

From his quick reading of the chapters, Steve could tell that the inquisitor wasn't very interested in or adept at political dealings, especially those with the Vatican. He was more interested in the purification of the souls for which he was responsible and never relented in his zeal.

He even ignored repeated consistorial decrees sent to him by the protonotary apostolic, the chief clerk of the Vatican court and a very powerful figure in the Catholic hierarchy. (The post was a stepping stone to becoming a cardinal.) The pope employed the protonotary apostolic at times to send messages through unofficial channels without having to utilize the authority (and exposure) of a papal bull, the official Vatican document signed by the pope. Employing the protonotary apostolic was a more discrete way to send a threat without having to make the entire Catholic world aware of it. The protonotary apostolic provided a layer of separation between a decree and the direct involvement of the pope.

The decrees sent by the protonotary apostolic from Rome to Dante at first were of an inquisitive nature. They requested that the inquisitor review his approach to helping heretics and blasphemers because Rome was hearing many rumors and complaints of brutality about the tribunal under his jurisdiction. Ultimately, they became more commanding and then combative in nature as each decree went unanswered. No direct threats were made, but the threatening tone of the communications from Rome was obvious.

The last decree Dante received was very direct:

> Cease and desist all actions being taken to purify your subject's souls for the Greater Glory of God. You have achieved the status of cleanliness of blood in your jurisdiction. To continue on the path that you are now proceeding upon, will be at the cost of your own soul. The Vatican wishes to thank you for all that you have done in the name of God and prays for you that you heed this Consistorial Decree. Amen.

He paid it no heed.

What had he to worry about? He had the blessing and backing of King Charles II. He had one of the most peaceful and controlled tribunals under the guidance of the Inquisition. The portions of the confiscated assets that he passed along to Charles were substantial. Besides, the Vatican was resistant at first to the Inquisition, so who cared whether it approved of his approach to the purification of his subjects? And most important, how dare the pope try to send a thinly veiled threat to him? The successor of St. Peter had no sense of the power of God that Dante yielded in his own hands—the power to personally purify lost souls, heretics, and blasphemers with his own life essence. The pope could not attain the understanding of the ancient texts on cleansing and saving of souls that Dante had attained. In his mind, Dante had no need to see the blessing of the pope.

In fact, Dante did not subscribe to the dogma of papal infallibility. He viewed the pope as a hypocrite who was guilty of heresy for using God's glorious name to collect vast sums of wealth and power. He believed that this accumulation of wealth and power corrupted the church and enslaved the entire institution of God into doing the bidding of the antichrist. Dante based this belief on his observations about wars started by the Vatican in the name of God, the huge accumulations of wealth by the supreme pontiff, the moral iniquities of the hierarchy of the church locally and abroad, and scandal after scandal after scandal involving local leaders of various churches. The worst of all insults to the house of God was the moral ambiguity of the church hierarchy regarding the souls for whom it was responsible.

The journal went on to reveal that Dante viewed himself as different, as superior in his vocation to everyone else. He realized that saving souls was of the utmost importance, which was why he did not mind so many dying under his authority. He knew he was saving their souls from the eternal torment of an afterlife in hell, so it was better for them that they died with a purified soul. None of the others in the Church realized this as much as Dante. That was why he did not care about the other clergy or the church hierarchy or even the bishop of Rome himself. None of them had done or accomplished this work as he had. So he did not concern himself with whether they approved of the very important work he had done. They were all hypocrites, blasphemers, and heretics that he would have liked to have had the opportunity to purify and release personally.

He did not ignore the final decree completely. He ignored the veiled threat. Then he did the worst thing he possibly could have done—he wrote a letter to the sovereign of the Vatican. He explained in very plain language all of his concerns with the hierarchy, the future of the church, and the supreme pontiff himself.

———◆———

Dante's letter was not received well in Rome. Innocent XII was a sedate, cerebral, and compassionate Pontiff. But the blasphemous communiqué that he received from Dante Torquemada so infuriated him that it awakened within him the inquisitorial personality that had been dormant since his time serving the Vatican in Malta. The reawakened wrath was to be brought down upon the mercenary Dominican who had delivered the accusatory epistle and was now standing before him.

With a mere look to one of his attendant Jesuit priests, the messenger was shown out of the pope's audience and instantly spirited away to a place with no hope or redemption. There the Dominican was introduced to a new and more intense version of limpieza de sangre that he had never before seen. He received his "cleansing" without being given the release that Dante had granted to so many of his flock. To the astonishment of the Jesuits, Dante's messenger took the limpieza without uttering a sound.

After rereading the letter he had received from the warped inquisitor from Spain, what infuriated Pope Innocent the most was that the very things Dante had accused him of were the very things he had been trying to change about the church. Innocent was known as a reformer of the church, seeking to save the church from itself. He was a Jesuit whose personal credo was "The poor are my nephews." In his eyes, there was no greater affront to his effort than the heretical and inaccurate accusations from the worst manipulator of God's will. For years, he had heard of Dante's abuses and brutality against the poor, the very people with whom Innocent had identified. Through discrete channels, he had tried to influence Dante to change his ways. Those efforts went unheeded.

With dread, Innocent realized it was time for him to take action before this inquisitor's blatant defiance would become known by others in charge of various tribunals and Rome would lose more of its crumbling power base than it could afford.

He had decided on a plan of action that would dispatch the disturbed inquisitor and all of his minions, while placing the blame on rogue heretic dissidents that had been creating havoc in Spain. Innocent could not afford a direct connection with this course of action. If a connection between this plot and the pope were to become known, it would be disastrous for the unstable relationship between Rome and the monarchy of Spain. It also would diminish the standing of the church in the eyes of the monarchies of the rest of the world.

An issue this important would require his best men. He had no doubt about whom he would call upon to complete his most discrete of missions for ad majorem Dei gloriam (the Greater Glory of God), the unofficial credo of the Jesuits, his own order. Their official credo was "to go without questioning wherever the pope might direct." Innocent had for years kept himself surrounded with his own special Jesuit attendants. The Jesuits were "foot soldiers of the pope," an appellation bestowed upon them in part because the founder of the Society of Jesus, Ignatius, was a soldier before he began to follow God and because the Jesuits were known for being soldiers as much as priests. Innocent kept his private complement of Jesuits secret and highly trained.

His covert agents would be under the direct supervision of the protonotary apostolic, also a Jesuit. They were instructed to follow his authority without question. They were to travel in two separate groups of three men, a few days apart, dress in simple garb, with no obvious weapons, and keep to themselves. It was imperative to the mission that they travel unnoticed to Catalonia. There they would come together again and covertly execute the pontiff's dark plan. The protonotary apostolic would travel with them, make sure the campaign was carried out completely, and report back to the pope.

INQUISITOR'S JOURNAL: THE VATICAN'S PLAN REVEALED

The last night of Dante's reign of terror was an ordinary evening. He had supper with his young son, had him put to bed by the nurse, and went unseen down to the chamber of the mistress for his assiduous nightly purification ritual.

As he closed and locked the door to the bound mistress's subterranean chamber, he though he heard something from the hallways above. It sounded like a soft clatter from a small bowl or something like it hitting the hard stone floor of the antechambers. He dismissed it as nothing.

He continued toward the vessel that had provided him with his son and withdrew his key from underneath his cloak. Something happened at that moment that he had not expected. The mistress welcomed the inquisitor forward for the first time ever. She spread her bound legs and encircled the demented holy man in a tender embrace.

I have finally reached through to her, he thought.

For the first time, he looked into her eyes and allowed her to look back into his. They regarded each other for a moment. There was no hate or fear in the woman's eyes, unlike so many times before. There was just a woman. For the first time, he did not hate her or feel the need to punish her for her insolence. He felt what he thought to be a small amount of compassion.

As he slowly pushed his key into her lock, he was overcome with feeling and decided to remove the ball of leather that he kept lodged in her mouth unless he was feeding her. He untied the binding behind her neck that held the ball in her mouth. He then did something that neither he nor the mistress expected; he gently wiped the hair out of her face. She looked at him in amazement and appreciation. Not a word was spoken between them.

The inquisitor went about his business of "internally cleansing" the mistress, and that was when everything changed between them. Just as he was delivering his "life essence" into the bound mistress, with his eyes clamped shut, she chomped down onto his ear like a rabid wolf and would not let go. Dante screamed in ecstasy and agony. He wrenched his head back, tearing a piece of his ear off in the process. He opened his eyes and saw to his horror a large chunk of his bloody flesh in the grinning mistress's mouth. He reeled back in agony as she spat the torn lump of meat onto the soiled floor and laughed out loud.

She screeched, "You will never have me!"

Then he gave her what she was truly looking for. In a fury that the inquisitor had never felt before, he reached into the sleeve of his robe, retrieved his pearl-handled dagger, and proceeded to release the mistress from her services to the greater glory of God.

As he repeatedly inflicted his fury upon her, she laughed louder and more maniacally. By the time the tempest of his ferocity had passed, Dante was exhausted. He was lumped against her suspended body, heavily breathing in exhaustion. It dawned on him that he had been cruelly manipulated into giving the Mistress of Bondage the release she had sought for so long.

As he was catching his breath and regaining his composure, he heard a metallic crash from another room in the underground chambers. Dante was furious, and someone was going to pay for this insolence. When he reached the door to the chamber, he heard on the other side of the locked door a muffled grunt from one of his guards. It sounded as if his body hit the floor and did not rise again.

Dante froze in place. He looked down at the door and saw the release latch to the chamber silently rise and then lower. He still had the only key for the lock to the room. No one would be able to enter. He put his good ear to the door and listened. He heard two men whispering in Italian.

"Leave him. He's done. There are many other rooms to search for the inquisitor in this labyrinth of a building."

The inquisitor heard the two men quietly pad off toward the dungeon. He comprehended the dire situation immediately. After gently unlocking the heavy door so as not to draw any attention, he slipped stealthily up the dark stairway to his private chambers, using a hidden door he had had built into the palace during its construction.

As he quietly slid into his sleeping quarters, he entered behind a heavy velvet curtain in his massive bedroom, which was at the back wall of the palace. A sitting room was between the bedroom and the only known entrance.

He heard voices coming from the sitting room.

"Relax, my child," said an educated voice. "I am the protonotary apostolic to Rome. No one has come here to harm you. To be completely honest, you and the child are quite a surprise to find here on these premises of iniquity."

"Thank you, Your Eminence, but why are you here?" Dante heard his blubbering nurse reply.

"Don't bother yourself with that, my dear. We are just trying to remove a scourge that has descended upon this area, and we will need to employ the inquisitor's assistance to accomplish our quest."

"Then why have all of the friars been killed, Your Grace?" she said, sobbing.

With that question, she sealed her fate in the protonotary apostolic's eyes.

"They were misrepresenting the greater glory of God and had to be dealt with. Don't bother yourself with that, my child. What you can do to assist the Holy Roman Church is to share with us the current whereabouts of Inquisitor Torquemada."

"I would gladly if I could, Your Holiness, but he moves about very secretly, and I never know where he is. I only know that I have to watch after his son with my own life and make no mistakes. He tolerates no mistakes, and his wrath is harsh. Myself, I have it better than most, but I have not seen my own family or left this palace for some time. The monks forced me here after I gave birth to my own son, and I have never seen him since. My husband was put to death for coming to the palace and making inquiries. It is dark times for this region. The inquisitor general rules this land with an intolerant iron fist. No one is ever released that comes here. No one."

As the nurse was telling the Vatican's emissary of her woes, Dante slipped out from behind the curtain, grabbed an enormous silver-bound, jewel-encrusted Bible, snuck up behind the protonotary apostolic, and knocked the unsuspecting cleric unconscious with one swift blow to the back of his skull.

The nurse stopped talking as if her brain had shut off, and she sat there with her mouth agape. Dante went over and locked the door. He turned to the nurse and asked, "How is the child? Is he still sleeping?"

The nurse was horrified. The inquisitor before her was covered in blood. He was missing half of one of his ears. His cloak was splattered in blood that was obviously not his. She began to tremble and cough.

"Be quiet!" he chastised her. "Is my son all right?"

"Yes. The boy is sleeping in his bed. He has not been stirred by the night's occurrences."

The inquisitor stood directly in front of the bereft nurse. "I overheard you say to this man that no one is ever released from this palace. For your unremitting service to me and my son, I shall release you from your obligations." He pulled the blood-covered dagger out of his sleeve and dealt with the nurse for the last time.

As the protonotary started to regain consciousness, his movement was restricted. Then with horror, he realized he was completely bound and immobilized in a small unknown chamber of the malevolent palace. He heard a voice speaking to him that amplified his dread.

"I have been receiving your eloquent communications, my dear protonotary. They have been very inquisitive and quite amusing, I must say. It's my understanding that all of my Albigensian guards have been slaughtered, and as we speak, your men are searching my palace for you right now. They will never find you. This room does not exist on any building plans of this palace. The man who secretly built it for me was put to death right after he finished. This room does not exist.

"I know who you are, and I think I understand why you are here, but I want the entire story, every detail. I want to know the extent of the pope's involvement and the extent of the problems I now face. If you do not cooperate, realize that I can keep you alive for days if I need to. I will extract the information I am seeking from you. It's up to you how easy you make your passage into the waiting hands of God."

Dante removed the blood-soaked knife from his sleeve directly in front of the apprehensive face of his prisoner, who responded defiantly: "I will tell you nothing!"

"Good."

Dante slowly sliced the protonotary apostolic's robe and pulled the material aside to expose the man's stomach. Then he slid the blade of the pearl-handled dagger over the man's plump abdomen. Rome's terrified envoy started to reveal the Vatican's plan as the inquisitor revealed the bound man's own organs to him.

INQUISITOR'S JOURNAL: ESCAPE AND EVASION

Dante found out everything he needed from the emissary of Rome. It did not take long. Having gathered the information, he then gathered up his son, some gold, and a coffer of valuable items. They slipped down a secret set of stairs, out to a loaded cart and horse. He and his child disappeared into the night; the entire process took less than thirty minutes.

From the intelligence he gathered from the protonotary, his situation was dire. When he found out that the pope himself was the initiator of his planned demise, he realized there would be nowhere in the world he could hide. With this knowledge of his new predicament, the inquisitor decided to make a stealthy exit into the dark night and make his way undetected to the underground network of Catharsian hideaways in Europe until he could hatch a more decisive plan.

Dante never mentioned the locations of the hideaways in his journal. He never mentioned his son's name, either. He wrote that he took these measures intentionally so that in case he was ever captured, the locations would not be revealed and his son would remain anonymous from the Vatican's wrath.

The father and son moved frequently about Europe, never staying in any town or any country for more than a month so as not to draw attention to themselves. Dante financed their secretive travels with the gold he took with him in his hasty escape. Once the gold ran out, he turned to the jewels encrusted on his "holy purification kit," which he carried away in his leaden coffer. Dante was amazed by the venality of both the local secular authorities and especially the Catholic officials, who were even easier to suborn.

After a few years, his wealth dwindled. Even though he had filled the pockets of many officials in many countries to ensure his and his son's protection and anonymity, Dante discovered through channels he had remunerated that the Vatican was closing in on them. No matter how many times they moved, how remote the accommodations, Innocent's Jesuits were never far behind.

He knew they had to go where the church had little influence, a place where he and his son would have new opportunities, where they could disappear and start over. The obvious conclusion was the New World. The potential opportunities were limitless. Most important, the Catholic Church did not have a stranglehold on the government or much influence over the people, especially in the northern regions of the Americas. It was perfect.

In the early spring of 1699, Dante booked passage to the New World for him and his son with a notorious "retired" pirate Capt. Samuel Burgess. His ship was the slaver *Margaret*. Captain Burgess's notorious reputation was earned from his time spent sailing with the dreaded pirate Capt. William Kidd aboard the *Blessed William*. Burgess "retired" when the *William* was seized in 1690.

This was the type of ship Dante was looking for—few questions, a captain and crew that valued being undetected in their travels, uncommon sailing routes, and most important, no ship's passenger list.

Dante heard of the ported ship while they were living on the Scilly Islands, off Cornwall, England. The area was known for its perilous sailing and the difficulty of reaching it. The ships that made the treacherous, rocky coast their homeport and the people who lived there were there for a reason—anonymity. Dante was one of them.

They set sail within the week.

During their evasive travels throughout Europe, Dante took the opportunity to begin his son's education. The boy had revealed himself to be highly intelligent, and his ability to learn and absorb information was impressive. In the few years that they were in Europe, the boy learned three languages, including all of their subtle nuances. The ex-inquisitor was currently working on the boy's English, and the lad was able to practice on the crew. By the time their voyage ended, and they reached the Province of Massachusetts Bay, the boy had not only mastered English but could speak in various accents and dialects. His amazing intelligence reinforced for Dante the notion that his son was an "ordained gift from God." "Ordain" was the root of the boy's name. Dante thought it was the perfect seed for a name of greatness, and so he named his son "Dain."

When they were dropped off at an unknown port in the mouth of the Penobscot River, Dante had all of the supplies he had purchased before they left unloaded. Then he purchased from Burgess with a few of the jewels that he had left ten of the best slaves on board. With the promise of a clean life and opportunity, he hired a few of the men from the ship's crew who were looking to retire from the pirate life. They packed Dante's three wagons of slaves and supplies and headed inland to start their new lives.

He used the last of the embedded jewels in his possession to purchase a tract of land near what would come to be known in modern times as the town of Beldon, Maine.

INQUISITOR'S JOURNAL:
MAP OF REVELATIONS

One of the last entries in the journal was a handwritten map of the tract of land from around 1800. It was more than a thousand acres at one point, more like an estate than a farm, and had its own village of support staff situated on the property to help run the day-to-day operations.

On the map, Steve noticed that the farm and village were situated near the old southern property line along Long Shadows Road and near a brook that was its water source. With an epiphany that was like a slug to the jaw, he realized that the main house and the little village were in the same location as the old swamp he had previously waded through to hide the inquisitor's coffer. In fact, he had hidden the coffer not far from the village, according to the map.

This map entry was one of the last few entries by Dante, who was very old by the date of the entry, 1847. By Steve's estimation, the man must have been around 180 years old by then. He wondered how that could be possible.

Dante wrote that he had been housebound for decades, and his son had been running the farm. Day by day, he sat up in the top window of the grand house and overlooked the farm and the fruits of all of his efforts. It brought him a sense of satisfaction and peace that he had never had before in his previous life.

In his last pages, Dante told how the villagers had slowly deserted the farm, leaving their small homes empty. No one ever came to replace them. He never understood why until his last servant in the house, an old black woman, confided in him that women of all ages had vanished from the farm without a trace. They disappeared at all hours of the day and night. It had been happening for years. The word in the area was that the farm was damned, and no one would come to fill the vacant positions.

Steve read the ancient inquisitor's second-to-last entry:

> "The water from the brook has slowly started to pool and rise in the hamlet below. It has actually crossed some of the doorways in the deserted village and flooded the lower lying areas in the past few months. I fear this to be the beginning of a slow death for the once prosperous Long Shadows Farm. This once great farm was a safe haven for myself and my son, Dain, having escaped from the most insidious and far-reaching of powers in the known world.
>
> "I believe it was a gift, our escape from the tyranny of Rome. An offering from God, as a form of his recognition for the 'Purifications' that I had performed in my previous life. I now know that I can release those that had been cleansed and purified into the hands of God. Having been up in this room for so many years, I have lost track of my sacred instruments that I brought with us from my previous life. I will need to employ the items and get my son to gather them for me and help me through my final Purification ritual. This must be done soon. Very soon. I am very aware that my own light is fading. I will no longer need the energy the Purified have provided me to fuel my prolonged mortality. The end is inevitable."

The final entry personally recorded into the journal by Inquisitor General Dante Perechine De Torquemada, regent of Catalonia, last direct descendant of Grand Inquisitor Tomas De Torquemada, was a statement written in what looked to be Latin: "In ordo pro animus futurus privatus ciphus must existo infractus."

In the next entry in the journal, Dain told of his father asking him to locate and retrieve the coffer that held the sacred instruments. His father told him of the ritual that the inquisitor would have to perform on himself in order to release the souls into the waiting hands of God on the following morning.

Dain then told of betraying his father by melting down the vessel-basin and reshaping it while his father slept. He did this because, unbeknown to his father, for the past eighty years, Dain had become a student of the ancient Bible, a primordial text that was scribed in ancient Latin at a time when pagan religions reigned. The ink on its pages was actually the blood of the purified.

Steve realized that the Bible Dain was referring to predated Christ. It was a copy of the Old Testament before there was even an *Old* Testament. It was an interpretation of God before Christ and told how to purify the unholy in preparation for being received by God, the wrathful God of the Old Testament.

The next note Dain entered boasted of having trapped his father in more than one way on the following morning.

———◆———

With a look of abject astonishment on his face, his father asked, "Son, what are you doing?"

Upon hearing those words, Dain bound his father by the neck to the rattan chair that he had sat in for the past seventy years and stuffed a rag in the old man's mouth.

The son (who revealed in the journal that he was about 130 years old and didn't look older than fifty) wrote at length of his response to his father's question.

"Because *I* need their energy *now*, old man! I found your leaden chest eighty years ago and have been a student of God's Preparation Bible since then. Your translation of the title as Purification Bible was incorrect. Many of your translations have been wrong. I have also read the journal you had tried to keep secret for so many years. In cross-referencing the Preparation

Bible to your journal, I noted what your mistakes were and corrected them for myself. For instance, you old fool, your translation of *ciphus* as 'basin' was idiotic. It meant 'cipher' from ancient Egyptian hieroglyphs. It looks something like this."

He held up a large silver oval to show his bound and gagged father.

"This is the true *sciphus* that was referenced in the book. I melted down your basin last night and reformed it into the proper shape you should have originally had it made into. With it, I will be able to keep the souls I will require for a life that will endure the oceans of time. I have had my own cypher for years. I fashioned it from the bodies of my own 'preparation' participants. It is in a hallowed place not far from here. The area is a catacomb of sorts. The bodies are arranged and presented according to the Bible.

"As you, yourself, focused mostly on females, I too have focused on women, but the difference in my rituals was that I would prepare only females, and I would take all ages. You will be my first and only male ever. You always told me that women were the reason man fell from the grace of Eden and robbed of immortality. That is why I also have made them pay for their transgressions over the years.

"You started losing time as soon as you stopped the purification rituals when we left Spain. When I was in my fifties, I found your materials in that leaden box. I studied them, and my life started to improve. Now with the more preparations I perform, the greater my power builds. When I finish with your preparation, I will gain all of your energy and whatever you have left from your 'harem of the confined.'"

He then stripped his father naked, bound him this time by his wrists and ankles to the old woven rattan chair. His next step was to lift both his decrepit father and the chair he was bound to and brusquely drop him with a heavy *thud* into the newly forged center of the cipher, which he had placed on the ground. He did this in order to encircle the old man and limit his power.

Dain positioned a chalice on the floor in the center of the newly remodeled oval for the collection of his father's blood and then carefully opened his father's veins around his crotch and scrotum. He watched the old man hemorrhage and weaken as his blood filled up the chalice placed under the chair. He then performed his father's own purification ritual for the aged inquisitor. He performed it without a flaw, right down to adding his own "personal ingredient" to the chalice. The final trap was closed for Dante when he was forced to partake "communion" from the chalice that Dain had personally prepared for his father. Dain had imposed this betrayal upon his father because he himself had been preparing the unclean souls of women for years, and he wanted his collecting to continue—indefinitely.

Dain had come upon the coffer decades before while searching for something in the attic. He delicately picked the lock to the leaden mystery chest to reveal its contents. Inside, he found what at first he thought were keepsakes of his father's past, but upon further inspection, they were revealed to be much more valuable in many ways. There was a silver-bound Bible written in old Latin; a cumbersome, sizeable silver basin; a silver chalice with very ornate etchings; another book bound in a black velvet-like material, which turned out to be a Spanish translation of the silver Bible; and a pearl-handled dagger. The silver Bible, basin, and chalice all were covered in pronged pock marks that were evidence of their jewel-encrusted past. All of the jewels had been removed, and the silver was tarnished, but they were still magnificent pieces.

Upon discovering the ancient relics, Dain was drawn most to the silver-bound book. The etchings on both covers were ornate and flowed back into themselves in a never-ending perpetual pattern. It was huge, heavy and beautiful. He never divulged his discovery of the leaden chest and its contents to his father.

The ancient Bible opened up a closet in his mind that had been shut for years. That closet held the Latin language that his father had educated him in during their early years while they secretly traveled around Europe. He was able to read the old text and became a ravenous student of the newfound Bible. He often delved deeply into the metal- bound book, without making his weakening father aware of what he had discovered from their long-ago past, a past he could barely remember.

In his study of the Bible, he became aware that his father had mistranslated quite a few words incorrectly throughout the text.

Making the translation even more difficult was that the original form of the Preparation Bible was a scroll written on papyrus, probably from around 300–400 BC. It had been carefully sectioned into pages in order for it to be bound. Besides the natural curling of the pages that had been flattened-out scroll pages and the Bible's some two thousand years of age when Dante first acquired it in the 1690s (from the assets of a wealthy family whose members he had both purified and released), the red ink of the Preparation Bible had faded to the point that some of the letters, words, and sentences were almost completely obscured.

The most critical word that his father had mistranslated appeared to be written as ciphus in the Preparation Bible. This was incorrect. Dain observed that his father had not been able to see one of the very faded letters in the word. The correct spelling of the word in question was sciphus. The missing letter *s* changed the meaning of the Latin statement. Dain noticed that his father had incorrectly interpreted the misspelled ciphus as the Spanish word cifras.

In Latin, sciphus literally meant "vessel," or figuratively, "cypher."

However, Dante had incorrectly read the word as ciphus, which he then errantly translated into Spanish as cifras, which means "basin" or "riddle."

That was why Dante incorrectly had a heavy, large silver catch basin in his hidden chest of religious relics from his previous life, instead of a large oblong loop, also known as a cipher, which should have been among the contents in his coffer of pagan artifacts.

———•◆•———

Steve could understand Dante's misinterpretation, which Dain had so thoroughly pointed out in his journal entries.

Out of curiosity Steve clicked the space bar of the computer and got back onto Google. He looked up "cypher" online. To his amazement, he found the origin of the word cypher could be traced back to ancient Egyptian script. Its modern definition: (1) an oval-shaped symbol; (2) a continuous interlocking design; (3) secret written code or riddle; (4) a receptacle of nothing, void.

Upon seeing the definition and the symbol for cypher, Steve's jaw dropped almost to the floor. At two different locations, he had seen that symbol before.

MEETING DENISE MOYNIHAN

Steve finished reading the disturbing journal around two in the morning. He stood up from the desk and with a big yawn stretched the kinks out of his back. He could hardly believe he had just finished reading such a twisted tale of a family's history. It was the stuff of horror stories.

He tried to shake off the disturbed images he had in his head of the atrocities the Torquemada family had committed under the guise of righteous religion. He also wanted to find out the meaning of the Latin statement that Dante had written in his last entries. Now, however, he was sick of reading, especially reading the journal, and wanted to go see Denise Moynihan.

It would be best to blend in with the hospital environment as best he could, he thought, even though he would be going to her room around two thirty in the morning. He grabbed his red flashlight and went to check the contents of the doctor's closets.

Upon opening a large closet and inspecting it with his red light, Steve chuckled.

"This guy must piss himself a lot!" he said.

The closet was loaded with neatly folded clothes, everything from socks and underwear to shirts and pants. There were even a few pairs of worn shoes at the bottom of the closet. He changed from his outdoor clothing into something more suitable for walking around in a hospital environment. Everything fit fairly well. Even the shoes fit, a little tight but not bad.

He retrieved the lab coat from the rack by the door. The nylon necklace with the hospital identification tags hung down by his stomach. In the pocket of the coat was a key chain of all of the keys he would need to move about the hospital. He started checking keys to see which one fit the lock on the door to the room he was in. Once he found the correct one, he went to the desk, retrieved some tape from one of the drawers, took a piece, and wrapped the head of the key in order to be able to distinguish it by touch from the others on the large ring, without having to look at it. He went online on the computer to find out the exact location of Denise Moynihan's room. She was on the third floor in the psych ward, room 312, in the midlevel security wing.

He slid his backpack and other items under the large desk, in the space where he had previously slept, and then went out the door.

Walking through the quiet corridors of the hospital made him feel very exposed. He was surprised there were other staff members moving about the hospital at this late hour. No one looked at him twice. He was dressed appropriately and had the proper credentials hanging from around his neck like everyone else that worked there. So as not to make eye contact with anyone, he pulled out a medical reference guide that was in one of the pockets of the lab coat and faked reading it as he walked along the hall to the elevators.

When the elevator doors opened at the third floor, he saw that the floor was very quiet. To his astonishment, there was an electronic swipe lock on a very modern glass door directly in front of him. For a moment, he panicked. He had not seen any swipe card on the doctor's desk and was starting to get worried when he remembered the credentials hanging from his neck. Sure enough, one of the cards had the telltale magnetic strip across the top of the back of the card. Apprehensively, he swiped the card, and the door slid open.

He breathed a sigh of relief. The hallway was dark except for the one small glaring fluorescent light on the desk of the nurse's station. No one was there at the moment, but he heard shuffling in one of the rooms down the hall. He heard the nurse gently speaking to one of the patients, then he went in the opposite direction from the room the nurse was in. Luckily, the room numbers were descending in the correct order. He was heading in the right direction.

———•·•———

Steve thought he would be mentally prepared for what he would encounter when he finally entered Denise Moynihan's room. He wasn't. Scrawled all over walls of the harshly lit room were thousands of renditions of the same symbol he had learned about on the computer in the doctor's office. A cypher was drawn any place on the walls there was a free surface. There were so many black ovals that the room was darkened even with its fluorescent lighting. The display spoke volumes to the depth of Denise Moynihan's broken sanity.

Steve was so struck by it that he lurched. He finally noticed the woman sitting on her hands on the edge of her bed, looking down at the floor. She was completely oblivious to him. Her stringy brown hair was hanging down around her face, concealing her identity. Her hospital gown was twisted all around her, exposing the top of her back. She just stared at a crumpled pile of bed sheets on the floor that appeared to have the contents of her dinner tray tossed on top of them.

He moved toward the motionless woman and in a gentle voice said, "Denise? Are you Denise Moynihan?"

Her only reply was to slowly start rocking in place, staying focused on the crumpled pile of her meal and the sheets. He slowly approached her and looked down at the pile that had her attention.

"I guess you didn't like the meal," he said softly.

She just kept slowly rocking. He looked down again and noticed something awry. There seemed to be a dried stain of blood on the floor under the pile of sheets and food. He knelt down to inspect the pile. Reaching across the soiled sheets, he grabbed the far side and slowly lifted the mass of food and linen to reveal what was underneath. With disgust, he saw the decapitated body of a dead rat. As he pulled the sheet back further, he saw written on the floor the same Latin statement he had seen at the end of the Dante's journal. It had been inked in blood, apparently the rat's.

As he pulled back in revulsion, he turned his head to the side and looked directly into Denise's haggard face from less than an inch away. Her mouth was filled with blood. Her cauliflower-patterned bloodshot eyes were looking directly into his.

She spat the head of the rat into his face and hissed to him with a hideous grin, "You are very close to being damned with the rest of us. Your quest is useless. As for your dormant wife, she is damned already. It's too late for her."

Steve stumbled back in abject horror. It was as if he had been hit with a two-by-four across the face. He scrambled to get to his feet so he could get away from her damning face. He felt panic and fumbled with a loud crash through the door.

Denise Moynihan never moved. She sat on the side of the bed, grinning at him with her evil grin.

By the time the irritated nurse arrived at Denise's room to check on the cause of all of the commotion, Steve had already sprinted wildly out of the unit and leapt down two flights of stairs in the emergency exit stairwell.

He did not like meeting Denise Moynihan.

SERGEANT ERDODY –
AN UNKNOWN ALLY

When he got back to his vehicle with Shultz, Sergeant Erdody was livid. He had dealt with assholes like Macfarlane his whole life and couldn't stand the type. He wanted to get ahead of him and stay ahead of him until Babin was safely remanded to state police custody. Erdody wanted to hear Babin's story himself. He was sure he knew the situation that the man had been forced into by Macfarlane, and it was making him sick. Nothing about Babin smelled like a murderous lunatic to him. From everything he found out from looking into the man's record and recent movements, Babin appeared to be clean.

He ran through the story in his mind.

Babin and his wife leave New Hampshire two days ago for a getaway weekend. They stay at Macfarlane's father's camp for the weekend. Babin and his wife, Carla, are in a hideous accident on Saturday night, and miraculously, both live through it. They're hospitalized, and she's still in an unexplainable coma. But her injuries are not severe enough to justify a coma. And why were they naked? Why were they traveling so erratically so late at night?

The toxicology reports on both of them showed no sign of narcotics in their systems. Babin's line of work is pharmaceuticals. He regularly gets drug-screened and has never had a problem. There were trace levels of alcohol in their systems, but nothing to hint at intoxication. They were both well below the legal limit. So why, after getting visited by Mason Macfarlane at the hospital, does Babin race out of there and go kill his good friend Mason Macfarlane. It just doesn't add up.

Then Macfarlane shows up from Aranville, and all hell breaks loose. Why would Babin break out of jail and call for an ambulance for a guy that was going to do him ugly? Why would Babin then take the time to bandage the wound of an asshole who is trying to frame him after knocking that asshole unconscious? And he left behind every firearm that he could have taken at his leisure.

The only reasonable conclusion is that he's no killer, and he's running from vigilante police justice.

That conclusion pissed Erdody right off.

In his newly invigorated state, Erdody called in for fresh SAR dogs to see if he couldn't find Babin out in the woods, and without drawing too much attention with this action, he would provide more troopers in the area.

Little did Steve know that he indeed had another ally as he was reading at a desk in an insane asylum twenty-some miles away about a woman who centuries before had been hung from a ceiling, bound, and repeatedly raped for months.

This new ally didn't resemble his other ink-covered lawless supporter on any level. This ally was the Yin to Dogtooth's Yang and was completely unknown to Steve. Sergeant Erdody of the Maine State Police would come to be a welcome advocate.

MASON'S LONG
SHADOWS CAMP

For the second time that evening, Steve found himself digging in the doctor's desk drawer for his bottle of booze. The last time he did it, he was apprehensive but fairly calm. This time he was frantic. He grabbed the bottle and guzzled down most of the remaining bourbon.

"Fuck this place!" he said with unsteady nerves and polished off the bottle.

It was about 3:30 a.m. by the time he started to settle down and regain his composure. The bourbon helped, but Steve couldn't feel anything. He was at a loss as what to do next. His nerves were shot by his encounter with Denise Moynihan.

How the fuck did she know something was the matter with Carla? He was completely puzzled.

Steve doubted she had read the Purification Bible or *The Inquisitor's Journal*, so how in the hell could she have the same Latin statement written on her floor? None of it made any sense whatsoever to him as he tried to think rationally.

He reopened *The Inquisitor's Journal* and went directly to the verse he had seen in both the back of the book and in Denise Moynihan's room. With no idea what it meant, he tried going online for a translation, but the search was fruitless.

Like never before, he felt the necessity to figure out the anomalous situation he found himself in. After his meeting with Denise Moynihan, he was motivated with a new fervor. He knew he had to decipher the mysterious Latin phrase that was such a riddle to him, but how? Who in the Beldon-Denton region of Maine would have the capacity to help him translate ancient Latin text? He was at a loss. He threw his hands up in the air in a frustrated motion then folded them behind his head and leaned way back in the overstuffed chair at the doctor's desk. He didn't know where to turn.

He slouched in the chair, disgusted and blankly staring at the knickknacks on the huge wooden desk. Aside from the computer and the phone, there were small framed pictures, a small clock, a UMaine penholder that was filled to capacity, and a small paperweight that had the letters *WWFD* pressed into it. Underneath the block lettering was the statement, "What would Freud do?" He also saw a small free-standing crucifix and a prescription pad. Then he had an epiphany.

He popped up in the large chair with a look of surprise and hope, quickly clicked on the keyboard, and typed in "Catholic Churches Maine." He clicked the mouse on one of the options, and a long list of churches appeared on the computer screen. He found what he was looking for in Derry, which was located between Denton and Beldon. In order to get back to the old Long Shadows Farm and decipher this ugly state of affairs, he would have to pass right through Derry.

He grabbed the small crucifix from on top of the desk, gave it a huge kiss, and said aloud with a big smile, "I was starting to lose faith in you after reading all of that, but thanks for showing me the way!"

First, he had to find a ride before he could seek help for his problem at St. Francis de Sales in Derry.

CALLED TO THE CARPET

When Ken walked into the Aranville Police Department at eight the next morning, he was in no mood for bullshit. He just wanted to work for the day and be left alone. He felt the looks of the other officers as he entered the locker room. As he was getting ready at his locker for his shift, he looked up and saw taped to the inside of the locker door the picture of him and his father at their camp. He remembered that they had just come in for lunch and that it had been lightly snowing. It had been a crisp, cool Maine morning. The photo was his favorite picture of them together.

Lieutenant Boudreau approached him and said, "The chief would like to see you in his office ASAP. By the way, I'm real sorry to hear about your old man. He was a good egg."

"Thanks," Ken replied.

When Ken walked into Chief Boehme's large office, Lucy, the secretary in the first room, whom he'd known for years, got up and walked around her desk. Silently, she reached up and gave the beefy Ken a huge hug of condolence. Lucy had known his dad since high school. She wiped a tear out of the corner of her eye as she pulled back. She looked Ken in his eyes, turned around, and went back to her desk. Ken had always liked Lucy, and her actions reaffirmed his thoughts about her.

As Ken closed the door to the chief's private office, he was surprised to see sitting there a man he did not recognize. He was dressed in a gunmetal-gray suit. He had tightly cropped hair and the telltale heavy black dress shoes that Ken had come to recognize as the state police.

This is going to suck, Ken thought.

Chief Boehme motioned him to sit down and started by saying, "I'm sorry to hear about your dad. Me and Mason went back a long way. We played football together back in high school. As a matter of fact, we were right next to each other on the offensive line. He was a tackle, and I was a guard. I have nothing but good memories about your dad. He was a good man. So that leads me into my next piece. I want to make sure the investigation of his death is carried out correctly. By that, I mean I don't want our department caught up in any more issues regarding your father's case."

He motioned toward the stranger sitting silently in the room.

"This man is Detective Lt. Leonard Coe of the Maine State Police Internal Affairs Division. He has not painted a very rosy picture of your last twenty-four hours. We all know and appreciate the loss you have experienced and the feelings you must have, but you got way too involved with yesterday's proceedings, and you are obviously not thinking clearly."

"You haven't even heard my side of the story, Chief. You're making assumptions about what happened based on what this dickhead here"—he pointed to Lieutenant Coe—"from the state rat squad is telling you. I mean, come on! Where is the due process?"

"That is the question exactly, Officer Macfarlane," Coe said coldly. "It seems from my conversations that I had last night with Sergeant Erdody that you already have Babin cuffed and stuffed for the murder of your father, yet no one has seen a crime and he was never even questioned. He was jailed and had obviously been brutalized. We checked it out also with the doctors that treated Babin in the emergency room after his accident. The injuries that Deputy Lynders described on Babin were not consistent with the injuries the doctors at the hospital observed and treated after the crash. So I will ask you, where is the due process, Officer Macfarlane?"

"Let me make it as plain as I can. Fuck you! You can take your snappy gray suit and your IAD methods and stuff them up your ass!" Ken seethed to Lieutenant Coe.

"Stand down, Officer Macfarlane!" Chief Boehme ordered. "These are only some of the reasons I have brought you in here. You are *obviously* emotionally involved with this case. Your being involved in this case breaks every investigative protocol. Even *if* Babin were completely guilty, it would never hold up in court if word got out that you were involved on any level. Believe it or not, Lieutenant Coe is here to help the department keep the case clean. The state wants to take this one. It is out of our jurisdiction. Your involvement in this investigation can only be detrimental to the case.

"As of this moment, you are on administrative leave. You will need to stay away from your father's camp because it is now considered a crime scene. Go take some time off. Spend some time with your mom. She's going to need some support to get through all of this. Mourn for your father. He was a good man."

Ken went to say something else to the chief when he was cut off in midsentence.

"I am chief of the Aranville Police Department. Know this. The only reason you are not in jail yourself this moment is because, back in the day, your father and I were very good friends. I will not tolerate insubordination from anyone in this department. You have used up your free pass. Now shut your mouth and leave my office before I change my mind. Are we clear?"

"Crystal," Ken responded. He rose to his feet, turned around, and left the room.

This was the absolute last thing he was expecting. Instead of being consoled by the chief one day after his father was killed, Officer Kenneth Macfarlane was, much to his dismay and for the first time in his twelve-year career, called to the carpet.

THE GOOD VICAR

It was eight on Monday morning, and Dr. Gerald Jorgensen was not feeling well, not well at all. His stomach wasn't right, and he had one hell of a headache. Once I get my things done, maybe I'll take a little nap on the couch this afternoon, he thought.

He had to put down the bag he was carrying, which was filled with replacements, in order to focus. He scratched his gray beard as he fumbled through his keys.

"Ahh, here we go," he said as he found among his personal keys the elusive key he was not supposed to make a copy of. He unlocked the door, stepped inside, and instantly heard a squishing noise as he closed the door and stepped onto the carpet of his room. Perplexed, he looked down at the soaked carpet and absentmindedly slid the bolt that locked the door from the inside, which he had installed himself.

"What the devil do we have here?" he said to himself, or so he thought.

"The janitor spilled something in the hallway last night. It washed under your door and soaked into your carpet. I heard him say he would be back this morning to clean it up," Steve said as he spun around in the doctor's overstuffed chair at his desk.

Dr. Jorgensen was dumbstruck for a moment.

In a very civil voice that was betrayed by the look of astonishment on his face, he asked curtly, "May I help you?"

"Yes, you may," Steve replied.

Later, as Steve pulled Dr. Jorgensen's car into the back parking lot of St. Francis de Sales Church, he was feeling a little guilty for what he had done to the doctor. He was a nice-enough man, but he wasn't very happy about being thoroughly tied to his over-stuffed chair with the nylon parachute cord from Steve's backpack. The doctor seemed most irritated not by the fact that Steve had pocketed his crucifix right in front of him, after snapping it from the plastic base, or even that Steve had intruded into his private office, but that Steve told him he had finished off the bourbon in his desk drawer. That was when Dr. Jorgensen started to get verbal. Steve had to put a balled-up sock in the doctor's mouth to keep him quiet.

On the way out of the office, out of curiosity, Steve searched through the rope-handled paper bag that Dr. Jorgensen had carried in with him. It was filled with more clothes, but at the bottom, there was another bottle of bourbon. He grabbed the bottle and walked over to the bound physician.

He knelt down and said into the doctor's ear, "If you promise not to yell or make a fuss, I will pour you a glass full of this and hold it for you to drink."

The doctor agreed with a nod, and Steve removed the sock.

"Good man!" Dr. Jorgensen said. "By my word as a gentleman, you have my oath that I will maintain my silence if you honor your part of the agreement."

Steve opened the bottle, retrieved the dirty glass from the drawer, and poured a long, deep helping of the doctor's panacea. He then held the glass to Dr. Jorgensen's mouth, and the liquid was gone in an instant.

"That was impressive," Steve said with raised eyebrows.

"Helps steady the nerves," Dr. Jorgenson said. He motioned with a nod of his head toward the empty glass, implying he would like another round, "If you wouldn't mind?"

Upon finishing the second full glass of bourbon in a gulp, the doctor opened his mouth for the balled-up sock.

"That won't be necessary," Steve said. "Just please keep quiet until the janitor comes to clean up the mess he made last night."

"Keep quiet, my dear boy? I'll be taking a nap, thanks to your help with my special elixir. It was much appreciated. And now if you don't mind, for the sake of propriety, could you please stow the glass and bottle back down in the drawer where they belong? Thanks much."

Steve put Dr. Jorgensen's private stock back where they belonged in the drawer, grabbed his pack, and headed out the door toward the doctor's waiting car. He stopped after one step, spun around, reached over to the desk, and picked up the phone. He made a very important call.

———— • ————

After Steve had thought about it for a minute, he didn't feel quite as guilty. He pulled up next to a car parked at the rectory behind the large church. No other cars were in the parking lot. This was a good sign. It was exactly 9:00 a.m. No mass was being celebrated, and it looked like the priest was in.

He hitched up his backpack as he knocked on the door of a large white house behind the church. After a few moments, he was greeted by a man in his early sixties.

"I'm sorry to bother you, Father, but are you the church's priest?" Steve asked.

"Yes, I am. What can I do for you?"

"I was wondering if you couldn't help me with a Latin translation that I believe might have some religious significance."

"Can't you just get a translation from the library or on a computer or something?"

"I tried to check online, but it was a dead end. I think the reason for that is because of the religious significance of the verse."

That statement gained the priest's attention.

"Come on in, and let's see if we can't figure this thing out for you. My name is Father Larivee. Why don't we go sit in the study and try to translate this for you."

"Thank you, Father. My name is Stephen."

The two men walked down a dark hallway of heavy oak paneling to the back of the house. The study was composed of rich dark mahogany bookcases and wainscoting that covered the walls and ceiling. The bookcases were loaded with every size of text imaginable. For a small private library, it was well stocked. In the center of the room was a simple mahogany desk that two people could sit at across from each other. On top of the desk were a lamp and a few religious mementos.

The priest motioned Steve to the closer chair, then went around the desk to the overstuffed leather seat. Steve took off his pack as he sat down and placed it on the floor next to his seat.

"Let us see what we can find out about this unknown passage," the priest said.

Steve reached down into his pack, then he realized with apprehension that he would have to expose *The Inquisitor's Journal* to the holy man.

"I'm wondering if you have a pen and piece of paper I could borrow, Father."

"Oh, of course. We'll be needing them, won't we?" The priest then dug around in his desk and retrieved two pens and pieces of paper.

Steve reached into his pack and retrieved the leather-bound journal. He made sure to keep the book below Father Larivee's point of view. He opened the journal to the pertinent page and copied the statement. He handed the sheet of paper to the curious cleric, who accepted it with a slight expression of disappointment. Steve could tell that he wanted to see the original text.

As Father Larivee looked at the words Steve had transcribed, he had a puzzled look on his face.

"This is a very old form of Latin that has mostly died out. I haven't seen it since my time in the seminary and then only sparingly. The verses back in the days when this form of Latin were used were very contextual and relied heavily on the exact layout of the words. There was no punctuation back in the days of the scribing of this doggerel. It could mean multiple different things. I would need to see how it was originally recorded."

With a sigh, Steve realized he would have to let the priest look at the disturbing journal. Before he relinquished the volume, he asked, "Please keep the existence of this journal in your confidence, Father. Can I have your word on that?"

"As long as it does not document your guilt of a crime, I have no problem giving you my word on that," the priest replied.

"It doesn't. There is nothing in here about me, whatsoever."

Steve then handed over to the unknowing priest one of the most hate-filled records of some of the worst documented atrocities that had been committed upon humanity.

"Please turn to the second-to-last written page of the journal," he said. "The Latin verse is at the bottom of the fourth paragraph."

Father Larivee had not even opened the black journal in his hands. He was inspecting the rich leather of the covers and the binding that had held steadfast against time. He slowly transferred the book from hand to hand gently, flipping it from the front cover to the back cover as he did so.

"Do you have any idea what kind of leather this is, Stephen?"

"No. I have no idea. I came upon this book quite by chance and have been caught up in it ever since."

"The leather is made from human skin, and I know this to be true for two reasons. First, I was an attendant to Pope Paul VI back in my early days after the seminary. I was a page to the Vatican Library and have seen and held books in my own hands that were made of the same leather. Second, this leather has the signature sporadic little bumps or goose-pimpled texture that comes only from human skin. This is a very rare book, indeed. Now I understand why you want to keep its existence very discrete.

"As you can see from the contents of my own library, I have a passion for literature and books. I prefer ancient books if I have the opportunity. There are a few books in my collection from the 1600s, and I even have a shipping log that dates back to the late fourteenth century. It is my crown jewel, but none of them are an example like this. This 'journal,' as you call it, must have been for someone very important. How did the book come to be in your possession, if you don't mind me asking?"

Steve sensed something else in the priest's question.

"Please don't be insulted, Father Larivee, but I would like to keep that information to myself. Suffice it to say, I did come across it legally."

"Good enough, then," the priest replied. "Every man is entitled to his privacy."

Steve could see that he was absolutely brimming with excitement to see the inside of the book. Father Larivee flipped directly to the second-to-last page and began to examine the chronicle.

"My Spanish is a little rusty, but the verbiage around the verse in question seems to have no bearing on it. Hold on a moment. Let me see if I have something that may help," Father Larivee distractedly said as he scanned the bookshelves with his fingers. "Ah! Here it is. This book was written to help the clergy understand old Latin so that they could translate some of the passages into modern sermons. It could probably help."

Steve sat and observed the priest move at his frenetic pace. Father Larivee scribbled something on his paper, then reread the verse, comparing it to the book he had pulled from the shelf. Then he scribbled something else, compared it to the book, crossed out what he had just written, and then started the process again. Sitting in silence, Steve observed this process for about fifteen minutes. The priest was so deeply involved in his translating that Steve was quite convinced that the old priest forgot he was even there.

Finally, Father Larivee sat up with a look of accomplishment on his face. He looked down at the translation he had just completed and said, "I think I have it. The translation might not be 100 percent, but it's probably 99. That didn't take so long, only about a minute or so." Then he looked at his watch and realized how much time had passed. With a sheepish grin and a shrug of the shoulders, he said, "I told you ancient text was my passion."

"So what is the translation, Father?"

"From what I could make of the verse and from cross-referencing, I understand the statement to be as follows, 'In order to release the confined souls from perdition, the perpetual cypher must be rent to ruin.'"

"Do you have any idea what that means, Father Larivee? Is there any religious significance?"

"I don't know for sure," the priest replied. "But it sounds Old Testament to me. Talk of cyphers and ruin—those are pre-Christian terms. Like the days of Sodom and Gomorrah." The priest quoted the Old Testament, speaking in a stormy fashion, "Then the Lord rained brimstone and fire on Sodom and Gomorrah, turning the cities of Sodom and Gomorrah into ashes.' That's a quote from Genesis 18 and 19. The stylings sort of remind me of your verse in the journal."

"Thank you so much, Father. I don't know how I can express my thanks to you," Steve said.

Father Larivee looked him right in the eye and said, "You can start thanking me by turning yourself in to the authorities."

Steve's jaw dropped in shock.

Father Larivee went on, "I have seen your face all over the television for the last two days. How can you be surprised? When I first answered the door, I recognized you instantly. I thought you had come to confess your sins for killing your friend. I thought you would eventually come out with your desire to confess, but once I saw the book, I was so distracted that I got caught up in the translation. So I will ask you directly, do you have anything you would like to confess to me?"

Steve snapped back to a reality that made him aware of how recognizable he was in public.

He looked directly at the priest and said, "Father Larivee, I have nothing to confess regarding my friend's death. He unfortunately was in that condition when I found him. However, I did defend myself from the two lawmen and broke out of jail. I cannot say it any plainer. I did not kill my friend Mason Macfarlane, nor did I have anything to do with the circumstances surrounding his untimely death. The reason I have asked for your help with this Latin verse is because I believe it will play a key role in my exoneration. That's why I was so interested in the translation. That's why I'm here now. Think back, Father. Everything I've told you has been the truth, even before I realized you knew who I am. I'm not a liar, and I won't start now."

The priest calmly deliberated over what he just heard, then replied, "Okay. You seem to me like a man of virtue. I don't understand how the Latin verse can help you, but that is not of my concern. You do know that as soon as you leave, I will have to call the authorities myself, don't you?"

"I understand that, and I do not fault you for it, but I think I can motivate you to maintain your silence in a way that will harm no one, and we will both benefit. I know you're a fan of ancient text, and I need a clean exit from this area. I was lost and didn't know what to do next, but because of you, I now know the path I must take."

Steve offered the good vicar a proposal.

PERSONAL, PRIVATE
HUNTING SEASON

Fuck Chief Boehm! Ken thought as he pulled his truck off of Route 77 south. That bastard isn't going to tell me where or when I can go to my own family's place!

He knew there was an old barn about a half-mile north of Long Shadows Road that he could hide his truck behind while he went on his private hunt.

When he pulled up to the overgrown dirt driveway of the barn, he heard police sirens blaring off in the distance to the southeast of him. He looked at his watch. It was 10:08 a.m., a perfect day for hunting.

He drove around the far side of the barn and parked his truck out of view from the road.

Ken was dressed completely in hunting camouflage; he had camo gloves to conceal his skin on his hands. When he clicked on his newly recharged police scanner, he heard a lot of chatter on the air about a motorcycle-gang shooting everything up out on Long Shadows Road and at his father's camp and about all of the cops pursuing them up the road, heading east and, most importantly, away from the camp.

"That should keep those fuckers busy for a while! I don't know how you did it, Steve, but it sounds like you pulled every cop away that was involved with the case," he said aloud to the back side of the abandoned barn.

Next, he pulled a nickel-plated .357 Desert Eagle Mark VII handgun out of the bag on his front seat. This gun was a killing machine. It could carry ten rounds—one in the chamber and nine in the magazine—and had a six-inch barrel for longer-range shooting. It was a massive weapon, but still concealable, although not easily. It did not exist in any records anywhere in the world. Ken had found it in a perp's residence during a drug raid earlier in the year and had stolen it. No one had seen him take it, and because the serial numbers had previously been filed off, no one was going to claim it as stolen.

Ken pulled back the slide to make sure he had one of his "special" rounds in the chamber, the same type he also kept loaded in his police sidearm. After grabbing another nine-round magazine from the bag, he tucked the Desert Eagle inside a concealed pocket he had made himself in his camo vest and stuck the extra magazine in the left back pocket of his camo pants. He gave the car one last check for anything else he might need.

He really didn't need much gear for this hunt. Once he encountered his quarry, he would dispose of it in the swamp when he was done with it. He wasn't going to mount it, and he sure as hell wasn't going to eat it. No Steve Babin was going to be on tonight's dinner menu. Babin would be hunted for retribution for what he had done to his dad and, most importantly, for personal satisfaction.

As Ken walked along the barn away from his car, he did not look into the dilapidated structure. If he had, he would have easily seen a hastily concealed vehicle that belonged to a hospitalized sheriff's deputy. But nothing was going to distract him from his own personal, private hunting season.

THE CAVALRY

At 9:40 a.m., as Steve stepped out of the doctor's car, which he had just moved to the next parking lot over from the church, he never thought he would be so happy to see a wild motorcycle gang waiting outside of a building just for him. When he was walking to the car after leaving the rectory, he could hear them coming from miles away. There were about twenty of them, more than enough for what he would need for his plan. Their bikes were all shut off, and they were all starting to light up their smokes and look around. As he walked by the church, Steve saw Dogtooth and his gang brothers looking at him like he was a hero. Dogtooth must have been telling them about their encounters together.

As Steve walked toward the grinning Dogtooth, his guardian angel said with a smirk, "You didn't make a fuckin' confession or nothin', did ya?"

"Fuck no! What better place to hide out than a fuckin' priest's house? He's locked in the cellar inside. I had to get the hell out of the asylum. There were too many people coming to the goddamn place. Thanks for answering my call from there and coming. I just ditched the car I lifted from the hospital two lots over."

"I told you he was our type of fuckin' guy!" Dogtooth exclaimed as the other bikers roared in heavy laughter.

"Are you guys okay with our little scheme me and Dogtooth came up with? You guys are going to catch some heat if you get caught," Steve said to the other riders.

A bunch of different answers came Steve's way from the rough men on the bikes, all leading to one conclusion—these guys weren't afraid of anything.

The biggest guy there, who looked like a scarier version of Bigfoot, hopped off of his bike, clapped Steve on the shoulder with an arm that weighed about eighty pounds, and said, "Any motherfucker that can bust up two fuckin' cops and then bust his way out of jail, without even using a goddamn gun, deserves my fuckin' respect! Bro, I'd help your crazy ass out anytime. Especially after what Dog over there said about you. Everyone calls me Yeti!"

Yeti stuck his hand out and shook Steve's hand biker style. Other riders either slapped Steve on the back or nodded to him in approval. He felt like a celebrity.

"I told you these were my bros," Dogtooth said. "They been dyin' to meet you ever since I told them you called this morning and asked for my help. They all volunteered. By the way, you know your face is all over the TV, right?"

"Yeah. I found out this morning the hard way. That's why I had to lock the old man down in the cellar in there." Steve motioned over his shoulder back toward the rectory. "I'm ready to get rollin' whenever you guys are," he said.

"You ride with me," Dogtooth said, "and give me your friggin' bag. Do you have to carry this thing with you every-frigginwhere you go?" He affixed the bag over his "ape hanger" handlebars, and it slid down over his headlight.

"Do you have that thing I asked you for on the phone earlier?" Steve asked.

Dogtooth pulled a model 1911 .45-caliber out from under his belt and handed it to Steve.

"I don't need to knock over a moose, for Christ's sake. I just need to blow a couple of rounds into the air," Steve said with a grin.

"I'd rather you had too much than not enough. If the chips are down, and you have to use it on some shithead lawman, I don't want the fucker gettin' back up," Dogtooth replied.

Steve realized with some uneasiness that his biker friend meant what he said. He was not kidding. That's when it really hit him that the men in this church parking lot were the real deal and not just a bunch of posers.

"Thanks, man. I appreciate that!" Steve replied.

"No sweat, brother. No sweat!" the big blond biker replied as he started up his massive Harley FXR. "Get on! Let's get to doin' what we gotta be doin'."

◆

As bikers were rolling along near some houses on Route 77 northbound, about eight miles away from the entrance to Long Shadows Road, Steve pulled the .45-caliber out of the waist of the pants that he had stolen from the doctor, gave Dogtooth a light jab in the back to let him know what he was about to do, and then fired three shots into the air about three seconds apart as they rode along. He wanted to start the diversion before the bikers reached the road. The shots were clearly louder than the deafening pipes of the rumbling motorcycles. There was no doubt as to what the three explosions were.

That should let anybody know we're around, Steve thought.

He saw people running into their houses and ducking for cover behind their cars.

As planned, Dogtooth pulled the bike over about a mile south of the dirt road that Mason's camp was on. Steve had noticed when he had come here from this direction in the past that there wasn't a dwelling for about five miles from the entrance to the road.

Steve climbed off of the bike and grabbed his bag from the bulky blond rider holding it out to him.

"Best of luck from here, brother," Dogtooth said. "You're on your own on this piece. Me and my boys, we'll be okay. I know those trails well enough out there. I'm pretty sure we'll be able to give those law fuckers the slip.

"Ain't nothin' been dull while we've hung out. You've got balls that clank. Now finish this shit and get your name clean!" He grinned broadly.

Steve reached into the bottom of the bag and fished out the police radio. He handed it to Dogtooth, saying, "You can use this more than me. It's one of the cop's radios." Then he reached into the exterior pocket of the backpack and retrieved the pearl-handled dagger. He handed it to his inked up guardian angel and said, "From what I've read about this dagger right here, it has killed well over a hundred people. This is what I cut that cop with yesterday. It's yours if you want it. It's definitely a killing blade. I think it would fit better on a warrior like you than on me."

With a shocked look of appreciation and gratitude, Dogtooth pursed his lips and nodded his head. He wrapped his beefy hand around the sheathed blade and gently removed it from Steve's grip. "Thank you, my brother. Roll safe." The grateful rider tucked the dagger and scabbard under his belt.

Steve took off toward the woods while he still had the cover of the biker gang. At the edge of the wood line, he stopped and yelled back to Dogtooth, "I'm going to need five minutes."

Then he ran about two hundred yards in a northeast direction. That was the way toward many things—Mason's camp, clearing his name, saving Carla, and whatever else lay before him.

Steve made sure he was well into the woods before he stopped to change out of the doctor's ill-fitting clothes. He pulled his own lightweight shirt and cargo shorts out of the backpack and changed back into them and the hybrid lightweight hiking shoes he had worn earlier. He knew he only had so much time and had to get a move on to get to the camp. Under a rotten log, he buried his second set of stolen clothes within fifteen hours of when he had buried the first set. He then disassembled the .45-caliber gun, buried the bullets under a rock, and moved on. As he ran through the woods to try to make time toward the camp and his planned diversion, he looked at his watch. It was ten. All hell was about to break loose.

———◆———

After five minutes, Dogtooth and his boys hammered up Route 77 North to the turn off onto Long Shadows Road. As they approached the dirt road, they blew right by the roadblock that the state police had set up at the old three-way intersection, riding past the screaming troopers. One of the riders drew a Micro-Uzi out from under his vest and fired into a state-police cruiser that was part of the roadblock. He pumped enough rounds into the parked vehicle that it looked like metallic Swiss cheese when he was finished. Troopers were diving in every direction.

Now that the bike gang had the law's undivided attention, they drove up the dirt road, heading east. Dogtooth had a grin that spread from ear to ear. Their plan was coming together perfectly.

———◆———

The SAR team had picked up the fugitive's track at five thirty that morning. They had just discovered, buried under a stump, the clothes that Steve had liberated from the deputy the day before. They were right near Route 77, a few miles north of the roadblock. It was 10:05 a.m. when they received the emergency call about the gang of bikers.

"All units, be advised. We have shots fired. A motorcycle gang times twenty members. They broke through our roadblock at Route 77 and Long Shadows Road. They are now in our perimeter and headed east on Long Shadows. Every available unit maintain visual contact but make no attempt to stop them."

Sergeant Erdody was with the SAR team when the call came. The three men looked at each other in amazement. Erdody moved into action.

"You two call to get picked up. This trail dies here, I'm sure of it. Route 77 is right over there. He obviously changed clothes and hitched a ride before we could corral him. I'm going to backtrack just to see if anyone circles back through the woods in an attempt to avoid us. Hurry up! This sounds like quite a shitstorm. We've dealt with this particular bunch of biker bozos before, and it's always ugly."

The two subordinate troopers and their K9s moved toward the road while calling on their radios for retrieval.

Erdody turned around and headed back into the woods. "Let's see what happens next, Mr. Babin," he said.

———•———

As Steve reached where he wanted to cross Long Shadows Road, he heard more police-cruiser sirens heading off toward Dogtooth and the boys. The dust was still hovering in the air from all of the commotion of the passing bikes and state-police vehicles. He crossed the road cautiously but quickly and headed toward the swamp in the southwest corner of Mason's land.

———•———

Dogtooth heard the wail of closing sirens as he and his brothers charged up the dirt road. As they were reaching the old camp on the left that Steve had described, he reached under his vest and grabbed another .45 (his favorite caliber). He could see eight to ten cruisers from various police agencies lining the road. With a large throaty war cry, he fired into two vehicles until his weapon was empty. Troopers and police officers scrambled in every direction toward their cruisers. The other riders took Dogtooth's cue and riddled the two cars with their own weapons. It sounded like the Guns of Navarone at the height of the gun-blast crescendo.

With that accomplished, and every cop in the central Maine area chasing them, Dogtooth sped past the camp and rode off into the waning afternoon light. He felt like a Viking on his way toward Valhalla, hoping to be chosen by the Valkyries, and behind him was the cavalry.

THE SWAMP

Once Steve crossed the road and trekked up into the woods, he headed due west so that he could approach the camp from the swamp, which he figured would be the safest way to get there. If his ploy worked as he hoped it would, Dogtooth and the boys were leading the police off into the woods, away from Mason's camp, for a fun-filled afternoon of escape and evasion.

As he started getting into the muddier ground, he came across a structure that explained a lot. It was a huge old beaver dam that had been built up over the generations to about ten to twelve feet high and at least 150 feet across. It was a huge and perfectly maintained (by beaver standards) wall of mud and branches of all sizes that had been cleaned of all of their bark and twigs. Steve guessed it must have stood for at least a century, maybe more. The dam's existence went a long way toward explaining the origins of the swamp, and its obvious age explained all of the overgrowth.

The earthen barrier sloped up toward the top. Steve decided to climb and survey the body of the swamp that had to be on the other side of the enormous natural wall. As he got to the top rim of the dam, he made sure to stay low so as not to be seen by anyone who might be in the area looking for him. He took off his pack and reached in an interior side pocket for a small pair of field binoculars. Lying on the beaver-built embankment, he peered into the swamp, which was huge. Dead trees and massive entanglements of green thorny vines were everywhere. The swamp was also deep. The pool of muddy water in front of him was at least ten to twelve feet deep. From the top of the dam, he threw the rest of the pieces of the .45-caliber into different areas of the black water.

What he could see from his vantage point was a vast classic New England swamp. All of the overgrowth interfered with making out anything discernible at a distance, even though the view must have been two hundred to three hundred yards. Steve grabbed his binoculars and took a look around. Way out in the swamp, three hundred, perhaps four hundred yards away, Steve thought he saw something that just didn't look right. It was a section or piece of something tall that didn't fit in with the rest of the landscape—a straightedge line at a forty-five-degree angle, about fifteen feet off the ground. He wasn't sure, but it looked like the rake (angled outer edge) of a roofline.

"It couldn't be!" he said aloud, in half-denial. As much as he tried to confirm his suspicions, he just couldn't get the correct angle to make out clearly what he was looking at. He would have to go and check for himself.

He slid down the earthen ramp with his binoculars secured in his pack and decided to make his way around into the swamp, intending to inspect the thing he couldn't believe was out there.

As he waded through the waste-deep murk, he hoped he would not step on any more unexpected bodies. The two from the day before were more than enough to fill his nightmares for a lifetime. Or so he thought.

When he was about a hundred yards from the area he was aiming for, he caught his first true glimpse of what he thought he had seen from on top of the dam. It was an old house. The swamp water had swallowed the house up to the bottom of the downstairs windows. The wood was rotten on all sides. From the remnants that were left, Steve could tell that the house had once been painted white. He had no explanation of how it had stood for so long. The front door was gone, but the glass of the windows was mostly intact on all three floors. He found he was wrong in his estimation of the rake as being fifteen feet high; it was more like twenty-five feet high near the bottom.

The rotten old farmhouse was of grand size and must have been something to behold in its heyday. As he got closer to the waterlogged edifice, he noticed that the clumps of thorns and briars were actually growing up from collapsed out structures. The smaller buildings were not nearly in the shape of the main building, but it was still amazing to Steve that there were any traces of them at all.

Although he had already realized in his gut where he was, a final piece of the puzzle fell into place that left absolutely no question in his mind. In front of him and directly in front of his view of the house was an old vine-covered archway made of field-stone. It was about thirty feet from the front of the house. Carved into the single piece of granite spanning the stone columns were the words "Long Shadows." Even though he had already suspected it, he still couldn't believe what he was looking at. The discovery of the archway made very real to him everything he had read about Dante and his twisted life.

At that moment, he saw the gaunt, pale-white face of an old man dressed in work overalls looking at him from the highest window of the old farmhouse. He jumped so suddenly at the sight that he lost his footing and flopped backward into the water. He scrambled in the murk to find his feet. The added weight of the now water-filled backpack was not helping. He splashed up and out of the water less than five seconds after he fell, wiped the water out of his face, and looked back up at the window with disbelief, but the figure was gone. There was just a reflection of the clouds in the glass where he thought he had seen the old man.

Steve was not going to stick around to see if the ghoulish white face would return. He knew that no one that old could be living in this place. He knew that no man that old could have got himself up into that rotten old house in the middle of this swamp. He knew that deep in his heart, and he would not admit to himself what he had just seen.

In a frenzied panic, he got out of there. Running as fast as he could in the waist-deep water, he splashed past the old house and buildings and headed northeast toward dry land and Mason's cabin. He never looked back. Instead, he started to believe the denial that he so wanted to accept about the old face in the window. He repeated to himself in a form of mantra: "It was just a reflection. It was just a reflection. It was just—"

Steve was happy to be leaving the swamp village.

DARK DESTINY

Soaked and exhausted, he finally reached the northeast corner of the eerie swamp and flopped down on dry land. Steve could tell immediately that he was very close to the area where he had his liaison with the two putrefying swamp sirens. He felt ill just recalling the encounter but couldn't keep from wondering who they were and how they fit into all of this.

As he lay on the dry earth catching his breath, he realized that almost every memory of his time since the accident was awful, with the exception of his anomalous guardian angel Dogtooth and the strange Dr. Gerald Jorgensen.

He looked down at his watch and saw that it was just past noon, Monday still. The last thirty-six hours had been surreal. It seemed that thirty-six days had passed rather than just thirty-six hours. In disbelief, he took stock of his activities in that period of time.

It seemed more and more likely that his wife had probably been possessed. They had been in a horrendous accident and had been hospitalized. He had illegally left a hospital and hitched a ride back to the camp. His dear friend had died in his arms. He had been arrested and savagely beaten by a policeman. Then he had brutally assaulted, bound, and gagged a deputy while escaping from jail. He had stolen a deputy's car and hidden it.

He had found an ancient book of the worst perversions of man on man and ancient dark religious relics. He had encountered a two-hundred-year-old crime scene—with bodies. He had found the body of his missing dog. He had found two more dead bodies and re-hid them. He had assaulted another policeman with a weapon, knocked him out, and bound him with his own handcuffs. He had hitchhiked with an outlaw biker who became an ally.

He had broken into a mental hospital, impersonated a doctor, and got a severed rat head spit into his face by an insane and also probably possessed mental patient. He had bound another person to a chair and stolen another car. He had locked a priest in a cellar. He had ridden with an outlaw biker gang and shot bullets into the air. He had discovered in the middle of a swamp a house that was probably haunted. He was now trying to escape and evade the police while trying to save his wife's soul from eternal bondage, not even really sure if his plan would work. But it was the only plan he had.

"It would make a great book," he mused after recapping his activities.

He was feeling the most guilt about the priest. Steve didn't have to force him down into the cellar at all; he didn't have to use physical coercion on any level. In fact, it was Father Larivee's idea to go down into the cellar. Steve recalled with embarrassment his conversation with the priest a few hours earlier as he was about to leave the rectory.

———•—•———

"Father, I understand that you're bound by a moral code, and I'm not asking you to impugn that in any way, but to quote you directly, 'Every man is entitled to his privacy.' I could really use some of that privacy now. I need some time to do what I need to do in order to clear my name and help my wife. I'm not setting out to hurt anyone or exact any kind of revenge upon any person, so rest assured, Father, I'm not going to harm anyone or break any major laws. It's just that it would help me enormously if you just didn't actively draw any attention to my visit here today. My thanks to you for your help today and your discretion in the future."

Holding up *The Inquisitor's Journal* in both of his hands with the cover facing the priest, Steve saw the priest's eyes fixate on the black leather and his mouth slightly gape open. His eyes slightly dilated, and he slowly reached out for the black journal without hesitation.

Steve no longer had any need for the grotesque ledger and was happy to be rid of it. He had read the entire thing. With the help of Father Larivee, he was able to figure out the remaining piece of the puzzle he needed. He had come up with a course of action that he hoped would work.

Getting up from the overstuffed chair, he said, "Thank you very much for your help, Father."

Father Larivee was inspecting the leather covers of the book so intently that at first he didn't hear Steve getting up and thanking him. The priest snapped to as if coming out of the dark and looked up at Steve, who was now standing on the other side of his desk.

He warned the priest, "That journal is a gruesome chronicle of very twisted men and the grotesque atrocities they imposed upon humanity. Beware reading it, Father. It is very descriptive and very disturbing."

"Thank you for the book and for the warning. I have read many disturbing works during my time at the Vatican. You could not perceive some of the things that are inside the Catholic Church's most sacred dwelling. By the way, my son, do you feel the need to be blessed before setting out to do whatever it is you need to do?"

"No thank you, Father. There are those out there who need blessing more than me, but if you could, with all of your power and might, could you please say a prayer of hope and blessing for my wife, Carla, to help her through what she's battling right now? That I'd appreciate!"

"I can do that. In the interim, why don't you lock me in the cellar so that I don't errantly feel compelled to call anyone and speak too soon of your visit? My cleaning lady will be in tonight around five, and I can keep myself busy with this until she comes."

"Are you sure about that, Father?"

"Positively."

"Can I bring a chair down or something?"

"No. I'll be fine. There are chairs down there. Now get moving before I change my mind."

He stepped through the cellar door onto the landing and clicked on the light. Turning to Steve, he put a hand on his shoulder and said, "Be careful in what you're doing, and don't take anything lightly or for granted. This is more than you and your wife's lives you are risking to accomplish whatever task it is you have in front of you. I don't know exactly what you have to do, but from your demeanor and the passages in this journal that I was able to read, you have a mighty undertaking in front of you. Godspeed."

"Thank you, Father."

The good vicar descended the staircase holding *The Inquisitor's Journal* out in front of him in both of his hands and examining the binding.

———————•◆•———————

As Steve lay on the dry ground near the swamp reminiscing about his bizarre experiences in the past day and a half, the priest's parting words shook him back to reality.

"I can't believe I bribed a priest," he said to himself, shaking his head.

When he got to his feet, soaked from head to toe, his pack felt like it weighed about five hundred pounds from getting soaked in the swamp. He wasn't too far from Mason's camp, he knew, but he had to lie low and move toward the cabin undetected in order to accomplish what he had in mind. He was pretty sure not every trooper would have chased after Dogtooth and the boys, and if they all did, he was sure more troopers would be coming, so he had to get moving soon. He had to get to the cabin and ultimately to the old, rusted oval that hung over the front entrance of Mason's cabin. That rusted old oval was the very cypher that Dain wrote about in *The Inquisitor's Journal*, and it was the key to this whole mess. Steve was sure of it.

It was his date with a dark destiny, and it was right where he was headed.

LETHAL CHESS MATCH

Steve opened up his waterlogged backpack for what would be the last time during the entire ordeal, although he did not realize it. He dug down into one of the inner pockets and pulled out a camouflaged jungle hat. It had a brim that went around the entire hat, was about a foot across, and hung low around his head and face (mostly because it was wet).

Steve's plan was to slide through the thick overgrowth and head eastward toward the cabin. He was trying to conceal as much of himself as he could. His shorts were black, and his shirt was olive green. Both were stained brown from the swamp. His white socks were charcoal gray because of trudging through the swamp. Only his calves and shins were exposed. They were pasty white, but that would have to do. He had no more clothes in his pack—or tricks, either. The pack had served him well. The last things he pulled out were his compass, his Leatherman, and his binoculars.

He stowed the backpack under some thick brambles and concealed it as best he could. He knew where he and it were, and it would just be getting in the way if he would need to move fast.

———◆———

At the same time Steve was hiding his pack in the brambles, Ken was situating himself in an excellent location for what he was trying to accomplish, and it wasn't Steve's apprehension. He had something far graver in mind. He was up on a knoll that was covered in thick brambles, about fifty yards due south from the front door of the cabin. The location gave him a vantage point over the entire yard of the camp. He was completely concealed, and the sun was behind his left shoulder. Even if the state troopers came back, and Babin tried to turn himself in at the cabin, he would be well within the lethal range of the Desert Eagle that Ken had inside his vest.

———•———

When all the hell had broken loose a couple of hours earlier, Sergeant Erdody had ordered the SAR team to exit the woods and be retrieved. He then found and backtracked Babin's tracks to the point where they had discovered the unconscious Officer Macfarlane.

"I hope Babin kicked the shit out of Macfarlane earlier," Erdody said aloud. "What an asshole!"

The sergeant was looking around the area where they had found Macfarlane the night before. He was hoping to find any clue that might give him some insight as to what was going on. That was when he heard loud splashing about thirty yards away and took cover. He was about to march over to where the noise came from and let his presence be known, but a thought came over him. He would probably have a more solid case if he observed who or whatever it was making all of the splashing and see if it had any bearing on, or could help explain, what was going on. There was silence for a few moments, and then Erdody clearly heard a human voice mumble something about "a priest" and then chuckle quietly.

Erdody knew it had to be Babin. He wanted to take him into custody, but he also wanted to find out more about what was going on. So he quietly approached the commotion, just in time to see Babin put a camo hat on his head and stuff what looked to be a knife in one pocket and something else in another pocket. The last thing Babin did was put a small pair of binoculars around his neck, and then he hid his bag under some thorns and brush.

Babin stood up and started to look around. Erdody ducked and took cover so he wouldn't be detected by the man he knew in his gut was probably innocent.

He heard Babin move off in an eastward direction. When he could no longer hear him (which wasn't long—Babin could move pretty quietly when he wanted to, Erdody noticed), he went to Babin's backpack and pulled it out of the brambles for a quick inspection to see if there was any clue in it. There was nothing remarkable inside the wet pack. Just a headlamp, a first-aid kit that had been opened (*probably for Macfarlane's dumbass*, Erdody thought), and some outdoors gear. The most remarkable thing in the pack was a small plastic crucifix that looked like it had been snapped off of its base. No clues.

Erdody closed up the pack and put it back under the brambles. He knew Babin wasn't going far because of the direction he had heard Babin go and because he had left his pack behind. He knew exactly where Babin was headed; he just didn't know why. That's what he was going to find out. Babin had gone east. Erdody was going to sweep south out to the dirt road and head east to the cabin to observe from a distance. Once he knew what was going on, he would make his move.

<hr />

After being in his ambush position for about an hour, Ken was starting to second-guess himself when he spotted something slowly moving about a hundred yards away in the woods to the north. It was slow but very deliberate, coming eastward to the far side of the camp. Ken could not make it out until it stopped. It was a man, well-camouflaged, who was peering through a pair of binoculars toward the cabin. It was Steve, completely oblivious to his presence.

Ken was so filled with hatred at the sight of him that he could barely sit still. His fury pulsed through him like a wave, and he felt the effect of his white-hot hatred for the man who had killed his father. He was quaking with rage. It took every bit of control he had to not open fire on Steve from there and then chase after him into the woods. He had to stand up. In the process, he pulled the Desert Eagle out of its interior pocket in his vest and took the safety off.

Ken did not know he was not the only one searching the woods that day for Steve or for anything out of the ordinary. Another pair of eyes—not Steve's—observed Ken's movement. As well as Ken was concealed and camouflaged, he was observed getting to his feet on the overgrown knoll and pulling a gun out of his vest. The lethal chess match was about to begin.

CRESCENDO

Steve stowed the binoculars in his cargo shorts while he was crouched down in the bushes. He took a deep breath and braced himself. "It's now or never," he said quietly. He slipped from the cover of the bushes he had been hiding in and observed the area to make sure it was safe, then walked toward the back of the cabin where this whole bizarre turn of events had started three nights earlier.

———•———

Moving up the road toward the cabin from the west, Erdody witnessed Ken move slowly off the knoll toward the front of the cabin, which was out of his view. He knew it was there from being there earlier. If Ken had just looked to his left westward, he would have seen Erdody plain as day, 150 yards down the road. Instead, he was fixated on something that was out of Erdody's field of view. It took Erdody every shred of self-restraint to not yell, "Freeze!" Ken moved rapidly and smoothly from the knoll and brought a handgun up in front of him as he moved. As Ken moved forward out of sight, Erdody ran up the road toward him as quickly as he could.

———•———

At the same moment, unaware that he was being observed, Steve reached the back wall of the cabin and flattened his back against it. He was trying to move as quickly and stealthily as possible because he didn't know if any of the state troopers were around or when they would be back. He wanted to do what he had come to do and get out of there. Sliding west along the back of the camp, he rounded the corner, heading toward the front. He saw the tool he would need to complete his job ten feet from the front corner of the cabin. Sticking out of a large wood-splitting stump was the double-edged stainless steel axe he had purchased for Mason on the way up here. He would need it for the task at hand.

———◆———

Unbeknown to Ken, another observer saw him moving from the knoll and heading toward the front east corner of the cabin opposite Steve, pausing there with his gun up and his head cocked as if trying to listen for something. He was frozen at the front east corner of the cabin with his gun pointing along the east wall toward the back. It's getting time to make a move, Ken's observer thought as he drew his weapon.

———◆———

Steve reached the front corner of the cabin and slowly peered around it into the front yard. One last check before I slide out there, he thought. No one was in the front yard, but there were footprints and tire tracks everywhere. He saw that all of the things that had fallen off of the porch were still in disarray from his hasty exit two nights before. The thing he saw that hit him the most and that he wasn't expecting was Mason's dried-up blood off the western side of the driveway. It caught him off-guard, and he froze in his tracks for a moment. Anguished, he turned his head away from the spot where Mason had died in his arms. As he did, he saw the cursed object in the front yard about fifteen yards away, in the same spot where it had always managed to come to rest. Without hesitation, he moved toward the malevolent oval, sweeping out toward the stump and angrily grabbing the axe.

As Steve grabbed the axe, Ken saw movement out of the corner of his left eye in the front yard of the cabin. He swung around blindly toward whatever the movement was and brought his gun to bear.

———◦———

Ken's observer saw Steve come out into the yard from the far side of the cabin. He watched Steve grab an axe out of a stump and head out into the front yard, oblivious to the man holding the gun, thirty feet away at the front corner of the house closest to the observer. At that same moment, he also witnessed Ken swing the gun around toward the unsuspecting Steve. The hidden observer made his move and raised his weapon as he quickly approached the evolving scene.

———◦———

As he approached, Steve saw that a section of the cypher was on top of a flat rock that was barely peeking out of the ground. It gave him an aim point for his next move, which he hoped would put an end to the horror story in which he had become so enmeshed.

———◦———

Ken saw Steve walk out in the front yard with an axe in his hand toward the relic that had always beckoned to him since his youth. He had always been aware of its power on a subconscious level, but never as clearly as he felt it call to him now.

The power of the metal oval had come to him in his dreams in his youth when he stayed at the camp with his father. It had motivated him to "explore" and mutilate the females of small animals, which he would toss into the swamp after he was done with them. He saw this as natural kid stuff in his youth.

His childhood friends who came to camp with him and his dad were repulsed by his treatment of the poor creatures. They were sworn to secrecy. If they didn't comply, they were told, they would receive the same treatment as the animals. The friends never came back, no matter how much Ken pleaded with them. Back in Bangor, he actually couldn't remember what they were talking about when they explained their refusals as he asked them to come back to camp. They were all frightened of him and his horrendous actions. In time, no one would even speak to him anymore. He grew bitter and isolated.

The only place he felt better was at camp with his father. He always thought it was the time he spent with his father and the attention he got from him, but it was really the land itself and, even more so, the cypher that had reached out to him in his youth and made the misery of his isolation fade away.

It was all crystal clear to him at that moment. The power of the cypher pulsed out to him on an imperceptible level, frantically yearning for his protection. In a trance-like state, filled with an inhuman fury, Ken pulled the trigger of the massive automatic in his hand.

———◆———

Steve became aware of Ken's presence at the front corner of the cabin a nanosecond before Ken pulled the trigger of the enormous Desert Eagle pointed at him. Everything seemed to be moving in slow motion. During the splinter of a second the bullet traveled the thirty feet from Ken to Steve, Steve had already begun to reflexively duck his head to Ken's movement. The bullet passed by his skull so closely; it actually burned the skin of his scalp on the way by. Deafening thunder followed the searing hot sensation on the top of his head.

Steve believed he had been shot and thought, *I expected that to hurt more.* He didn't turn to look at Ken. He knew what Ken was there for and knew he had only one chance at this before he was dead. More important than that, he knew Carla's very soul was at stake, and she mattered a lot more to him than his own life did. With that renewed motivation, he ran toward the cypher and raised the axe high over his head, hoping to get one attempt at the miserable thing before he was dead. It was all or nothing.

As the observer saw Ken miraculously miss Steve from ten yards away, he raced the remaining steps to Ken for what he knew was going to be a bloody encounter. He saw the man with the gun get a dead bead on Steve for the next shot. This time, he knew, Steve would be killed.

Ken no longer existed. His sole function was to protect the cypher at all costs. Nothing else mattered—not his family, which he could no longer remember, and not his life. Nothing. The sanctity of the cypher was all that mattered. He raged out loud in ancient Spanish as he took dead aim at Steve, "No se arruina ningun hereje la cifra de almas!" He started to pull the trigger.

When Dogtooth, the other observer, reached Ken, he slashed down toward the wrist Steve had slashed the day before. He slashed with such might that he hacked right through the outer coat and sleeve on Ken's arm, going down into the bone. Ken let out a shrill scream of agony and rage. He spun toward his attacker and pumped two rounds from the .357 Desert Eagle directly into Dogtooth's chest. The biker fell to the ground with the bloody inquisitor's blade straight up in his hand as if he was still ready to fight. Instead, the light was almost completely gone from his eyes in an instant. He was on his way to be judged by the Valkyries.

Instantly, Ken swung the gun back toward Steve and had him in the sights.

Steve heard Ken scream at him in Spanish. He instantly translated the shrieked statement of his adversary, "No heretic shall ruin the cypher of souls!" It made a lot of sense to him, considering his current situation.

He was aware of some sort of scuffle taking place to his left but did not take his eyes from the foul oval that lay on the ground in front of him. With the free second that Dogtooth bought Steve with his life, Steve plunged the stainless steel axe down on the cypher with a wild-eyed ferocity that could have cleaved a boulder in half.

───◆───

As Sergeant Erdody rounded the bend of the driveway to the cabin, he witnessed Ken shoot at Steve as he ran into the front yard of the small cabin. He saw Dogtooth attack Ken with a knife and get shot twice in the chest. He also witnessed Steve run, raise an axe over his head, and chop down at something in the front yard of the camp. What he witnessed next he would never be able to accurately describe in any sworn testimony or police report. As Steve made contact with whatever he was trying to strike in the front yard, something happened that had never been witnessed before.

───◆───

As Steve cleaved into the hideous cypher, a two-inch piece of the axe blade broke off and ricocheted off his forehead above his left eye. As the broken steel sliced through his skin, the blade sliced through the cypher, severing the oval. A cataclysmic explosion of lights and screams shot up into the air like a gigantic roman candle. It gave off a blast wave that knocked Steve and Ken off of their feet.

———•———

At that very instant, far away in an asylum in Denton, Denise Moynihan was heard by the orderlies at the nurse's station down the hall screaming in searing pain as if she were burning alive. By the time they reached her room, she was sitting up in her bed, looking around bewilderedly as if she had no idea where she was. She asked in a confused young woman's voice that was not her normal gravelly hiss, "Where am I?"

———•———

Carla's eyes opened up in the hospital bed at St. Bartholomew's in Derry. She asked the nurse in her room the same question.

———•———

Sergeant Erdody witnessed Steve get blown off of his feet to the ground. He also witnessed Ken get blown off of his feet and fall backward onto the upright dagger that was still in the dead biker's hand. What he did not witness was the inquisitor's blade sever Ken's spine and pierce his heart, killing him instantly.

———•———

As Steve watched the cataclysmic light show in front of him, blood poured from his wound into his eye. It stung as he wiped it away. He wasn't sure what he was seeing, and the whole event lasted only about ten seconds, but he thought he could make out female forms rushing up through the illuminated torrent as if soaring off into freedom. One last pulse wave of pastel fluorescent green marked the end of the event. A vapor cloud rose out from the center of the fractured cypher and dissipated into the air. Just as it disappeared, Steve could have sworn he saw the same old man's face that he had seen in the window of the old house out in the swamp. Steve's head flopped back on the grass, and he passed out cold.

EPILOGUE

The evening brought a beautiful breeze, which was the end to a perfect summer day. Steve appreciated them more now than ever before. The freedom that he almost lost, the life, or more accurately, the lives, he almost lost in those trials and tribulations up at Mason's camp seemed like a lifetime ago. As he stood there on the balcony off of his and Carla's bedroom, breathing in the fresh warm day, he couldn't believe it had been only one year, one year to the day, since those strange events started to unfold in that old cabin at Long Shadows Farm. Steve dropped his head in sadness as he remembered the loss of his old friend Mason.

What a waste.

"I'm still not sure what happened, and I'm not sure I really want to know, but it sure did leave a mark," he said aloud as he rubbed a pink scar above his left eyebrow.

He spun on his heels and headed back through their bedroom and down to see Carla, who was in the kitchen preparing dinner. They were staying home tonight to enjoy each other's company and take it easy. They had made a conscious decision to stay home on this oddest of anniversaries and let today be the beginning of allowing the macabre memories of that strange weekend start to fade away.

Carla really didn't have any memories of that weekend, which Steve saw as a blessing. Steve always described what he witnessed occur in her as a "seizure" because he knew if he described what he really saw, he would have been locked up in Denton, Maine, as a newly diagnosed patient of Dr. Gerald Jorgensen.

"I wonder how that guy is doing?" he said aloud.

———•———

During the inquest, Dr. Jorgensen never said a bad thing about Steve, just that he tied him up and that the doctor "lent" him his car.

"I never felt threatened at all," he said. "And I should know. I have dealt with psychopaths and sociopaths constantly in my professional career, and Steve never exhibited any of those behaviors. It seemed to me he was earnestly trying to get out of trouble without any help from the authorities, whom he could not trust."

The doctor's testimony went a long way in motivating the state and local police departments that were involved to drop whatever legal issues they had with Stephen Babin and sweep this one under the rug and out of the public eye in a quick and timely manner.

But Steve's most powerful ally was a man he had never met before the inquest. His testimony secured Steve's freedom and exonerated him of all wrongdoing in any matters related to that weekend. It was the testimony of State Police Sergeant Steven Erdody that really cleared him.

Erdody spoke of Steve's spotless record before the weekend.

He told how Steve called in medical assistance for Sheriff's Deputy David Lynders after the deputy had tried to scald him with hot coffee.

He told how Steve bandaged Ken's wound after Ken had tried to kill Steve the first time.

He told how Steve never took a gun to arm himself when they were readily available in the jail and never took Ken's gun after he had incapacitated the officer at the camp.

He told how Ken turned into a rogue vigilante officer, disobeying direct orders to stay off of the property that was now a crime scene.

He told how Ken illegally beat, tortured, and jailed Steve without due process. Experiences like those would have made any man turn away from the authorities for help and fair treatment, he told the inquest panel.

He testified how he saw with his own eyes: Ken try to ambush and kill Steve, then kill another man an instant later, slip and get killed himself by falling on a knife that was in the hands of the dead man.

There was an awkward moment at one point during Erdody's testimony. It was when he tried to describe the "flash explosion" of sorts that he witnessed when Steve broke the cypher with the axe. He said the explosion looked like the result of a booby trap incendiary device that had been left as an ambush, but there was no scorching or other physical evidence to corroborate that possibility.

The more Erdody spoke, the more dread washed over the faces of the members on the inquest panel and the prosecutors who were building their case against Steve.

When questioned about the circumstances of Mason's death, Erdody responded that his wounds were indicative of an animal attack, most likely that of a bear. It had looked like he had fallen into an old cellar hole during the attack. He was impaled on an old pitchfork that was down in the rubble during the fall. His wounds were consistent with trying to fend off a large animal and with the evidence at the scene. No bear or animal was ever found, but when examined, the blood on Mason's clothes was consistent with animal blood.

When asked about the incident with the motorcycle gang and the leader known as Dogtooth, whose name was Tom Dennel, Erdody responded that no link could be found between Steve and the renegade gang of bikers. No direct connection or secondary connections through work, family, social, or geography could be established. No one from the biker gang who was captured during the day's events said anything, and Steve denied any contact whatsoever.

Erdody said he could only surmise that longstanding, violent antagonism between the bike gang and all levels of law enforcement in the State of Maine was the reason for the bikers' involvement. He believed they must have heard on a police scanner what was going on and came to disrupt the investigation. Another state trooper had reported that he had checked Dennel's truck at the roadblock on Route 77. This was most likely the connection.

Steve was in shock at the inquest upon hearing all of this. He didn't know how he would ever be able to thank Erdody for all of his help, but he knew he stood a very good chance of staying out of jail after that testimony.

Of course, the state and the municipal authorities dropped the case. Steve and Carla were in shock. They wanted to get home and start putting it all behind them as soon as possible. The nightmare that had started during that strangest of weekends was over.

———◆•◆———

Steve walked down the stairs from the bedroom. As he came around the corner, he saw Carla sitting at the countertop island slowly twirling a glass of red wine in her hand, with her mind off somewhere else. She was staring out the sliding glass doors, which were open and letting in the mild summer breeze. She looked beautiful.

"What're you thinking about?" he asked as he quietly slid up behind her and gently kissed her neck.

"I'm not really sure. My mind was a thousand miles away. Just kind of enjoying the nice quiet moment, I guess. The breeze feels like a gentle bunch of fingers blowing by. It feels kind of nice."

"I have to go downstairs to my office to do a few things. When do you want to eat?"

"Whenever," she responded. "It's a beautiful evening, and I'm in no rush. Did you want a glass of wine?"

"After I do my things and come back up. I shouldn't be too long. Maybe we could take a stroll around the neighborhood before dinner. It is a beautiful evening."

On that note, he opened the cellar door with a little more energy in his step. The last few steps he was taking the stairs two at a time, saying to himself while wearing a Cheshire-cat grin, "Daddy's gettin' lucky tonight!"

He went to his desk in his office and grabbed a key that he had hidden under the bottom right drawer, taped to the outside of the drawer. Next, he went over to his gun closet, which Carla never went into because she found its contents completely droll and boring. The gun closet was a full double sliding-door closet that held all of his firearms and other important items. He opened the lock and left the key in it, opened the doors wide, and pulled up a chair to the open closet. Once he rolled the chair to where he wanted it, he sat down and reached into the closet and pulled back a sheet to reveal the same lead coffer that he had left on the swamp island on Mason's land, the same lead coffer that still held the silver-bound Bible and the chalice. His mind raced back to the day he went to get the leaden box.

During one of his fall sales trips through Maine, Steve had retrieved the coffer after the investigation and inquest were over. In order to account for the muddy clothes he would be bringing home, he had told Carla that he needed to get the backpack he had left there. He had slipped in and out of the swamp in under thirty minutes. The coffer was still up on the island exactly where and how he had left it. He had avoided the area of the swamp where the old farm was standing and the area where the two swamp ladies were resting at the bottom.

After shaking the memories of his experiences out of his head with a shudder, he reached into the closet and opened the coffer for the first time since he had placed it on the island. This was the first time he was able to work up the nerve to open it. The moment he lifted open the top, there was a loud *klang* from upstairs. Steve jumped out of his skin and headed toward the stairs. *Oh no, please not again!* he thought as he started to panic.

As he reached the bottom step, the top door to the cellar swung open, and Carla stuck her face through the door with a smile and said with a false apprehension, "Sor…r…r…ry, honey. I just dropped the colander with our pasta in it all over the floor. I was just rinsing it before I set it aside to make lasagna."

"No problem. We'll just have something else. I jumped out of my skin, though, from the bang. Damn, that was loud down here."

"Don't be a weenie and get your butt up here so we can take our walk. I'm growing impatient," she said with a mock furrowed brow. "If you make me wait too long, you won't get your dessert." She spun around, looking him in the eye the entire time, slapped her own butt, closed the door hard, and walked away.

"Ooooo, do I love that woman!" he said, smiling to himself.

He went back to his office, sat down in front of the coffer of artifacts, and thought aloud, "How do I find out how much this stuff is worth, and how do I sell it under the radar? Maybe I can take it to the *Antiques Roadshow*. They'll probably know. I can tell them I found it at a yard sale. It'll have to wait, though. Mumma's calling, and she means business."

That evening was wonderfully relaxing—a nice walk, a fine meal, a very nice roll in the hay, and a drifting off into peaceful sleep entwined in each other's arms. Just as he fell asleep in Carla's warm embrace, Steve thought again about how much he loved her.

Shuffling. Darkness. Steve was awakened by something he thought he heard in their room, but he wasn't sure. It wasn't loud. He thought he heard the words "with me" whispered in the dark. He clicked on the light on the nightstand just in time to see Carla sink into the side of her neck one edge of a double-edged stainless steel axe, whose other edge was broken.

AFTERWORD

It seems that many of the finest thriller/horror stories, books, and movies are based out of Maine. The master of all things thriller/horror himself resides in Maine and has based what I feel are his best stories in Maine.

The setting of this book and some of the references to towns are a definite homage to the aforementioned "King of horror," and I, in all ways, will defer and tip my hat to this man because I have always enjoyed his works.

However, I must mention that the impetus of this story being based in Maine was quite incidental. This is due to the facts that the central locations, the back history of those locations, and the cypher are all very real and exist—in Maine.

REFERENCES

American Heritage Dictionary, Third Edition. Boston, MA: Houghton Mifflin, 1994.

Chapman, Robert. •*The Concise Roget's International Thesaurus, Fifth Edition.* New York, NY: Harper Collins, 1994.

May, Herbert, and Bruce Metzger. *The New Oxford Annotated Bible With The Apocrypha, Expanded Edition, Revised Standard Version.* New York, NY: Oxford University Press, 1962.

Sumption, Jonathan. *The Albigenisian Crusades.* Farber and Farber, 2000

Wikipedia, inquisition, auto da fe. Wikipedia, 2009.